THE ARMAGEDDON VIRUS

A TOM BLAKE THRILLER

ADRIAN WILLS

The Armageddon Virus

Copyright © Adrian Wills 2015

To my family for their continued support and devotion.

ONE

Tom Blake shook the rain from the sleeves of his coat and combed the moisture from his hair with his fingers. It was a grey, autumnal afternoon that had dampened his mood long before the message had chimed on his phone and intruded on his day. The instruction was unequivocal. Drop everything.

His decision to use public transport had been a mistake. The mortuary was on the far side of town but the fug of stale carbon dioxide on the Underground had made his head buzz and his eyes sting. All he wanted was to lie down in a darkened room. It didn't help that he knew what was waiting for him behind the double doors. A soulless square room, tiled in white under unforgiving strip lights. And the smell. The sweet, rotten stench of corporeal mush. The memory of it from medical school made him feel green.

He took a deep breath and crashed through the doors.

The body was lying on a cantilevered table under a thin sheet with only the feet, head and shoulders left uncovered. A cardboard tag with a name scribbled in black ink had been tied with string to the big toe. It was the body of a man, a little older than Blake, maybe in his early fifties. His hair

1

was bitumen black, receding over a dark skull. A rash of salt and pepper bristles masked sallow cheeks. His skin was puffed and bloated. Someone had arranged his arms at his sides and his legs out straight so his feet fell away at the ankles. Blake stepped closer with his top lip curled and his nose wrinkled, like he was inspecting the remains of an animal at the side of the road.

'Who was he?' he asked.

The pathologist on the other side of the slab stretched his back. He looked tired, like he'd worked through the night and been called back to cover the next day's shift.

'You don't know?'

Blake shrugged. The message said to take a look at the body but he wasn't sure what perspective he could bring. Anatomy wasn't his speciality. They knew that. But a twenty year military career had left him pre-programmed to follow orders without question.

The pathologist unhooked a metal clipboard and read from a handwritten form. 'Javed Rahimi. Forty-eight years old. Five feet eight tall. One hundred and eighty-six pounds.'

'Cause of death?'

'Multiple organ failure and severe internal bleeding. He had haemorrhaging around his lymph nodes, heart, kidneys, stomach and intestines.'

'What's your supposition?'

'That he was poisoned.'

'Murdered?'

The pathologist's eyes flitted over Blake's shoulder to the woman standing at the back of the morgue. She'd been waiting in the corridor when Blake arrived and followed him in. No welcome. No introduction. But he had a pretty good idea who she was.

'It looks suspicious,' said the pathologist. 'His white

blood count was incredibly high although toxicology came back inconclusive. No trace of anything in his blood, urine or tissue samples.'

'You don't think an external trauma could have caused the haemorrhaging?'

'Possible but improbable. We found no bruising. I would speculate it was something he either ingested or inhaled.'

'So why do you need me?'

The pathologist looked at him blankly. 'I've no idea who you are or why you're here,' he said. 'I was told to give you the facts. That's all.'

The click of high heels echoed off the tiled walls as the woman stepped forwards.

'He was a political refugee.' Her voice was deeper than Blake had expected and carried an authority he found appealing. 'He came here five years ago from Iran seeking asylum after being arrested and tortured for his involvement in protests following the disputed election of President Ahmadinejad. When he was released he fled the country, made it across Europe and into Britain clinging to the axle of a lorry.'

'So?' said Blake. He caught a breath of perfume as she breezed past. It was subtle and expensive. He wasn't sure why he was surprised that an MI5 field agent should be wearing scent.

'For the last three years he'd been working as a cleaner for the Prison Service.' She stopped on the opposite side of the table so Rahimi's body was between them. She had delicate features, paper-thin, almost translucent skin and tight, corkscrew hair the colour of autumnal oak leaves.

'So call the Met,' said Blake.

She gave him a weak smile. 'A few weeks ago the Pentagon issued a general alert through their Iranian Directorate after intercepting a series of calls made from the UK. They were placed to an agent on their radar.'

'And you think Rahimi made them?'

'We don't know for sure. The Americans say the calls were made from inside the prison.'

'Where he worked?' Blake raised an eyebrow.

'The Prime Minister's furious. God knows how GCHQ missed it. There'll be an inquiry, of course, but for now he's demanding a quick investigation and whatever was being planned shut down.'

'So Rahimi *was* murdered?'

'We don't know but it seems a likely explanation. It would help to find out if he made those calls.'

'Why would he?'

'We don't know.'

'What do you know?'

'That he had a good job as a computer programmer in Iran but took a cleaning position here to make ends meet.'

'And now he's dead. Do you have any evidence he made the calls?'

'Not specifically but the facts are straightforward. A series of phone calls made to an Iranian agent were intercepted and an Iranian cleaner at the prison winds up dead.'

'People die all the time. Doesn't mean a thing.'

'Unexplained internal haemorrhaging and possible poisoning. You don't think that's even a little suspicious?'

Blake wiped his nose with the back of his hand. His skin was cool. Even on a dull autumn day it had been like walking into a chiller cabinet. 'It's still quite a leap of imagination.'

'But nonetheless a possibility we need to investigate.'

'Where was he found?'

'He rented a room not far from where he worked. A

shared house, mostly occupied by other immigrants. They raised the alarm when they hadn't seen him for a few days.'

'Had he tried to get any medical help?'

'We don't think so.'

'Well, that's curious.'

'Why?'

'Because death by poisoning is a slow, agonising death. He'd have been cramped up in pain, possibly for days. If that had been you, would you have called a doctor?'

'Maybe he didn't have one? Or perhaps he became ill so quickly he didn't have the strength to call for help?'

'Maybe,' said Blake. He pulled the sheet covering the body down to expose a line of ragged stitches running from his sternum to his stomach where he'd been carved up in post-mortem. Blake grabbed a wrist. Lifted it to inspect the skin from the shoulder then repeated the examination on the other arm.

'Did you look for puncture wounds?' Blake asked. The pathologist had wandered to the far side of the room and was busying himself at a worktop. 'It's possible he could have been injected.'

'Of course, but we didn't find anything.'

With two straight fingers, Blake rolled Rahimi's head to one side, the stiffening effects of rigor mortis having long since vanished. He checked his neck on both sides then set his head straight again.

'No other marks or bruises?' asked Blake.

'Nothing out of the ordinary.'

'Anything in his stomach?'

'No.'

Like a plasterer checking his work for imperfections, Blake scrutinised every inch of Rahimi's skin. He pulled the sheet away from his legs and set it in a heap over his pelvis.

He ran a careful eye over both legs then lifted his knees to check the back of his thighs.

'What's this?'

The pathologist shuffled back to the table, dropping a pair of wire-rimmed glasses onto his nose. He screwed up his face as Blake pointed to a tiny blemish. 'An insect bite. Probably a mosquito or a bed bug. Nothing more.'

'It's worth a closer look. You should carry out a biopsy.'

The pathologist took a step back and lifted his glasses. 'A biopsy?'

'Do as he says,' said the woman.

'Have you searched his room?'

'We didn't find anything,' the field agent replied.

'What about a mobile phone?'

'It was sent to the lab but they've already confirmed it wasn't used to make the calls.'

'Who did he last call?'

'It hadn't been used for more than a week before his death.'

'I see,' said Blake.

'You think it's significant?'

'I've no idea, I'm not a detective. You should try CID.'

'We can't leave it to them. This is a matter of national security.'

'You don't know for sure.'

'We can't take the risk.'

'So what happens next?' The woman didn't reply, letting Blake work it out for himself. 'I need to know what you need from me,' said Blake.

But even as he formed the words he sensed he already knew the answer.

TWO

Her car was parked in a leafy avenue a few minutes' walk from the mortuary. The paintwork of the sporty two-seater was so highly polished that it reflected the branches of the trees. She unlocked the doors remotely and Blake folded himself into the passenger seat with his knees up to his chest. Inside was immaculately clean. Almost obsessively spotless. It could have come straight from the showroom apart from the hint of perfume that hit him as he opened the door.

The woman smoothed out the legs of her trouser suit and adjusted her jacket as she climbed in beside him. She tucked a stray strand of hair behind her ear and checked her make-up in the rear-view mirror. When she slotted a key into the ignition, she left one hand on the wheel. No wedding ring. Not that it was unusual for MI5 agents to be single, particularly those who worked in the field.

'I'm Alex,' she said as she started the engine.

'Doesn't sound much like a spook's name. I thought you got to choose a pseudonym? I imagined you'd have picked something more sophisticated.'

'Like what?'

'I don't know. Eloise or Paris?'

A smile crept across her face. She checked over her shoulder and pulled out. 'What's wrong with Alex?'

'I didn't say there was anything wrong with it. Is it just Alex?'

'Mortensen. It's Danish, on my grandfather's side.'

'I'm guessing you already know my name?'

'Blake,' she said. 'Although I thought you'd have chosen something more sophisticated.'

'They tried to fix me up with a new name but I didn't like it.'

'When?'

'It's a long story.'

The car rumbled through the smart commercial districts of the city and swept over the River Thames, leaving behind the tourists and well-heeled businessmen on the north bank. They were heading for the ugly, post-war blocks of flats on the outskirts. Blake reached for the lever under his legs but found the seat was already pushed back as far as it would go.

'Is it far?' he asked, the dashboard digging into his knees.

'You're taller than I thought,' said Mortensen.

'What were you expecting?'

'The agency doesn't usually recruit tall guys. They tend to stand out in a crowd.'

Blake didn't consider himself particularly tall but even at a fraction under six feet he'd been a giant among the squat NCOs of the SAS.

'I'm not like you,' he said.

'What do you mean, not like me?'

'I'm not a spook.'

'Well, you work for MI5 and I think that's pretty much the only qualification.'

'You know what I mean.'

'I don't think I do. If you're not a spook, what are you?'

It was a good question. Blake's transition from the military had happened so quickly. When they announced his unit was being disbanded, it came as a complete surprise. A victim of a nervous government and budget cuts. Somehow his commanding officer, Harry Patterson, had convinced MI5 to bring the unit under the auspices of the service. Told the Deputy Director General straight that Blake's skills, honed as a military psychologist, would be an invaluable asset for an organisation battling against a mounting home-grown terror threat.

'Did Patterson send you?'

Mortensen ignored the question. 'I was told to meet you at the morgue and fill you in on Rahimi's background, that's all. They said you had some medical knowledge and that you might be able to help with the case.'

'I don't think I can.'

'Your boss has a different opinion.'

'So Patterson did send you?'

'He was confident your expertise would prove valuable.'

'With what exactly? A spurious link between a dead refugee and a supposed phone call the Americans think was made in the prison where he worked?'

Mortensen kept her eyes on the road, unmoved by Blake's outburst. They pulled up outside a Victorian terrace in a scruffy street stippled with litter. Weeds had woven themselves around an iron fence set into a low wall. A bored-looking police officer was standing with his hands clasped behind his back in front of a blue door. Its paint was cracked and peeling.

'I was told you'd have a unique perspective on the case and I was to offer as much assistance as you needed. That's it. Now do you want to take a look at Rahimi's bedsit or not?' said Mortensen, ratcheting on the handbrake.

Blake peered up at the building. 'How long did he live here?'

'For the last eighteen months. It's privately-rented, like most of the places in the area. They've mostly been converted into flats and filled with low income benefits claimants.'

Blake trailed Mortensen up five crumbling steps to the front door. Mortensen flashed an identity card and the police officer stepped aside. Rahimi's room was on the ground floor along a narrow corridor adjacent to a flight of stairs that disappeared up to a gloomy landing. The door was hanging off its hinges. The frame was splintered and sealed off with strips of blue and white police tape.

'Put these on.' Mortensen tossed Blake a pair of latex gloves and ducked into the room.

The foul stench of death hung in the air, lingering on nicotine-stained walls and the dirty carpet. Mortensen flicked on a light and disturbed a squadron of flies that had gathered on the exposed bulb hanging from the ceiling. The room was small. Big enough only to accommodate a bed, a wardrobe and a table. There were traces of white forensic powder on some of the surfaces. A pile of soiled bedclothes lay in a crumpled heap on the mattress. A grubby sink was tucked against the wall next to a uPVC door that led out to a concrete courtyard.

Blake was drawn to a faded photograph with dog-eared corners stuck to a wall over the bed. He peeled it off and studied the three smiling faces. An older woman, her head covered by a black headscarf, was flanked by two girls. One looked to be in her late teens, the other a few years younger. Each had lustrous brown eyes and thick lashes. No mistaking they were a mother and her daughters. The similarity between them was striking.

'Is this Rahimi's family?' asked Blake.

'His wife, Niyoosha, and his daughters. Alaleh's fourteen. The elder girl, Yasaman, is seventeen. Their current whereabouts in Iran is unknown.'

'He left them behind?'

'I guess he had his reasons.'

'Do they even know he's dead?'

'The embassy's been notified. It's up to them to pass on the information.'

Blake dropped the photo on the table and poked around a pile of books and newspapers. A plastic lighter was balanced on top of a packet of foreign-branded cigarettes. He picked out a stubby butt from a mound of ash in an overflowing ashtray and sniffed it like a connoisseur selecting a fine cigar. He pulled a face and dropped it. Moved lightly across the floor towards the wardrobe. Stopped to rock back and forth on a board that creaked under his weight. The wardrobe was pathetically bare. Three cotton shirts and two pairs of beige polyester trousers were hung from the sort of wire hangers given away at dry cleaners' stores. The sum of Rahimi's belongings swinging sparsely on a metal rail.

A limescale-encrusted razor and a can of shaving foam were lined up around the sink next to a toothbrush with splayed bristles and a dried sliver of soap. Blake ran his fingers around a mirror splattered with white toothpaste flecks, feeling for anything hidden behind it, then tried the handle of the patio door. It was locked and there was no key. Outside, concrete steps led into a shady courtyard pebble-dashed green with moss and algae. Blake shaded his eyes with one hand and peered out at dirty puddles that had formed in the depressions of a sunken patio.

When he turned back into the room, his gaze fell on the dishevelled bed. He fished under the cheap pine frame with a flailing arm and pulled out a canvas travel bag in a cloud of dust. He unzipped it, found it was empty and slung it back. He slumped to his haunches and peered around, looking for something, anything, he might have missed.

He was slowly rising to his feet when he heard it. Or maybe it was something that he'd felt. He wasn't sure.

'Listen,' he said.

'What?'

'Can you hear it? It's only faint.'

Mortensen cocked her head to one side. They listened together but heard only the drone of a frustrated fly trying to break out through the glass of the patio door.

Blake fell on his hands and knees, moving away from Mortensen. At the far side of the room he picked at a frayed edge of carpet until he'd teased a section free. He rolled it back to reveal a crumbling foam underlay hiding stained floorboards running the width of the room. One of the planks had been sawn through in two places. A knot the size of a large coin had fallen out leaving a hole just big enough for a finger. Blake tucked the carpet under his knees and was about to hook the loose plank free when he froze.

'What now?' asked Mortensen, leaning over his shoulder.

'It's stopped,' he whispered.

He jammed a thumb into the hole. Pulled out the plank and peered into the cavity between two joists. There was something in the darkness. A rectangular lump of plastic. He reached in and pulled out a mobile phone. An old model. Thick and heavy with an old-fashioned number pad. The screen was alight, bright enough to illuminate his hand and lower arm. It was displaying a message. Two words. Mortensen read them out loud.

'Missed call.'

THREE

Blake tried the keypad, prodding at the buttons with a thick finger, but the device was locked by a passcode. The phone was like a technological relic. A brick designed only for placing and receiving calls, unlike the hand-held super-computers that now masqueraded as phones. It was no doubt a pay-as-you-go device. An over-the-counter purchase that could be bought without any documentation. Untraceable.

'We should get it over to the lab,' said Mortensen. The note of hesitation in her voice wasn't lost on Blake.

The lab could wait.

There are ten thousand possible permutations for a four digit code and the chances were high the phone would auto-disable after a number of failed attempts. But people rarely use random codes. Most choose numbers they can easily remember. Sequences with a personal significance.

'What's Rahimi's date of birth?' asked Blake.

Mortensen screwed her eyes shut as she tried to recall the information she'd seen on a file. 'March the twenty-third.'

Blake punched in the date as four digits.

2 - 3 - 0 - 3.

The phone chirruped. An incorrect code. He tried it in reverse.

3 - 0 - 3 - 2.

Wrong again.

'What about trying the month first, the way the Americans write their dates?' Mortensen suggested.

Blake tried again. 0 - 3 - 2 - 3.

'No, that's not it either.' He looked around the room seeking inspiration. 'What year was he born?'

'Nineteen sixty-four,' said Mortensen, this time without hesitation.

Blake tapped in the numbers and the screen turned blue. A handful of icons appeared on the display.

'We're in,' he said. He navigated his way through a series of menus to the call register and was surprised to find no calls had been placed on the phone but there were two numbers in the list of calls received.

'Mean anything to you?' Blake passed the handset to Mortensen.

'No,' she said, frowning. 'But if this was the phone used in the prison then the times should match up with those of the intercepted calls. Come on, we really ought to get it over to the technical lab. Have you seen enough?'

Blake stood up and balled the latex gloves into his pockets. They'd made his hands sweaty despite the powder on the inside. 'Yeah, let's go.'

Mortensen's car had attracted the attention of a gaggle of greasy youths cooing over its sleek lines. They dispersed briefly when Blake shooed them away but re-formed as Mortensen fired up the throaty V6 engine. The bravest ones hollered a volley of wisecracks. Mortensen floored the accelerator and pulled away with a squeal of rubber which provoked a sarcastic cheer.

'What did the other tenants tell you about Rahimi?' Blake asked.

'He was a loner who left the house at around six every morning and was home after five. Regular as clockwork. He spent his free time on his own in his room.'

'When did anybody last see him alive?'

'Five days ago. One of the tenants passed him as he was going out. He said Rahimi was a little agitated but didn't think much of it.'

'And no one saw him after that?'

'Not in the house. It looks as if he took himself to his room when he fell ill and stayed there until he was carried out.'

'What about the prison? Didn't they notice anything suspicious?'

They pulled up in a queue of traffic on a bridge behind a red bus with a rattling engine spewing out dirty diesel fumes.

'We've not spoken to them yet.' Mortensen threw Blake an awkward glance.

'Why not?'

'Operational reasons.'

'I thought this was an urgent matter of national security?'

'Blake, you'll have to trust me on this, okay?'

'So, let me get this straight. You suspect Rahimi was making calls to an Iranian terrorist from inside the prison where he worked. A few days later he ends up murdered but you didn't think it was worth speaking with the prison staff?'

'We don't know he was murdered, or whether that phone belonged to him or even if he made the calls. It's all conjecture.'

'But I'm not getting the full picture, am I?'

'Everything will become clear in time, I promise.'

They were moving again but the traffic was heavy. They rolled on a few metres and stopped. Mortensen had the heater on, blowing hot air, trying to keep the windscreen clear. A nausea swelled from the pit of Blake's stomach. It was uncomfortably warm and he craved the taste of a cool, fresh breeze.

Another five metres. Mortensen jammed on the brakes, a little too sharply. They both jolted forwards in their seats.

Blake

Blake stared out of the window with dead eyes at the stream of shoppers drifting from store to store. Too many questions, not enough answers. It all felt wrong.

His left hand fingered the smooth plastic of the door handle.

If Mortensen was serious about getting to the bottom of Rahimi's involvement in some kind of plot, speaking to staff at the prison should have been top of her list. She was hiding something. He was sure of it.

'You're playing games with me,' said Blake.

The car crept moved forwards a few metres until the brake lights of the truck ahead flashed on and Mortensen stamped on the brakes again.

Blake let his right hand fall casually to his side and in one movement unclipped his seat belt. He was out of the car before Mortensen knew it, striding along the street with his hands in his pockets.

Mortensen swore under her breath, pulled off the road and mounted the kerb.

'Blake, wait!' she shouted as she jumped out of the car, forcing a white van to swerve. She mouthed an apology and ran after Blake, bowling through startled pedestrians.

She caught up with him as he was turning into a side street.

'Listen to me,' she said, grabbing his upper arm from behind.

He spun around on his heel. 'I told you, start talking straight or I walk away.'

'Just calm down, okay? Let's get this phone to the lab and I'll tell you everything I know. We'll find somewhere quiet to talk. Please, get back in the car.'

'Let's talk now.'

'Later.'

'Fine.' Blake found his phone and dialled a pre-set number. It rang twice before diverting to an answerphone. He decided not to leave a message.

'Who're you calling? Patterson? You know it was his idea for me to work with you.'

Blake hands balled into fists. His jaw was clamped so tightly that a vein behind his ear began to pulse. Every instinct told him to keep walking. This wasn't how he operated. Patterson should have known better.

'You want to be reassigned?' Mortensen asked.

'Murder mysteries aren't really my thing.'

'Patterson thought we'd work well together. At least give it a chance.'

'He knows I work alone.'

'He said you could be a bit of a cold fish. Cantankerous I think he said. Maybe he knows you better than you think.'

'I work alone,' Blake repeated.

'You didn't operate solo in Echo 17 though, did you? Or did I get that wrong?'

'That's classified information. What do know about the unit?'

'A Special Forces deniable asset, acting under the direct authority of the Prime Minister?' said Mortensen. 'I read the files. The unit is still operational, only now it's run by

MI5 under Patterson's direct command. Want me to go on? You're currently the only active operative...'

'Enough,' Blake snapped.

'Come back to the car. We'll find somewhere to talk.'

Blake's shoulders slumped, his will to protest evaporating. He trudged back to the car behind Mortensen like a defeated man.

'I was given special clearance to read those files, just so you know.'

'By who?'

'The Deputy Director General.'

'The existence of the unit is known only to a handful of people, and for good reason.'

'But it's not run by the military any more is it? It's an MI5 asset. Things change. Get used to it.'

'It's still a covert operational unit that has to stay off the grid precisely because of what I do.'

'And what is that exactly?'

Blake ignored the question, watching the road ahead snarling under the weight of traffic.

'Your job was never to work alone. So what changed?' Mortensen asked.

'I did.'

'Why?'

'I don't know.'

'Do you miss it? The Army, I mean?'

'I miss the unit as it used to be, before the Ministry of Defence shut us down and consigned a dozen good men to the scrapheap. One up to the accountants, but life goes on. I'm happy enough.'

'I read something about a Deep Sleepers programme. What is it?'

'I thought you'd read the files?'

'There were holes.'

'Probably for good reason.'

'Patterson said you can get inside people's heads. What is it, some kind of mind control?'

The cause of the heavy traffic revealed itself as a set of roadworks that blocked one side of the carriageway. Traffic flow was being controlled by temporary lights.

'It's not something I can talk about,' said Blake, crossing his arms. He wasn't supposed to have a history or a background beyond his supposed fatal shooting in Afghanistan by a Taliban marksman. He lived his life in obscurity. A ghost. The fewer people who knew of his existence the better.

Mortensen took the hint and sat in silence drumming her palms on the steering wheel.

When her phone rang it made them both jump. It was connected wirelessly to the car's stereo system so the sound reverberated through the speakers. Mortensen answered with a push of a button on the wheel.

'Can you get back to the mortuary urgently?'

Blake recognised the voice of the pathologist.

'We can be there in fifteen minutes,' said Mortensen, glancing at a clock on the dashboard. 'What's wrong?'

'There's something you should see. I don't know how we missed it before.'

'We're on our way,' she said.

FOUR

The pathologist led them along a corridor to an office cluttered with paperwork and ushered them into chairs opposite a desk. Faded yellow paint was flaking from the walls and a florescent tube flickered overhead. A narrow window letting in virtually no natural light gave views out onto the dirty bricks of an adjacent wall. Three long shelves groaned with the weight of serious-looking medical textbooks on anatomy, surgical pathology and microbiology.

The pathologist sat down, gathering his lab coat around his body. With a frown he reached into a drawer and produced a plastic pot, sealed with a white screw-on cap.

'We found this after some further exploratory work,' he said.

He swept away some loose papers and set the pot on the desk. It contained a tiny sliver of metal. Blake picked up the pot and rolled the shard around.

'We found it in Rahimi's leg under the surface of the skin near a blemish we thought was an insect bite,' the pathologist said, lifting his glasses and perching them in a crop of sandy-coloured hair.

'What is it?' asked Mortensen, as Blake handed her the pot.

'A poison pellet, we think. Are you familiar with the Georgi Markov case?'

'The Bulgarian Secret Service assassination?'

'It has the hallmarks of a copycat killing,' said the pathologist.

'You think Rahimi was killed by someone with a poison-tipped umbrella?' said Mortensen. 'That's a bit fanciful.'

'But a plausible explanation at this stage. I'd like to run some more tests but it looks highly likely the pellet was filled with a powerful toxin and injected into his thigh.'

'I've pulled bigger splinters out of my thumb. Could something that small really have killed him?' Mortensen rolled the pellet one way and then the other.

'That's the interesting thing. It's actually less than two millimetres in diameter. A precision-engineered piece.'

'Which suggests we're looking at a sophisticated assassi-nation,' said Blake. 'Do you have any thoughts on the poison they used?'

'Something fast-acting. My guess is ricin. It would certainly account for all the symptoms - the haemorrhaging and the high white blood count, for instance.'

'But the dose must have been miniscule,' said Mortensen.

'Even very small amounts of ricin can have fatal conse-quences once it gets into the bloodstream,' the pathologist said.

'It's exactly what the Bulgarians used in the Markov assassination in '78. He thought he'd been stung by an insect as he crossed Waterloo Bridge,' said Blake.

'And a few days later he was dead,' said the pathologist. 'And the thing about ricin is it's so easy to come by.'

'An extract from caster beans, if I remember rightly?' said Blake.

'Simple to obtain but deadly because it has two toxic elements. The first penetrates cells to create a passage for the second toxin which attacks the cell itself and stops it being able to produce proteins. The effect is the cells die off one by one leading to a painful and protracted death.'

Mortensen set the pot back down on the desk with a shudder.

'The question is, who's behind it?' said Blake. 'It would have required highly-specialist laser-cutting technology to drill into a pellet this small. And it would have to be constructed out of a very hard material to stop it distorting when it was fired into the body.'

'I made a point of looking up the Markov case before you arrived. That Bulgarian pellet was made out of platinum and iridium, which are both biologically inert,' said the pathologist. 'They coated it with a wax that dissolved at body temperature allowing the toxin to be released. Very clever and brutally efficient.'

'And unless Rahimi sought immediate medical help, his death was inevitable,' said Blake.

'But not instant. The poor bugger would have been in agony for days.'

'The question is, who has the capability to produce something like this?' asked Mortensen.

'The KGB had labs working on this sort of thing at the height of the Cold War but who knows who they might have sold the technology to,' said Blake.

'The Iranians?' suggested Mortensen. 'They've always had a cosy relationship with Moscow.'

'True, and it would fit your theory that Rahimi was communicating with Iran.'

'But it doesn't explain why they had him killed. The PM needs to be informed.'

'That's your department, I believe,' said Blake.

'Of course, the coroner will also have to be told,' said the pathologist. 'There'll have to be an inquest.'

'How soon do you have to let him know?'

'It's a possible murder case. He already has the preliminary paperwork but I need to let him know about the pellet.' The pathologist swept up the pot and returned it to his desk drawer. 'It does somewhat change the complexion of the case.'

'Yes, of course,' said Mortensen, standing up. 'Just how soon would you let him know? Is it reasonable that perhaps it could take a few days for the information to filter down, if you catch my drift?'

'Are you suggesting I withhold information?'

'Not at all, I'm suggesting this is a serious matter of national security. If you could give us a couple of days to make some inquiries before the coroner is notified, that would be helpful.'

'That would be very irregular. If it was discovered I failed to disclose...'

'You won't be failing to disclose anything. You'll send your updated report to him, but not for a few days. We need at least forty-eight hours head-start. As soon as the coroner's office is informed there's a risk of the information leaking out. You do understand, don't you?'

The pathologist slammed the drawer shut. 'You don't leave me much choice do you? Okay, I'll hold off for two days. That's it.'

'Thank you,' said Mortensen, turning to leave the office.

Blake followed her closely out of the building. He caught her by the elbow as they stepped out onto the street.

'You promised me some answers,' he said, spinning Mortensen around.

'Not here,' she said.

'Then where?'

'My apartment's not far. Come back with me and I'll fill you in on everything I know.'

'Everything?'

'Everything.' Mortensen sighed. 'There's something else you really need to know.'

FIVE

Her apartment was on the third floor of a modern fortress of steel and glass on the banks of the Thames with views across the river. She showed Blake into an open-plan living space with white walls and sparse furniture.

'Make yourself comfortable, I'm going to freshen up,' she said. 'Help yourself to a beer. I'll be out in a minute.'

Blake found the fridge and grabbed a bottle of lager as the sound of a shower running drifted through from an adjacent room.

He stood by ceiling-height windows where rivulets of rain clung to the glass causing the lights opposite to shimmer and watched the ebb and flow of early evening activity. Tiny figures darting through the rain on the opposite bank and cargo-vessels struggling against the tide.

His warm breath fogged on the cold pane.

'Can I get your help for a second?' Blake spun around at the sound of Mortensen's voice.

She was framed in a door wearing a red dress that clung tightly to her slim frame. 'Could you do me up?'

She held the front of the dress to her chest with one hand and was half-turned with her back towards him, the material puckering open. Blake's eyes lingered on her naked skin, pale and unblemished save for a peppering of freckles across her shoulders. His eyes ran along the sharp prominence of her shoulder blades and traced the dual tracks of muscle that ran the length of her spine.

'Come on, I won't bite,' said Mortensen. Her face was glowing. 'I love this dress but it's so difficult - ' she said.

Blake's cheeks flushed.

'What's wrong?' Mortensen swept her hair away from her neck. 'I thought I'd treat you - to dinner, I mean,' she said. 'I thought it would be good to get to know each other better.'

'Not a good idea.'

'I thought you wanted to know about the Rahimi case, but if you've changed your mind?'

Blake looked up at the ceiling as if seeking divine inspiration. 'I'm sorry. It's just been a while.'

'Since a woman's asked you for help dressing for dinner?'

He walked across the room, grasped the silver zip between meaty fingers and inched it upwards, careful not to catch her skin.

'There,' he said.

Mortensen adjusted the tightness around her chest and floated back to her room. 'I won't be long.'

Blake noticed his own worn jeans and crumbled shirt. 'I'm not really dressed for going out,' he shouted.

'Don't worry, you'll be fine.'

They ate at an intimate Italian restaurant with red chequered tablecloths and wicker chairs. The owner, an avuncular man with pipe cleaner-long legs, tried to seat them in the window but Mortensen insisted on a table at the back with unobstructed views across the room.

'Routine caution,' Mortensen said, as she allowed Blake to pull out her chair.

She dropped a clutch bag at her feet. It hit the floor with a noticeable thud.

'We want you to go into the prison undercover,' she said as a young waiter stepped out of earshot with their order scribbled on a pad. 'Find out what you can about what Rahimi was up to.'

'Into the prison?'

'It's technically two prisons, a category-A jail for regular and remand inmates and a high security unit, mostly full of murderers and terrorists, within the compound. You'll have heard of a few of them thanks to the tabloids.'

'And that's where the calls were made?'

'Yes, but we don't know how Rahimi smuggled in a phone. Security is incredibly tight. The only access is through the main prison, passing through a series of gated entrances independently controlled by a central locking system overseen by a command hub. There are more stringent measures protecting access into and out of the unit, full body scans, physical inspections and banks of CCTV cameras. Frankly, it'd be easier to break into the vaults of the Bank of England.'

'So why didn't you tell me earlier you wanted me inside?'

'Patterson's decision. He wanted you to take a look at Rahimi's body and get a feel for the case first. He was adamant I wasn't to tell you.'

'What's the plan for getting me in?'

'We're still working on that.'

Blake swirled his wine around the inside of his glass, gripping its stem between his finger and thumb. He'd only seen the inside a prison once before. They'd hit it hard and fast. A standard four-man team tearing into the town in the dead of night under a plume of desert dust. They'd ripped the door off its hinges with blocks of C-4 and filled the bunker with assault rifle fire, quickly overwhelming the poorly disciplined Iraqi guards. Most had died before they'd reached their weapons. Those who'd been asleep died in their beds.

It took less than three minutes. In the haze of smoke and dust filtered green by their night-vision goggles they'd found the racked and broken bodies of prisoners lying on stone floors. More than twenty skeletal scraps on the verge of death, caged behind bars and with hopelessness in their eyes. Victims of one of Saddam Hussein's notorious hidden detention centres.

'Sir, you need to see this,' the message had crackled through an earpiece in Blake's ear.

At the far end of a corridor they'd found a room.

He recalled two of his men standing at the entrance with their rifles poised. The ground had been caked in blood, rusted shackles bolted to the walls. A metal bedframe had been placed in the middle of the room with scarlet-stained leather straps tied to each corner. Two electrical leads with crocodile-jaw metal clamps had been attached to a car battery next to a wooden chair.

Blake had ground his teeth and gripped his Carbine tightly.

'Sir, I've found al-Sadr,' said another voice in his ear. There'd been a pause, filled with static crunch, then, 'He's alive. Just.'

He'd been cowering in the corner of a dirty cell. His body bloodied and bruised. At least they'd reached him before he made it to the hangman's noose, the usual punishment for suspected informants.. He could barely stand, let alone walk so they'd carried him out on their shoulders. The best they could do for the rest of the prisoners was to set them free, smashing open their cell doors as they left.

'I still don't understand why you haven't talked to the prison staff, or the Governor at least,' Blake said, draining his glass and ordering another bottle of Tuscan red.

'You're assuming Rahimi's contact inside Marshside is a prisoner. But until we can prove otherwise everyone in that prison is under suspicion.'

'It doesn't make sense for a prison officer to be involved? Why would Rahimi risk smuggling in a phone for a prison officer?'

'We're not making any assumptions. I take it you don't have a problem with going in?'

'It's what I do. How soon can you make the arrangements?'

'We need a day, maybe two. You won't get much notice.'

'Not a problem.'

'You don't have commitments?'

'No,' said Blake.

'Family?'

Blake finished a mouthful of pasta and wiped his mouth with a napkin. Folded it on his lap. 'No.'

'I thought you might be married, that's all. I don't think I'd appreciate it too much if my husband disappeared in the middle of the night without so much as a goodbye.'

'You're married then?'

'I meant it hypothetically.' Mortensen pushed her plate to one side. She had only picked at her food. 'No one special waiting at home?'

Blake shifted in his chair trying to think of a way to change the subject. 'No.'

'Wedded to the job?'

'Like I said, I prefer to operate on my own. Life's easier that way. Anyway, I don't make great company.'

'I don't think you're as cold as you like to make out.' Mortensen crossed her legs, brushing her foot against Blake's calf. He flinched. 'So which is it, never found love or bitten so badly you've told yourself you'll never love again? I bet it's the latter.'

'Not even close,' said Blake.

'So come on, who was she?'

'Who?'

'The woman who broke your heart.'

The restaurant was filling up and the noise of sociable chatter growing loud. Blake watched an elderly couple greeted by the owner with warm handshakes and kissed cheeks. He made such a fuss of them they must have been regulars. They took a table at the back, near the kitchen. Blake acknowledged their friendly smiles with a nod. They were easily in their eighties, dressed in their finest and still enraptured by each other's company. Blake imagined they'd enjoyed a long and happy marriage.

'Stop being coy,' Mortensen said.

'Can we talk about something else?'

'I was right. There was someone.'

'A long time ago.'

'So how did you manage to let her go?'

'It doesn't matter. Anyway, what about you? You must have plenty of admirers?'

Mortensen feigned embarrassment although the glint in her eye suggested she was pleased by the suggestion. A waiter moved in to clear their plates before she could reply. 'It's complicated. Currently single and enjoying it.'

'Dessert? Coffee?' said Blake.

The waiter stood poised with a pencil hovering over his pad.

'Just the bill,' said Mortensen. She watched the waiter move away. 'Come back to mine for a nightcap.'

'Is that a good idea?'

'Of course.' Mortensen leaned across the table with wide eyes full of innocence. 'We should discuss how we're going to get you into Marshside.'

'Do you ever think of anything other than work?'

Mortensen rocked back in her seat and laughed. 'Come on, let's go.'

SIX

It was a cool night, fresh from the earlier rain. Mortensen took Blake's arm as they walked along the riverbank. Like two lovers on an evening stroll. Her dress accentuated all her best features. Tight in the right places, pinched at the waist and short enough to show off toned legs. They fell into a natural rhythm, matching each other's stride.

They stood side-by-side in the lift up to the third floor of Mortensen's apartment block, staring at their distorted reflections in the polished metal doors. It came to a halt with a gentle bump, and as they slipped out into the corridor, Mortensen gave Blake an encouraging smile.

Her apartment was in darkness. Blake's hand hovered over the light switch but she stopped him, her fingers falling over his.

'Leave them. I like to watch the river at night. It's better in the dark. Sit down, I'll fetch us a drink.'

Blake fell onto a sofa and watched Mortensen float around in her bare feet. She had the poise of a ballerina, her back arched and her toes pointed. As she leaned into a sideboard, the hem of her dress rose high up the back of her thighs.

'Whisky?' she asked, producing a bottle of single malt and two glasses.

Blake caught himself gazing at her thin waist and the swell of her calves. He chastised himself, stood and moved to the window. Somewhere outside a siren wailed and through a break in the cloud a luminous moon appeared.

'Amazing views,' said Blake, as Mortensen handed him a glass filled perilously full.

'Are you trying to get me drunk?'

'Now why would I want to do a thing like that?'

They chinked glasses and Blake took a large gulp, the liquid burning the back of his throat.

Blake noticed for the first time the colour of Mortensen's eyes. Emerald green. They seemed to sparkle in the moonlight, drawing him in. He leaned closer until their heads were almost touching. Her breath on his cheek was warm and sweet. He moved a hand to her waist but Mortensen turned away with a knowing smile. She drifted to the sofa. Smoothed her dress under her.

'Come, I want to know more about you. You're an enigma,' she said.

He sat so their thighs touched, drinking in her perfume, like jasmine on the morning rain. 'What do you want to know?'

'Who is Tom Blake?' she whispered.

He raised the back of his hand to touch her cheek and blinked hard.

He couldn't focus on her face.

Her delicate features swam around her face, lost in a blur. His head felt light and he struggled for breath. He leaned forwards to put his glass on the table but misjudged the distance. It fell to the floor, splattering the carpet.

'Don't worry, it's okay,' Mortensen said, her voice pulsating in his ears.

'I don't feel so great. I need to....' But he couldn't finish his sentence. Searing pain shot through his brain. He flushed hot and cold, a sweat breaking out on his brow. The room was spinning. The brush strokes of an abstract painting on the far wall swirled and merged into a hideous maelstrom of colour.

'You look a little pale,' Mortensen's voice sounded distant, like she was calling to him from the far end of a tunnel.

He heard another voice beckoning him. It was a woman he recognised from a long time ago, buried in the recesses of his memory. But when he turned to look there was no one there.

He tried to speak but the words came out of his mouth only as strangulated noises. He needed air. When he tried to stand his legs buckled. He slumped in a heap on the floor, clattering against the edge of the coffee table.

'Let me open a window.' It was Mortensen's voice but he failed to comprehend her words. 'You'll feel okay in a minute.'

He tried to move his leg, an arm, a hand, but nothing worked. It was like the connection from his brain to his muscles had been severed. His cheek was pressed into the deep pile of the carpet, soft and coarse at the same time. He couldn't see anything other than the weave of the carpet and the tacks that pinned the fabric to the sofa.

His breathing came quick and shallow. 'Help me....' he croaked, his eyes flickering wildly, his pupils wide opals.

Mortensen moved across the room. He heard a rattle of a key turning in a lock and the sounds of the city rush in. The hum of traffic sounded loud after the tranquility of Mortensen's apartment. A salt-crusted breeze washed in from the river, cooling Blake's back.

'Alex?' he groaned.

Darkness was crowding his vision, creeping around the periphery of his sight. A thin, needle-like pulse ticked rapidly in his wrist and under his jaw, quickening as he fought unconsciousness.

And then all hell broke loose.

The door splintered in its frame and the windows flew open. The floorboards shuddered with the weight of heavy boots and screaming voices filled Blake's head.

'Get down! Stay where you are! Don't move!'

Over his shoulder, a table was tossed to one side and a heavy hand grabbed his collar, hauling him over. His eyes opened wide and his jaw fell slack at the sight of a dozen masked men. They wore dark jumpsuits and helmets, balaclavas and respirators concealing their faces. The barrels of twelve Heckler and Koch MP7s were trained on his body.

A boot kicked an arm away from his body. He glimpsed Mortensen by the window where a curtain was billowing. Her arms were crossed, her face unreadable.

'Right, get him up,' a gruff voice barked. Two of the gunmen slung their weapons over their backs and dragged Blake to his feet.

Blake focused on Mortensen's face.

'I'm sorry, Blake' she said. 'Get him out of here.'

SEVEN

Blake woke in the back of a van. His head struck the jagged edge of a wire mesh, rousing him from semi-consciousness, his mouth dry and his brain dull like it had been stuffed with rags. He raised a hand to his temple to check for blood and found his wrists were cuffed. He blinked sweat from his eyes and tried to focus as the vehicle lurched on its axles through a tight corner.

He was inside a cage. Trapped like an animal. The air was a bitter fug of urine and stale sweat. Through a darkened window he glimpsed unfamiliar buildings flashing past in a blur.

They passed through gates in a high brick wall. Came to a halt with a jolt. Boots hit the ground. Two men in uniform threw open the rear doors, grabbed him by the arms and marched him through a walled courtyard. They dragged him into a dreary reception area that smelled of disinfectant, checked his details against a computer, bagged his clothes and inspected his hair for lice.

They made him change into jogging bottoms and a grey t-shirt. White socks and a pair of black shoes with self-fastening straps. Two prison officers with stony faces escorted him through a bewildering labyrinth of corridors of white painted walls, steel gates with solid locks, high ceilings and polished floors. They emerged into a quad formed by the towering walls of the surrounding buildings. It was open to the elements apart from a wire netting that formed a protective ceiling below the second-storey windows. Cameras were mounted on poles and powerful floodlights turned night into day.

The High Security Unit at Marshside was a squat hexagonal building on the far side of the courtyard. Blake sensed the hopelessness as he was led inside.

'Blake, Tom. Remand prisoner. Awaiting trial,' said one of the guards to a man behind a counter.

Cold adamantine eyes drilled into Blake. 'Remand?' He said it like it was a novelty word.

'Recommendation of the Home Office, Sir.'

'Tough guy are you?'

He stepped out from behind the counter and stood eyeball-to-eyeball with Blake. Ramrod straight. So close that he could smell the coffee on his breath. Blake recognised the air of military authority. Maybe a former sergeant major. They tended to end up in places like this at the end of their Army careers.

'Whoever you are and whatever you've done outside, forget it right here. You've just walked into the dragon's den and home to a nastier bunch of bastards you wouldn't want to meet. Unpleasant men, aggressive men who've done unspeakable things and are paying their dues. They're in for the duration and they don't care about life because no one's given them a reason to care. That makes them worse than dangerous. Stay out of their way and don't upset them. Don't share your business with anybody and don't ask them theirs. Do you understand?'

Blake wondered what Patterson had let him in for.

'My domain and my rules,' the officer continued, 'whether you're here for life or waiting for trail. I don't care.'

He drove a tightly-clenched fist into Blake's stomach. A deft blow he didn't see coming. It doubled him over, forcing the air from his abdomen and made his lungs feel like they were collapsing.

'Keep your head down and your mouth shut and you'll get along fine.' He stretched his fingers and rubbed his knuckles.

They passed Blake's shoes through an X-ray machine and shoved him under a security arch. They prised open his mouth and peered under his tongue with a penlight torch. They checked the soles of his feet and the palms of his hands. Just like Mortensen had said. Security tighter than the Bank of England.

His cell was at the end of a corridor alive with night-time babble. Men restless in their beds. Snoring, coughing, chattering and whimpering. Bed frames squeaked and pipework clattered.

There wasn't much to his cell. Brickwork and concrete with just enough room for a metal sink, toilet bowl and a bed fixed to the wall. The door slammed behind him and bolts snapped into their housings. He tried the mattress. The sheet was thin and the blanket coarse but they smelled clean enough. He folded a pillow under his head and lay down. He didn't bother to undress. His eyes were sore and his head still spinning from the effects of whatever Mortensen had slipped into his drink. All he wanted to do was sleep.

It came easier than he'd imagined but was less restorative than he'd hoped. His dreams were filled with vivid images. Rahimi's body laid out on a slab, his eyes wide open. Thousands of flies pouring from a wound in his thigh, filling the room with the drone of sibilating wings. Three women hovering over his body wiped tears from their eyes with the loose ends of their headscarves. Their wailing soared to a crescendo until Blake had to cover his ears.

He woke with a start drenched in sweat as electric lights pulsed into life. He sat up and realised there were no windows and no natural light. The day was regulated by an automated flick of a switch. Under the stark reality of a fluorescent tube, his cell looked even less inviting than it had in the dead of night. And smaller. Barely ten paces long and half as wide. Thick paint slapped on brick walls and a ceiling that was oppressively low.

A metallic clunk followed a short buzz as the lock on the door was released. The cell filled with the sounds of a prison block waking. Shuffling and banging. The chatter of early morning banter and cat calling. Blake swung his feet off the bed and ran his fingers through his hair. Rubbed his eyes with the balls of his hands. The few hours of snatched sleep had done little to revive his senses. Full-consciousness seemed out of reach somewhere in the back of his mind.

The sound of the door thudding open against a rubber stopper caused him look up. He'd expected visitors. Maybe not so soon. Word would have travelled of a new inmate. They'd want to check him out. Put him in his place.

He forced himself to remain seated on the bed. Tried to look relaxed. Calm. If he was going to earn status he needed to set his stall out early. Show no fear. Stand his ground. Let them see he wasn't afraid.

'Where's Ray?'

Blake stared at the diminutive figure who shuffled into the cell. Thinning grey hair fell over his shoulders and his clothes hung limply from his skeletal frame.

'Who are you?' said Blake.

'What are you doing in Ray's room?' If he'd have been standing, the man would have barely reached his chest.

'What have you done with him?' he hissed. 'Cat got your tongue?'

He skulked to the sink, ran a bony finger around the bowl and licked it like a chef tasting a sauce. Smacked his lips. Pondered for a moment looking to the ceiling, then cocked his head as if he'd reached an important conclusion.

'Why did they put you in here?' he asked.

Blake didn't have a cover story. His entry into the prison had been so sudden he'd not had the chance to think it through. No good making one up either. Patterson must have arranged a pretence. He decided to say nothing.

'You don't say much do you?'

'I don't have much to say,' said Blake.

'Ah, it speaks!' The man stepped towards the bed. Leaned in close, nose to nose, violating Blake's personal space. His breath was like sour milk. The man snatched a towel folded on the end of the bed and ran a bristly cheek across it. Held it to his nose and breathed in its fragrance. Put it down and reached for Blake's prison-issue toiletry bag.

'Touch that and I'll break your arm,' said Blake. He tried to sound matter-of-fact. Didn't want to start a fight but had to lay down some authority.

The man pulled back his hand like he'd been burned. 'Think you can touch me? I'll kill you! I'll fucking kill you!' he screamed, his pupils growing large and black. Thick veins pulsed on his forehead. 'I'll snap you like a puppy's neck!'

Blake rose from the bed. Drew himself to his full height and pushed the man away.

'Don't touch me!' the man howled.

'Leave my things alone,' said Blake, shooting a glance at the door. The rest of the block would find out soon enough they had a new neighbour. No good getting them all excited so early in the morning.

'Okay, okay, I'm fine,' said the man, panting.

Blake let him catch his breath, watching his chest rise and fall as he brought his anger under control. It disappeared as quickly as it had flared. 'I meant what I said. I could kill you right now if I wanted.'

He perched on the end of the bed. Turned to Blake and held out a bony hand. His fingernails were long and yellow. 'Name's Walt,' he said.

'Blake,' said Blake, refusing to shake his hand. 'Been in long?'

'Fifteen? Twenty? I forgot. But they're never letting me out. So what's the point in trying to remember?'

'What did you do?'

Walt noticed his hand still hanging in mid-air. He withdrew it with a slight shake of his head and tucked it into his lap.

'Shouldn't go asking people their business. Didn't the guards warn you? No ask, no tell.' He looked Blake up and down. 'They'll like you, you know.'

He gave a phlegmy laugh, reached over and squeezed Blake's bicep. 'Strong too. Do you have kids?' His eyes opened wide.

Blake shook his head.

'Pity. I miss the sound of them playing most of all.' His eyes fluttered shut. 'Chasing around with their chubby arms and pink knees, smelling of talc.'

He licked his lips and wiped a globule of spittle from the corner of his mouth.

'Did you do something to a child?' Blake's blood ran like ice through his veins and revulsion rose from the pit of his stomach. He wanted him off his bed and out of his cell.

'As if they'd let you anywhere near children again, you

filthy nonce.' The voice came from the corridor. A giant with glistening ebony skin filled the doorway. A bleached-blond Mohican brushed the top of the frame. Bulging shoulders and rippling biceps glistened where he'd ripped the sleeves from his t-shirt.

Walt jumped up and cowered in the corner.

'Get back to your dirty little hole,' said the man in the doorway, raising a hand as if to cuff Walt on the back of his head as he scuttled past.

'They found the bodies of six kids in his loft,' he said when Walt had gone. 'Cut out their hearts and livers once he'd had his fun. They reckon he cooked them up and ate them.'

A second man squeezed into the cell. If anything he was bigger than the first. Blue veins ran like the tributaries of a river down the length of muscular arms. His hands, the size of plates, fell at his side. He had piggy eyes set into deep sockets and the skull of a Neanderthal. Round and thick and heavy.

Blake suspected he knew the reason for their visit. Time for an education in the rules. No doubt prison was like the military. It had its own order. And right now the new guy needed putting in his place. Make sure he realised where he stood in the food chain. Right at the bottom.

Only Blake wasn't ready to take a pasting. With only a few days to find out what Rahimi had been up to he was banking on fast-tracking his status application. He stood relaxed, running the scenarios through his mind and plotting his moves.

The cell was cramped and his only exit was blocked. But in his favour the two men in his cell were all vanity muscle. Pumped up on steroids and serious hours in the gym. They looked tough but that didn't make them fighters. Blake had training and experience on his side.

He set himself so that he was comfortably balanced on the balls of his feet, ready to react. He relaxed his hands at his sides and rolled his head to loosen his neck. He made a bet with himself that the white guy would come first, charging like a rhino, all power and no finesse. The Mohican would follow with fists swinging wildly, using brawn over brains.

He waited.

He looked the men in the eye, watching for the inevitable flicker that would signal the launch of their assault.

They stared back but didn't move.

Then the Mohican spoke.

'There's someone wants to meet you,' he said.

EIGHT

They led Blake from his cell and along the corridor with their rubber soles squealing on the tiled floor. Haunted-looking men lining the route fell silent as they passed. Men with abandoned hope in their eyes, more irritated than intrigued by the new arrival disrupting their pointless daily routines.

The Mohican pushed Blake into a cell where a man naked from the waist up was sitting on a bed. He was the size of a bear with a barrel chest and a plump stomach, a man whose youthful muscular frame had been lost to middle-age. His head was hairless, smooth and round, his torso covered in tattoos, elaborately-scrawled words and enigmatic hieroglyphs.

He looked up as if from a trance, noticed Blake and beckoned him in.

'Come,' he said in a low murmur.

The cell was stale with sweat. It was identical to Blake's apart from a table with a melamine top and metal legs. On it lay a gilt-edged bible longer than Blake's forearm and thicker than his fist. It was open at one of the books from the Old Testament.

The man on the bed drew a deep breath and let it go slowly, straightened his spine and stared at Blake with black, impenetrable eyes.

'Are you a killer?' he asked.

'I've not been convicted of anything,' said Blake, 'I'm on remand.'

'Don't lie to me. The wing doesn't take remand prisoners.'

Blake shrugged. What was that accent? He put it as mid-European, maybe Slavic. 'I was caught up in something, that's all. It's a misunderstanding.'

'So you're innocent? Join the club. Everyone's innocent in here, Mr Blake,' he said with a phlegmy laugh.

'You know my name?' said Blake a little too urgently and instantly regretted it.

'I make it my business to know what's going on.'

'Then you have the advantage over me.'

'Dragoslav.'

'You're a Serb?' Dragoslav's eyes narrowed. 'The tattoo,' said Blake, nodding at the man's neck. The emblem was a black scorpion with a barbed tail and pincers poised to strike. Blake knew it from a long time ago but it hadn't lost its power to repulse him. The symbol of the feared paramilitaries who'd operated a reign of terror during the Balkans War.

The Scorpians were the most of brutal of soldiers in a conflict that had plumbed new depths of inhumanity. Torture, rape and mutilation were their weapons of terror. They'd first risen to prominence in the besieged town of Srebrenica, butchering their way to notoriety and slaughtering more than eight thousand Muslims under the noses of United Nations peacekeepers. Their killing was indiscriminate. Men, women and children all suffered at their hands. The foreign correspondents coined the term 'ethnic cleansing' to describe it, managing to sanitise in pithy journalese the horrors Blake had heard about in appalling first-hand testimonies from those who'd survived. He'd been part of a coalition hunter-killer unit made up of British and American Special Forces tasked with bringing as many of the perpetrators to justice as they could find. But in six months they'd located less than fifty men. The rest had vanished back to their previous lives protected by people who either loved them or feared them too much.

To find one sitting an arm's reach away twenty years later but still untouchable was a blow that hit Blake hard.

'A distant memory of my past,' said Dragoslav, touching his neck lightly where the tattoo was fading.

'Were you at Srebrenica?'

Dragoslav replied with an almost imperceptible nod and Blake willed himself to remain calm.

'So you were at the massacre?' His throat tightened and he swallowed hard.

'It was necessary for the future of my country and my people.' His mouth turned up in a malevolent grin.

Blake tried to look impressed, against his instinct to step forwards and throttle the life out of him. 'So how did you end up in Britain?'

'My wife was British. I'm a UK citizen now.'

'Was British?'

'She died,' Dragoslav said without emotion or elaboration. 'Enough questions about me. I'm interested to know about you. Tell me, what's it feel like when you kill?' He steepled his fingers over his stomach.

'What makes you think I'm a murderer?'

'I can see it in your eyes. It's intoxicating, don't you think? That moment when you hold the absolute power of life and death in your hands?'

Blake had been a soldier for most of his life. There were

times he'd had to be a cold and ruthless killer. But only when it was necessary to preserve the lives of others. Never for pleasure. 'I don't know what you're talking about.'

'Everyone is a killer in here. A wing of men who delight in the suffering of others. But let me give you some advice. Trust nobody. Understand?'

'I can take care of myself.'

Dragoslav grimaced. 'I've heard that before. He bled dry before the guards found him.'

'You're trying to intimidate me?'

'There are more than thirty men on this wing. Vile creatures locked up together twenty-four hours a day. What do you suppose they do for amusement? We're one of a kind, you and I. We should be friends.'

Dragoslav rose from the bed with a supple fluidity that seemed unlikely for a man of his size. He padded across the floor and flicked through the pages of the bible.

'Are you a religious man?'

'Not really,' said Blake.

'You don't believe in one omnipotent being who controls our fate and judges our lives?'

'I believe we hold our fate in our own hands.' Blake had formed an early view that life was for living. Live it hard and live it well. But when it was over, it was over. There was nothing else. No heaven and no hell. When it was time to go, there wasn't much religion or a god was going to do about it.

'This book used to give me peace but now, I don't know. I believe true omnipotence comes from being able to decide who lives and who dies. What could be more powerful than that?' Dragoslav looked up from the page, stood still for a moment like he was running an internal dialogue through his head.

'I want to show you something.'

He banged on the door twice with his fist. The Mohican appeared.

'Fetch him,' Dragoslav said, before turning back into the cell and sweeping up the bible.

He laid it on the bed, pulled the table up to the sink and unfolded a face cloth. Soaked it under the tap. With a powerful twist of his hands, Dragoslav squeezed the cloth dry, straightened it out and soaked it again.

The sight and sound of running water reminded Blake of his raging thirst and his throbbing head. He licked his lips. They were cracked and dry.

The door crashed open and a slight figure with terrified eyes bulging from their sockets was thrust into the room, half carried by the Mohican who had an arm across his chest and a hand clamped over his mouth. The Neanderthal was behind them.

'Hemingway,' said Dragoslav. Blake could smell the man's fear.

The Mohican lifted Hemingway off his feet and dropped him on his back on the table so his head fell over the sink. He fought against their attempts to pin him down with erratic twists and jerks. A pathetic plea for mercy escaped from the back of his throat. Not a full-bodied cry but a whimper muffled by the wet cloth Dragoslav draped over his face. It moulded to the point of his nose and cratered over his mouth. His breathing came quick and fast through his nostrils like a steam train building speed. Every muscle in his body went taut.

Dragoslav fetched a bucket from under the sink, filled it with water and held it over Hemingway's head. Slowly he poured a stream of water over the cloth that covered the man's face. It wasn't much more than a trickle, hitting him between the eyes and around his nose. It ran down his neck and drenched his t-shirt. It seeped into his throat and sinuses and leached into his trachea. Hemingway kicked and bucked like a wild stallion, as with each ragged breath, he drew the fluid down into his gurgling lungs. Sensing he was drowning, an uncontrollable panic racked his body and a primeval instinct to survive kicked in. It took all of the strength the two giant men to hold him down.

Dragoslav kept pouring, prolonging the agony, until the bucket was empty. He threw it to the floor and grabbed a handful of Hemingway's hair, hauled him and ripped the cloth from his face. Hemingway sucked in gulps of air. He coughed and spluttered, stalactites of spittle oozing from his mouth.

'First and final warning. Next time I'll take an eye,' said Dragoslav, running the back of his hand along Hemingway's cheek. 'Get your affairs in order by the end of the week or face the consequences.'

Hemingway slumped from the table in a trembling heap and was dragged out of the room. Dragoslav wiped his hands dry on a towel and calmly folded it over a rail under the sink. He smoothed out the creases and checked it was hanging straight.

'Are you familiar with the method?' he asked. 'I'm told it's widely used by American interrogators.'

'So I've heard,' said Blake. He knew all about waterboarding. But the thought of ever using the technique to elicit information sickened him.

He'd seen it used once before, by CIA interrogators at an American safe house on the outskirts of Islamabad when he'd been a guest of a unit of US Navy Seals. They'd arrested a young man, not much more than a boy, suspected of running messages for insurgents. The CIA agents were tired-looking men with blood-shot eyes, thick beards and leathery skin who stripped the boy naked, blindfolded him and strapped him to a sloping wooden board. For three days they repeatedly took him to the point of drowning, using a running hose and a cloth over his nose and mouth until he was ready to confess to just about anything.

It was horrific to watch and produced nothing more than an unsafe confession from a youth barely old enough to shave. Later Blake had questioned the interrogators, intrigued by their reliance on such a seemingly barbaric practice. They explained that carried out correctly the technique brought on a controlled death that could be repeated over and over to great effect. And if done incorrectly? Terminal hypoxia, the brain fatally starved of oxygen, they said.

'The Americans don't consider it to be torture but a legitimate interrogation method,' said Dragoslav.

Blake shrugged as if he didn't hold an opinion. 'So what was that all about?'

'I deal in personal insurance. Hemingway defaulted on a payment.'

'A protection racket?'

Dragoslav sucked in a breath through pursed lips. 'An ugly description. I provide security services.'

'And you want to make me an offer?'

'I have a straightforward proposal. There will be no negotiating or cutting deals. A one-time only offer. For two hundred a month I guarantee you'll not be harmed while you remain with us at Marshside.'

'You're having a laugh, right?'

'Do I look like I'm joking?' Dragoslav's face clouded.

'Nobody has access to that sort of cash locked up in here, surely?'

'Most are sitting on sizeable bank accounts, even if they can't access them while they're inside. And they can always ask for help from friends and family. It's a small price. I expect one payment into a specified account every month. No defaults and no excuses.'

'And if I refuse?'

Dragoslav straightened himself to his full height and stepped up close to Blake so his enormous bulk bore down on him. Blake stood his ground, focusing on a vein in the Serb's neck pulsing with a slow and regular rhythm.

'A one-time offer, Mr Blake. Be careful you make the right decision.'

'I'll pass. Thanks all the same.' Blake turned to leave.

'Maybe I'm not explaining my proposition very well,' said Dragoslav, his cheeks flushing crimson. He pushed past Blake reaching for the handle of the cell door, as if he meant to pull it open and summon some assistance.

It was time to seize the initiative. Three against one in the tight confines of the cell was not a fight Blake relished. He dipped his shoulder and sprang forwards, catching Dragoslav with full-force between the shoulder blades. The Serb's head catapulted forwards and thudded into the steel. His legs buckled and he dropped to the ground.

NINE

Blake held his breath, listening for movement outside the cell. He counted to ten but no one came. Dragoslav groaned and rolled onto his back. Blake could have finished him off. Wrapped an arm around his neck and snapping his spinal cord with a quick jerk of his skull. Game over. But he wasn't a murderer. He needed to make a statement of intent. That's all. To earn some respect, a little status to move freely around the prison without interference. And no better place to start than with the guy running a protection racket.

Dragoslav sat up on his knees, a wounded and dangerous animal. A lump on his forehead was swelling into an ugly bruise. Blake stood back and let the big man haul himself up, watching as he rose unsteadily, swaying from side to side. Dragoslav shook his head to clear the haze behind his eyes.

Blake reminded himself of Srebrenica and relaxed his shoulders.

With a roar, twenty-five stone of fat and under-used muscle shot across the cell. Blake stood his ground. Waited. Let the Serb build up a momentum and at the last moment sidestepped, letting Dragoslav fly into the wall behind, jabbing at his head with a wasp-sting punch as he went.

The Serb spun around, his face red. 'Stand and fight like a man,' he growled.

'You're slow and weak, old man. I doubt you could fight your way through a wet tissue these days.'

He came again, pawing the air with enormous fists, under the misapprehension his size and longer reach gave him the upper hand. But when he drew back his right arm it was with such exaggeration that his intention was hopelessly transparent. He was looking to land a wild right hook that could probably lay a man out for a week. But he was too cumbersome. Too obvious. Blake ducked under his fist and countered with blows to the Serb's torso, pounding the soft tissue of his liver and kidneys through a thick layer of loose muscle.

Dragoslav fell back. Came again. Throwing flailing punches while Blake bobbed and parried.

'You're nothing but a washed-up has-been,' said Blake. 'Without those two heavies out there you're pathetic.'

Dragoslav mumbled a reply. It could have been, 'Go to hell.' It might have been something else. It didn't matter. His bare chest, glistening with sweat, was heaving. He was flabby and unfit and despite his size, no physical match for Blake.

'Come on, is that all you've got?' Blake put on an expression of mock disappointment.

Dragoslav opened his mouth to speak but his words made it no further than his throat. Blake swung an elbow in a looping arc towards the Serb's head. The sharp tip of bone struck his skull like a hammer blow and sent him stumbling backwards. He recovered quickly, wiped the wound with the back of his hand and examined a sticky smear of crimson with disgust.

'You filthy dog,' he said, before launching an avalanche of uncoordinated punches Blake had no difficulty blocking.

As the lactic acid from the exertion seared his muscles, the Serb's arms sagged below his waist, his energy levels temporarily sapped. Blake whipped a sideways kick from his hip striking the Serb's ribs with the power of a baseball bat hitting a home run. He heard the bone crack. Dragoslav ignored the pain. The Serb saw the move coming. He wasn't quick enough to block the shot but managed to pluck Blake's ankle from the air. Twisted and pushed in the same movement and sent Blake sprawling across the floor, the wind knocked from his lungs as he landed heavily on his back.

The Serb was on top of him in a flash, hands grappling for his neck. Hot fingers gripped the cartilage below Blake's chin, squeezing and tightening, pressing harder and harder so Blake could neither swallow nor breathe. The edges of his vision clouded, losing his grip on consciousness. A few more seconds and he would be out cold. A minute more and he'd be dead.

Blake tried breaking the Serb's grip but his hands were vice-like around his throat, his face contorted in a grotesque snarl. In a last desperate attempt to save himself, Blake scrambled for Dragoslav's ears, took a firm hold with his fingers and jammed his thumbs into his eyes. He squeezed for all his life was worth, the soft orbs squelching and deforming under the pressure. Dragoslav howled, released his grip and allowed Blake to buck his hips and roll the heavy Serb away. Blake crawled across the floor gulping for air. Bright lights flooded his vision as he sat gasping with his back against the door, each strained breath a mixture of agony and relief.

The respite was temporary. Dragoslav recovered his senses and stood. His eyes were narrow, red slits. He lunged with a new-found energy, throwing a jab that missed its mark by an inch. Blake snatched his wrist as it whistled past his ear and twisted the Serb's arm until it was almost wrenched out of its socket. Blake kicked him across the room with a foot planted in the small of his back. Dragoslav stumbled, fell against the bed and smashed his face on its concrete base.

'Tell me when you've had enough and we can renegotiate the terms of your deal. Let's say five hundred a month and I won't come back and kick your ass again. I'll give you the details of my account,' said Blake, wiping sweat from his brow.

Dragoslav spat blood on the floor. His mouth was a pulped mess. 'Who are you?' he gurgled through the gap where his front teeth had been.

'Don't worry about who I am. Worry about what I'm capable of.'

'Keep your eyes open because you'll need to be looking over your shoulder for the rest of your life. I guarantee it.'

'Your threats don't wash, old man.'

Heavy, impatient footsteps stomped in the corridor and both men glanced at the door as if expecting it to be thrown open. Dragoslav seized the distraction and threw himself across the cell. Blake turned too late, felt the cold sting of a blade slicing through flesh. A lucky strike that caught him on his bicep a few inches below the shoulder.

He caught Dragoslav's wrist, ploughed his elbow into his nose and slammed the Serb's hand into the brickwork. Dragoslav dropped the improvised weapon with a howl and it clattered to the floor. A razor blade embedded into the handle of a toothbrush he'd secreted under his mattress and palmed when he'd fallen by his bed. Blake kicked it away and glanced at his wound. A deep gash the length of his hand oozing sticky blood down his arm. But the cut was clean. It should stitch up no trouble.

Blake slipped his uninjured arm around the Serb's neck, jumped on his back and squeezed hard, using his free hand as a lever to exert maximum pressure. Dragoslav thrashed and kicked, smashing Blake into the walls. But Blake's resolve only hardened. Through gritted teeth he hung on and, ignoring the agony from the wound on his arm, pulled tighter. It would have taken wild dogs to have dragged him off.

Eventually the Serb's movements slowed and his body went limp. Blake let him crumple to the floor and laid him out along the length of the cell. The Serb's mouth was a gaping mess and his nose bloodied and flattened where Blake had broken it with his elbow. He didn't look pretty but it was nothing that should cause any lasting damage. He'd be off the wing for a few days in a hospital bed. Out of Blake's way. The injuries a warning to anyone else looking to cause the new arrival any trouble. Job done. Almost.

Blake slumped on the bed, letting his heart rate come back under control. His blood-smeared hands were shaking. The after-effects of the rush of adrenaline. It would pass soon enough. Drips from the tap at the sink caught his attention. The steady plip-plop of beads of water forming and falling in a regular beat. Cool, refreshing water. Blake ran his tongue over dry, cracked lips. Jumped up from the bed, stepped over the body and turned the tap on fully. He gulped down hungry mouthfuls, hardly noticing the metallic tinge from the prison's network of pipes. He splashed a handful over his face and the back of his neck, washing away the sweat and blood. Rinsed the wound on his arm, cleaning off the caked blood, testing how deep the cut ran. He made a bandage from a strip of bedsheet, wrapping it tightly around the wound. Grabbed the towel from under the sink and dried his mouth as he turned back towards the door.

It was wide open. The Mohican and the Neanderthal were standing rigid staring at Dragoslav's body, their jaws slack at the horror they saw. Blake followed their gaze to the mess that had been the Serb's face. Splashes of blood stained the floor and the sheets were streaked red. The cell looked like a house of horrors. Blake folded the towel and hung it on the rail.

'Why are you standing there gawping? He needs medical attention. Get him out of here, quickly.'

One man grabbed the Serb's ankles, the other slipped his hands under his arms and between them they half-carried and half-dragged him out of the cell.

The corridor was alive with the sounds of men chatting and grumbling. But a hush descended over them when they saw the beaten, unconscious body of Dragoslav.

'Put him down,' said Blake.

'But you said...' the Neanderthal tried to protest.

'I said put him down.' The look Blake shot him was sufficient to quell the protestation. Blake drew back his shoulders, held his head high and scanned the length of the wing, making sure he caught everyone's eye. A hunter posing with his spoils.

'Is he dead?' someone called out.

Blake scanned the faces but wasn't sure who'd asked. 'He'll live. But he'll be sore for a few days.'

Blake had anticipated the sight of Dragoslav bloodied and defeated would attract a crowd. That they'd all want a close look, to see how he'd vanquished the bully who'd ruled over them with intimidation and fear. But none came. Even laid out cold, the Serb seemed to hold a power over them. For a while, the only sound was Dragoslav's burbling breath as he drew air through his blood-soaked mouth and nose.

Halfway along the corridor one of the prisoners emerged from his cell, a small man with slicked black hair and an eye half-closed in a permanent squint under hooded brows. His footsteps on the tiled floor sounded hollow. When he saw Dragoslav, he broke into a jog, fell to his knees and tilted back the Serb's swollen head

'What have you done? He's half dead,' he said, holding an ear over his mouth.

Blake peered at him through squinted eyes. His arm was throbbing and his head was light.

'Guards! Guards!' the prisoner shouted. He checked Dragoslav's breathing and hunted for a pulse. 'Medics!'

Blake felt as if he was drifting towards the ceiling, looking down on himself from above. His eyes were heavy and there was a dull ache in his back. He needed to sleep. He stepped over Dragoslav's body and headed towards his cell, his steps falling subconsciously one in front of the other. He ignored the calls of alarm from a scrambling force of prison guards. The sound of keys rattling in locks was distant and dull as though he was in the aftermath of a close-quarters explosion that had dampened his hearing. He had only one thought in his head, of collapsing onto his bunk, letting his eyes close and falling into a deep sleep.

Two sharp stabs in his back jolted him back to the moment. A sharp pain between his shoulder blades where two tiny barbs had pierced his t-shirt and attached themselves to his skin just out of reach no matter how far he stretched his arm.

'Stand still!' a voice barked.

A crackle of electricity signalled a jolt of nerve-twisting agony that ran through the length of Blake's body, cramping his muscles and clawing his hands and toes. His teeth clamped down on his tongue and he tasted the sweet, metallic flow of blood trickle down his throat. He collapsed to his knees and, unable to control his muscles, collapsed headfirst, his convulsing limbs dancing to the tune of fifty thousand volts. He imagined his inner organs being cooked and his brain being fried. He fought with consciousness, sensing it eluding him, until his eyes fluttered and fell closed.

TEN

The isolation cell was a cold and damp windowless box with a low ceiling and concrete walls. There was a dirty mattress on the floor and a slop bucket in one corner. Standing in the middle of the room Blake could almost touch both walls at the same time. A light behind a plastic cover never went out making it almost impossible to sleep or to delineate the day. With twenty-four hour artificial light, days and nights were impossible to distinguish. It was enough to drive some men mad.

But not Blake. He was well-versed in surviving isolation, a skill honed from days tucked up in concealed dugouts on observational duties. He'd learned how to combat the boredom by surviving in a trance, like a computer in sleep-mode ready to spring to life at the touch of a button. He kept his mind active by solving imaginary maths puzzles, designing architectural plans for buildings he knew well or challenging himself to list countries and their capitals in reverse alphabetical order.

For the first few hours he'd tried to sleep on the thin mattress but he was sore all over and no matter which way he turned he couldn't find a comfortable position.

He tried lying on his back, with his knees drawn up, but his muscles still fizzed from the electrical charge they'd tasered through his body. His tongue was swollen and tender and his head swam from a lack of food and water.

'You'll be best off in here for a while, for your own protection,' said one of the guards as he'd shoved Blake into the cell.

'I don't need protection,' Blake had protested.

'Trust me, you do. Let Dragoslav and his cronies cool off for a bit.'

'For how long?'

'Depends on the governor. Maybe when the excitement's calmed down on the wing and you're no longer considered to be a danger to anyone else.'

Food was delivered through a horizontal serving hatch in the door. His first meal was an inedible-looking pile of brown mush served on a plastic plate with a beaker of water and a brittle, plastic fork. An evening meal appeared five hours later.

'Hand me your dirty dishes,' said a voice through the hatch.

Blake's tray was snatched away. It was replaced by another that contained a half-full plate of slop and a mug of tepid, milky tea.

'Thank you,' said Blake.

'You're welcome.' The voice sounded familiar.

'What is it?'

'Stew, I think.'

'Another culinary triumph. What's your name?'

'I can't talk to you,' the voice whispered loudly. 'The food's supposed to be punishment rations. Sorry,' it said as an afterthought.

'I've eaten worse.' Blake recalled the countless packets

of Army rations he'd survived on. At least the prison meals were warm. 'My name's Blake.'

'Everyone on the wing knows who you are.'

'I like to make a first impression that lasts.'

'I've got to go.'

'Stay a minute. Please?'

There was a pause. Blake sensed the man on the other side of the door was keen to chat. After all, Blake must be the talk of the block after what he did to Dragoslav.

'If they catch me, they'll throw me in the box next door. I'm Sweeney.' A hand shot through the serving hatch. Blake grasped it. It was warm and calloused.

'I'm going mad in here on my own,' Blake lied. 'It's good to hear another voice.'

'It's not supposed to be a holiday camp.'

'You been inside long?' Blake drank thirstily from the mug of tea. It was warm but not sweet enough for his taste.

'Eight years, nine in April,' said Sweeney.

'What did you do?' Sweeney didn't reply. 'Sorry, I forgot, never ask, right?'

'Can I give you some advice? Be careful who you go around picking fights with.'

'You think I made a mistake with Dragoslav?'

'Some guys you don't mess with. He's one of them. A certified lunatic. You should have kept well clear. You don't know what you've done.'

'He should have stayed away from me. How is he?'

'They moved him to the hospital wing.'

Blake had a recollection of the prisoner with black, slicked back hair running towards the Serb in the cell corridor. Checking to see if he was alive. Feeling for a pulse. He recalled his voice calling for the guards.

'Was it you who came to help him? Called the medics?' said Blake.

'I thought you'd killed him.'

'I did you a favour. All of you. I don't know how many were signed up to that racket but it's over.'

'It's not over,' Sweeney snapped. 'You think just because you've turned up and knocked some heads together that's it? That we'll all just get on with doing our time in peace and harmony? Geezer, were you born yesterday?'

'He's finished. He's a bully, that's all.'

'He's not finished. After this it'll be worse. You humiliated him and when you get back they're going to kill you, for sure.'

'I don't think so.'

'You're a dead man walking.'

'He won't try anything again.'

'You got lucky this time, that's all. But it's not Dragoslav you need to worry about.'

'Those two muscled-up goons? I'm not worried about them. I've cut off the head of the beast.'

'You should be. They're going to catch up with you and then you'll find there's nowhere to run. The screws won't help. Don't think they will. Just watch your back. I've got to go before they send someone to find me. I'll be back in the morning.'

The hatch slammed shut and Blake finished his meal alone, draining the mug of tea and setting the tray at the end of the bed. He eased his aching body onto the mattress and sat with his back resting against the wall staring at the concrete opposite, visualising patterns and pictures in the textured swirls. After a while, he let his eyes close.

He replayed in his mind his arrival in the prison van and of being processed into the high security unit. He recalled in fine detail being led to his cell and the bed with its clean white sheets and pillow. The smell of disinfectant and the sound of water clunking through pipes. He fast-forwarded to the moment he'd had the Mohican and the Neanderthal dump Dragoslav's unconscious body in the middle of the wing. He'd taken a good look at everyone along the corridor. He never forgot a face. Or a name. The trick was simple mnemonics and scanning for three unique features. Three was the most workable number. Any fewer and his memory struggled. Any more and it was too difficult to assess at speed. It might be unusual physical attributes. A hooked nose, crooked teeth, blemishes or birthmarks. He looked at facial shape, lip size and the thickness of eyebrows, tagging each face with a unique name that connected with their features. It was an impressive party trick he'd developed during prolonged surveillance operations.

There had been twenty-four men on the corridor that morning and although he'd not had long, it was a straightforward task to index and file each of them. He shifted and sorted, reinforcing the memory. But something was bothering him. Something that didn't quite add up but that he couldn't put his finger on. The more he puzzled over it, the further it seemed from his grasp.

He replayed the moment he emerged from Dragoslav's cell frame by frame like he was running a roll of cinema acetate through his fingers. He reached the part where he was tasered by the guards and let the memory roll on. He remembered pitching forwards, unable to break his fall as his limbs locked out. The muscles in his neck contracted and forced his head backwards so that he was looking up at a throng of prisoners, jeering and shouting.

He remembered black leather boots with thick rubber soles and navy blue trouser legs. Vibrations of feet through the floor and rapid-response officers in riot gear towering over him, kitted up in dark overalls and full visor helmets, with batons tucked up against clear plastic shields. They were turned away from Blake and facing the other prisoners, formed up into a long line with shoulders tight together and their shields high.

What were they doing?

The guards must have seen the state of Dragoslav and over-reacted. Maybe their panicked arrival had sparked a riot. Blake remembered seeing punches thrown and kicks lashing out, angry voices galvanising into a roar.

But he'd been on the edge of consciousness. Nothing other than his own personal world of hurt had registered at the time. He'd tried to focus on something, anything that would stop him slipping away. His eyes had fallen on an object in the middle distance. A fleeting glimpse of something like a shadow created by the headlights of a passing car. He'd forced his eyes to open wide, trying to fix on it, to make some sense of what he was seeing. But the harder he'd tried to hold onto consciousness, the further it had slipped away. His eyes had closed once, twice and by the third time his lids fluttered shut, his conscious brain had shut down.

ELEVEN

Blake had been sleeping fitfully when the serving hatch crashed open and a tray with gloopy porridge in a bowl was thrust in. He rolled off the mattress but the hatch had slammed shut by the time he reached the door. Sweeney was his only source of information about what was happening on the wing while he was locked-up in solitary confinement and Blake regretted missing him.

He made sure he was waiting by the door when his lunch tray arrived. He grabbed it with both hands.

'Sweeney?'

'What?' an unfamiliar voice replied.

Blake recoiled to his bed with his tray and sat poking the food with a plastic spoon wondering about Sweeney's absence. When he failed to arrive with his evening meal, Blake feared there was something wrong. Maybe the guards had discovered he had been talking to Blake and punished him?

The following day Sweeney returned.

'Blake, are you awake?' he hissed through serving hatch.

Blake scurried across the dirty floor and sat with his ear

near the opening. 'Where have you been? I was worried I'd got you into trouble.'

'We've been in lockdown.' Sweeney took Blake's dirty dishes and passed him a bowl and a mug of tea. 'They didn't let us out all day yesterday.'

'Why?'

'One of the lads has gone missing.'

'Escaped?'

'The guards have been going berserk. It happened the night you attacked Dragoslav. His cell was empty when they called lights out. There's no sign of him anywhere.'

'Who is it?'

'Guy called Ricky Vaughn.'

'He's a thin guy, right? Boxer's nose, brown eyes? I saw him.'

'When?'

'After they sent in the riot squad. I was on the ground. I'm sure I saw him before I passed out.'

Blake was convinced of it. A dark figure noticeable because he was standing away from the rioting throng. His back against the wall, hands tucked into his pockets. He peeled away from the others, inching his way towards a staircase while the guards' attentions were otherwise occupied. He made it up the steps in four large bounds and disappeared.

'What's up the stairs at the end of the corridor?'

'The canteen. There're some pool tables and a bit of gym equipment. Not much else.'

'Is there a way out?'

'Not unless he had the keys to a dozen gates. And even if he made it out of the unit, he'd still be inside the perimeter of the main prison.'

'So the chances are he's still inside the High Security Unit?'

'I suppose,' said Sweeney. 'Why do you care so much?'

'I'm curious. Aren't you?'

'I guess. Look I'd better get going. I'll talk to you later,' said Sweeney. The hatch clattered closed and Blake heard his soft footsteps disappearing.

It wasn't long after Sweeney had brought breakfast that a key rattled in the lock and the cell door was heaved open. Two guards appeared with their jackets buttoned up and caps pulled low over their eyes. They clamped cuffs on Blake's wrists and shackles around his ankles.

'What's going on?' Blake asked.

No reply.

They marched him out of the cell, up two flights of stairs and into an interview room with a table in the middle and two chairs screwed to the floor.

'Sit down, you've got a visitor,' said the first guard, leading him to one of the chairs.

'Who?'

'Who're you expecting? Your mum?' the second man sneered. 'It's your lawyer, stupid. You're on punishment, so you don't get to see anyone else.'

They cuffed him to the chair and clamped his ankles to the legs, before retreating to the back of the room, standing to attention with their eyes fixed ahead. Blake flexed his hands against the cuffs. A mesh-covered window overlooked the exercise yard he'd walked through a few days earlier. It was the first time he'd seen natural light in days and his eyes were drawn to the sky even though it was a grey, gloomy morning. There were splatters of rain on the window and thick cloud enveloped the roof of the red-brick building opposite. He longed to be outside. To taste a fresh breeze and feel the rain on his face.

His attention was snapped back to the room when Alex Mortensen strode in looking every part the smart lawyer. Hair tied back, white blouse buttoned to the neck and a dark-coloured trouser suit. She had a briefcase in one hand and walked with a swagger that bordered on arrogance. He thought she was overplaying it a bit but the guards didn't blink. Her shoulders were back and her chin was up. She shot the guards such a look of disdain that Blake couldn't help himself but smile. He was loving the performance. She hadn't even looked him in the eye. It was like he wasn't there.

Her briefcase landed on the table with a thud and she was unfastening the catches when she noticed the guards still standing at the back of the room. She stopped mid-catch and coughed.

'Thank you, gentlemen,' she said with barely disguised impatience. 'You can leave us now.'

'Ma'am, we can't leave you on your own with the prisoner.'

'Are you being serious?'

'It's against regulations.'

'Firstly, stop calling me 'ma'am'. Secondly, screw your regulations. Lawyer-client privilege means this man is entitled to speak with me in private. So leave. You've cuffed him pretty well, so he's not going to be much of a threat is he? You can wait outside. I'll call if I need you.'

The guards looked at each other and shrugged. 'Your choice. We'll be the other side of the door. If you need us, shout.'

'Very authoritative,' said Blake, as the men closed the door behind them.

Mortensen sat, closed the briefcase and placed it on the floor. 'God, you look like crap,' she said.

He'd not seen a mirror in days but imagined how he

must look. A face ravaged by several days' beard growth and his hair a tangled mess. He'd not washed so figured he didn't smell all that great.

'Thanks, you still look pretty amazing. What's in the briefcase?'

'Anything I could find to steal from the stationery cupboard,' she smiled. 'Some paper, a notebook and some pens.'

'Nice touch.' Mortensen's arrival had lifted Blake's mood more than he'd expected. Her suit jacket was pinched in at the waist and tailored trousers emphasised her long legs. Her eyes sparkled green, picking up a hint of the gemstones she wore around her neck.

'I didn't get to say thanks for a great evening the other night,' he said.

'Just doing my job.'

'Seducing and drugging me? And I thought we were on the same side.'

'I didn't seduce you. As I remember, you were the one making all the moves. Besides, we had to make your arrest look convincing. I might have encouraged you back to the apartment but you didn't take much persuading.'

'And the drugs?'

'We couldn't have had you putting up a fight and making a scene.'

'Or we could have worked through a plan together.'

'We thought your reaction would be more genuine if the arrest came as a surprise. Think of it as helping you get into character.'

Blake shuffled on the hard, wooden chair but found it difficult to find a comfortable position with his arms and legs immobilised.

'How are you settling in?' Mortensen asked after a strained silence. 'All the other boys being nice to you?'

'What do you think?'

'I hear you have your own cell.'

'It's better than that, I have solitary confinement. But sadly, as you can see, and probably smell, the washing facilities are in short supply.'

'Solitary confinement?'

'It's a long story.'

'So you've not made any progress on the case?' she asked.

'It's been a bit tricky while I've been in a punishment cell.'

'I thought you were used to working covert ops and keeping a low profile? You've only been in five minutes. What did you do?'

'I needed to acquire some credentials, so I took down the toughest guy on the wing. Anyway, he was trying to tap me up for some kind of protection racket.'

'And there was me thinking that blending in and living with the enemy was your field of expertise.'

'Don't start lecturing me on how to do my job. I needed to establish a status otherwise no one's going to take me seriously. Now I've made my point, I can talk to a few people about Rahimi. What about you?'

'The lab came back with details of the phone you found under Rahimi's floorboards.'

'And?'

'The SIM card's interesting. A number of calls were made from it from inside Marshside.'

'Not the phone?'

'We think Rahimi smuggled in the SIM on its own,' said Mortensen.

'But he still needed a phone to use it.'

'And that still leaves the question of why he bothered

smuggling it out again, doubling his chances of being caught. None of it makes a great deal of sense.'

'So I need to crack on with finding out who Rahimi was associating with,' said Blake.

'That's the other thing. I've checked and he didn't have clearance for the High Security Unit.'

'So what the hell am I doing in here?'

'It's where the calls were made from. The Americans are adamant.'

'They've made a mistake,' said Blake.

'I don't think so. They were very precise about the location. Once they'd determined the number the calls were made from, they were able to accurately track the device. And it was in the HSU, no doubt. You need to concentrate on finding out who made the calls.'

'How?'

'I thought you'd be able to use some of your mind-control stuff,' said Mortensen.

'What are you talking about?'

'Come on, I know all about it. Coercive hypnotism, right?'

A trickle of sweat ran down the back of Blake's neck, soaking into his collar. The room was uncomfortably warm. 'You've read the files,' he said. 'You tell me.'

'You developed it to help in the interrogation of hostile witnesses. I know that much,' said Mortensen. 'I also know that Echo 17 specialised in the extraction of information from high value targets from inside non-friendly states and that your role was invaluable. Unique even. The files say you can bend people's minds to your will. Is it true?'

'Within reason. It can certainly help to loosen tongues.'

'Show me. Put me under,' said Mortensen, leaning forwards in her chair and resting her arms on the table. She looked at Blake with wide, doe eyes.

'Tempting right now but no, it wouldn't be ethical.'

'Don't be like that. How are those cuffs?' she said, nodding at his wrists. 'Tight enough? I bet you could make the guards remove them if you wanted to. Shall I call them?'

'This isn't a game.'

Mortensen was already on her feet. 'Guards!' she shouted.

'Alex, don't do this,' said Blake.

The two prison officers crashed through the door at the same instant an ear-splitting alarm, like an air-raid siren, sounded. A red light screwed into the ceiling flashed and radios clipped to the officers' belts crackled with distorted shouts. They stopped on the spot, torn between the alarm and Mortensen's cries for help. They looked first to Blake, then finding he was securely restrained, glanced at Mortensen. Finally their eyes were caught by something outside the window.

'Bloody hell,' said Mortensen, her jaw falling open.

The arm of a crane had been extended over the top of the outer wall of the prison. Beneath it an open-sided bucket dangled from a hook with a figure dressed in black overalls standing inside. His face was hidden by a balaclava. The bucket came to rest on top of the wire ceiling above the exercise yard and the man inside produced an industrial-sized pair of wire cutters. He leaned out and cut open a circular section, peeling it open with gloved hands. He shouted into a radio handset he snatched from his hip, and the pulley rope snapped taut. It lifted the container frac-tionally off the mesh and lowered it through the hole. Within a few seconds it had vanished from view, plunging to the ground below.

Nobody in the interview room moved. Four pairs of eyes were fixed on the drama outside, their brains unsure what to make of it. A shouted command over their radios jolted the two guards out of their inaction.

'Stay here with them,' the first shouted over the alarm. He turned and sprinted out of the door, slamming and bolting it behind him.

'Ma'am, the prison's going into lockdown. You'll need to stay here for the time being while we resolve matters,' said the second guard.

'What about him?' She nodded at Blake.

'He stays too. I'll keep him cuffed to the chair,' he said. 'You'll be safe, don't worry.'

Blake said nothing. He sat back in his chair and tried to make himself comfortable. Mortensen moved to the window.

'Ma'am, please sit down.' The guard stepped towards her but the look she gave him stopped him in his tracks.

The crane arm was fully extended at a sixty degree angle over razor wire that topped the perimeter wall. As they watched, the lifting cable snapped taut and the bucket reappeared with three people inside. Two prisoners had joined the balaclava-clad man in their distinctive regulation grey jogging trousers and t-shirts. The taller of the two had his arm clamped around his chest and a knife against his neck. The shorter man stood wide-eyed and motionless as the container swung up into the air.

Sirens sounded in the distance as the bucket rose. It ascended high above the roof of the adjacent buildings, swung over the top of the wall and dropped out of view while the alarms continued to ring at an ear-splitting volume.

'Hey, buddy, any chance of loosening these cuffs?' Blake gave the guard an encouraging smile. He was losing precious minutes to act while chained to the chair. The chances the escape wasn't somehow connected with Rahimi's murder were too slim to contemplate.

'Stay where you are, Blake. We'll get you back on the block as soon as we can but try to relax, okay?'

'Okay,' said Blake. 'I understand.' His head dropped and the guard turned his attention back to the window. 'Maybe I could talk to you privately for a moment?'

'I said relax, we'll get you back onto the wing as soon as we can.'

'I really need to speak to you. It's important.'

'For God's sake, what is it, Blake?' A frown clouded the guard's face.

'It's a bit awkward. I don't really want to say in front of the lady.'

The guard stepped closer, his hand on a baton in his belt, wary of the tricks the prisoners played. He knew to keep his distance even from someone secured to a chair. His was particularly cautious of Blake's head, knew the damage a skull could cause used as a weapon. A flex of the neck muscles was all it would take.

'What is it?' he said with a huff.

'I've got a really bad itch,' said Blake.

'What?'

'Top of my leg. It's driving me insane.'

'For God's sake.' The guard leaned forwards, arm outstretched, his eyes never leaving Blake's face.

At the moment his fingers brushed past Blake's hand, he snatched the guard's wrist like a viper pouncing on a mouse. 'Sleep,' said Blake, pulling the guard closer.

The man's eyes fluttered and closed. His shoulders relaxed and his head fell to one side. Blake spoke slowly and deliberately as if from a well-rehearsed script, his tone soft. His words were designed to burrow into the core of the guard's subconscious and reach the deepest depths of his psyche.

'You're going to do exactly as I tell you. I'm not a genuine prisoner so there's nothing for you to fear. I need your help, so you'll follow my instructions without question or hesitation. Do you understand?'

The guard nodded. Mortensen had turned from the window and was watching intently with her head tilted to one side.

'Still sceptical?' said Blake.

'It's really as easy as that?'

'When you know what you're doing. I don't normally work with an audience but needs must. Now grab your briefcase, I'm going to get us out of here.'

'Is he okay?'

'He's fine.'

'And he'll do anything you tell him?'

'I can't make him do anything that would inherently put him in danger but I can override his conscious decisions to an extent. He'll stop if I try to overstep his natural boundaries.'

'Which are what?'

Blake shrugged. 'Who knows? We're all different, different compulsions and different urges. No two people's boundaries are the same.'

'So what now?'

'Time to get out of this chair.'

Blake instructed the guard to release his cuffs and the restraints around his ankles, then stood and stretched his cramped muscles.

'And your next trick? A rabbit out of a hat?' said Mortensen.

'You said you wanted to see what I do. Now you know.'

A sudden silence. Someone had cut the alarm although the red light continued to flash.

'Did you recognise the men who escaped?' asked Mortensen.

'Only one of them. The tall guy with the knife was on my block. I didn't recognise the other one.'

'Name?'

Blake was certain it was the same man he'd seen disappearing during the riot. The prisoner who'd been missing for the last two days. Even from a distance he recognised his build and his flattened nose.

'Ricky Vaughn,' he said. 'I saw him on the morning they put me in solitary. Now come on, we need to get out of here.'

On his command the guard unlocked the visitor's door and Blake and Mortensen followed him into the corridor.

'Quickly, there's someone we need to pay a visit to,' said Blake.

TWELVE

It was turning out to be a bad day for Jim Mullins. He'd left his wife sitting at the breakfast table clutching the letter that had turned their lives upside down. Now he wondered if he should have stayed. They'd sat for a while lost in their own thoughts, that single sheet of paper between them like a hideous pustule. What was he supposed to have said? That everything was going to be fine? The toast had remained untouched in the silver rack and their mugs of tea had eventually gone cold. He'd made uncertain claims about the advances in modern medicine, partly to ease her concerns but mostly to reassure himself. He didn't dare think of a life without her. He'd never be able to cope. He didn't even know how the dishwasher worked. Margaret was one of life's copers, there in everyone's hour of need. After twenty five years of marriage he'd never seen anything shake her so badly.

He'd convinced himself he'd be no use at home. She'd be better off calling her sister. She'd have the right words to say. That was the thing about women. They were born with an empathic gene most men lacked. It would be better all-round if he carried on as normal. Besides, the prison wouldn't run itself. He had staff to lead and prisoners' welfare to consider. She was still in her dressing gown when he'd left, her eyes red and her cheeks streaked with tears. He'd kissed her on the head and told her he'd be home by seven. Then he'd left. Like any other working day.

As he'd driven, he couldn't shake the image of her sitting at home, ashen-faced, staring at the words and numbers as if by reading the letter over and over she could change their meaning. There would have to be an operation, of course, and treatment to poison her insides and make her sick. He knew that much. He'd wondered if she'd lose her hair. He'd pictured her wearing one of those brightly-coloured scarves.

He'd driven on auto-pilot, barely registering his route and had arrived at his office looking and feeling weary. His face was hollow and grey. He'd tried to busy himself with the routine of the morning, checking e-mails and signing off the overnight reports but his heart hadn't been in it. He'd tried to concentrate on the final details of a parole board report but hadn't found the focus.

When the alarm sounded, it was a welcome distraction. He looked up from his desk as if expecting someone to come bursting in with news. The wailing siren cut through walls and ceilings accompanied by the distant sound of pounding boots and strangulated cries. He couldn't remember if there was a scheduled drill but he wasn't unduly worried. He was confident his officers knew what they were doing. The procedure was standard for any incident. Prisoners would be locked in their cells and the jail would go into lockdown with the control room remotely sealing doors and gates.

Mullins prided himself on his record. There'd never been a break-out or any significant trouble in the five years he'd been governor. He suspected a minor incident which, under the rules he'd implemented to tighten security, necessitated the alarm to be raised. He'd know soon enough. Protocol dictated the duty control officer would contact him as soon as the details could be verified.

Realising the futility of trying to continue with his report while the sirens were raging in his ears, he swung his chair around to face the window behind. His usual view was of the exercise yard and the barred windows of the cells opposite, a scene he normally viewed with a certain satisfaction. But not that morning. He stood slowly and stepped closer to the glass. The bright, yellow arm of a crane spanned the top of the perimeter wall and was lowering an open capsule into the grounds. As it landed on the protective wire screen above the yard and a figure in dark overalls leaned out with a pair of wire cutters, Mullins snatched up the phone on his desk. He punched in a three-digit number and was connected instantly to the control room.

'What the hell's going on?' He tried to keep his voice even. No point panicking until he knew the facts, but he heard his words waver as he spoke them.

'Guv, there's an attempted break-out.'

'I can see that.'

'Sir, we also have a hostage situation.'

They were the words Mullins had dreaded to hear. 'An officer?'

'No, one of the men on the HSU's taken another inmate.'

'Right,' said Mullins with relief. 'Names?'

'We're still trying to find out.'

'And the situation, is it contained?' There was a pause on the other end of the line. 'Please tell me we have this under control.'

'We can't get to them. Not without putting the hostage in danger. One of the prisoners has a knife and he's making threats.'

Mullins turned back to the window as the bucket was winched up through the mangled wire ceiling. He had an obscured view of the three men inside but couldn't make out their faces.

'Have the police been notified?'

'On their way, Sir.'

The capsule swung into the air and over the top of the razor-wire capped wall, before disappearing from view.

'Shit!' Mullins slammed down the phone and immediately his mobile phone rang. He checked the number and dumped the call.

He knew the standard procedure. His next step should have been to alert the Home Office. They'd want the identities of the two escapees and an assessment of their danger to the public. It would determine not only the level of response but how much to reveal to the press. The recriminations and inquiries would come later. It wasn't something to worry about for the time being.

Mullins slipped his glasses from his nose and rubbed his eyes. He wondered if the day could get any worse. He dialled another number on his desk phone and reached the senior warden on the HSU.

'I need the names,' he said, as calmly as he could. It suddenly felt very warm in his office, the collar of his shirt tight around his neck.

'Ricky Vaughn, Sir,' he said. Mullins picked up a hesitancy in his voice.

'Are you sure?'

'Absolutely.'

'Who else?'

'A guy from A Block. Elias Pitts.'

'Christ, what a mess.'

Mullins hung up, rocked back in his chair and tried to compose himself. He needed to think carefully about his words before making the next call. He'd just become the first governor in the prison's thirty year history to have allowed a successful break-out. Not a record that was going to do his career much good. Someone silenced the alarms. He took a deep breath and picked up the phone.

THIRTEEN

Blake and Mortensen found the governor's office at the top of a staircase pungent with the aroma of disinfectant and polish. A brass plaque engraved with Jim Mullins' name had been screwed to the door. Blake knocked and walked in without waiting for a reply. He left the prison officer on guard outside.

Mullins glanced up. He was on the phone and stopped speaking mid-sentence. Mortensen pushed in front of Blake fearful his appearance unwashed and unshaven in his prison uniform might provoke some alarm. She flashed an identity card in a leather wallet.

'Sorry for the intrusion, Governor.'

Mullin's left hand had already disappeared under his desk, reaching for a panic button. It was no surprise. Blake couldn't have looked any less like an MI5 agent. His clothes were dirty and dishevelled and his knuckles grazed and bloodied.

'Please don't do anything rash,' said Mortensen. 'If you put the phone down, I can explain.'

Mullins took the receiver from his ear and looked at it as

if he'd forgotten he'd been on a call. 'I'll call you straight back,' he said, hanging up.

Mortensen pulled up a chair. Blake remained at the back of the office, leaning against a row of metal filing cabinets.

'MI5?' Mullins' eyes narrowed. 'Did you know this break-out was being planned?'

'We're investigating another matter but it could be connected,' said Mortensen. She crossed her legs and placed her hands in her lap.

'Tell me what you know about a man called Javid Rahimi,' said Blake. 'You employed him as a cleaner.'

Mullins threw up his hands in an exaggerated gesture of exasperation. 'We have lots of ancillary staff. I don't know them all. Why?'

'He was a political refugee from Iran.'

'So?'

'Rahimi was found dead a few days ago,' said Mortensen. 'We think he'd been murdered.'

Mullins fell back in his chair deflated, like a balloon pricked by a pin. 'How?'

'Poisoned, possibly because of something that happened in Marshside. We can't elaborate on the details but Blake's been inside the HSU trying to establish the circumstances.'

'On whose authority?' Mullins' tone hardened.

'I'm sorry, we had to keep you in the dark to make sure his arrival raised no suspicion.'

'Look, we have to assume the break-out was linked with Rahimi's death. It's vital we get as much background on the men involved,' said Blake. 'We need details of their convictions, names of their associates and everything else you have on record about them.'

'I can't give out that information. Not until I can confirm who you are.' Mullins reached for his phone.

'I don't suppose this escape is going to look great on your record, is it? Of course, if you were to help us recapture of these men, that could go some way towards mitigating what's happened. I'm sure the inevitable inquiry will take that into consideration,' Mortensen said.

Mullins withdrew his hand from the phone and put his fingers to his lips. He studied the two agents, his eyes moving from one to the other as if he was working out whether he could trust them.

'The men you're looking for are Ricky Vaughn and Elias Pitts,' he said at last, rising from his desk. He approached Blake who stood to one side and let him open a drawer in one of the filing cabinets. He pulled out two cardboard files. 'Vaughn's your main concern. You might have met him in the HSU?' He peered at Blake through finger-smudged lenses.

'What's he's in for?'

'Murder and armed robbery. It was a well-documented case in the press.' Mortensen raised her eyebrows, encouraging Mullins to continue. 'He was the mastermind behind a jewellery raid in central London,' said Mullins, sitting back at his desk and opening the file. He smoothed down a sheet of paper pinned inside the front cover. 'It ended in a shoot-out with police at a farmhouse in Wales.'

'I remember it,' said Mortensen. 'Remind me of his background?'

'He grew up on an East London housing estate. His mother's an alcoholic. He has a brother and sister, both from different fathers. His criminal career began when he was around thirteen with some low-level drug dealing, cannabis mostly but there was nothing significant until he was caught dealing steroids at a gym where he'd developed some talent as a boxer. He could have made something of himself there. By all accounts he had some talent in the ring but he became involved with a gang with some serious form for assault, robbery and firearms offences. At some point they came up with an idea to rob a jewellers in Bond Street. It was supposed to be a one-off big-time hit that was going to fund their early retirement.

'Four of them stormed the shop just before closing time, dressed in boiler suits and ski masks and armed to the teeth with handguns and semi-automatics. Vaughn was the ring-leader. They held the staff hostage, forced them to open display cabinets and safes and when they were done wiped the CCTV footage. Then they walked out of a back entrance with several million pounds worth of gemstones, gold and silver stuffed in holdalls.

'The alarm wasn't raised for nearly four hours when one of the shop workers managed to free himself but by then the gang had split their spoils and vanished. They should have got clean away but someone couldn't keep his mouth shut and word started to spread among the criminal underworld. Eventually someone coughed a name to the police and after that it didn't take them long to piece together who was responsible. They picked them up one-by-one until there was only Vaughn left.

'They tracked him to Wales where they think he was lying low before attempting a ferry crossing to Ireland. He found a remote farmhouse, broke in and murdered the elderly owners in their kitchen. The alarm was raised by a postman who was concerned when he saw the post piling up. Two police officers from the local constabulary who went to investigate were shot dead by Vaughn on the doorstep, and when armed response teams were scrambled, there was a long stand off. Three more officers were wounded and Vaughn was only finally apprehended when he'd spent all his ammunition.'

'What about his hostage, Pitts?' asked Blake.

Mullins closed Vaughn's file and opened the other. 'I take a special interest in our inmates in the HSU but Pitts was in the main wing so I don't know so much about him. He's serving eight years for fraud, so in many respects he couldn't be any more different than Vaughn. He's Oxford-educated and a banker by profession but lost a lot of money in 2008 during the global financial crash. Not only was he made redundant but discovered that many of his investments were worth next to nothing. That's when he became wrapped up in a sophisticated international pump-and-dump fraud scheme.'

'What's that?' asked Mortensen.

'With the money he had left, he and a number of associates invested heavily in worthless penny stocks, often taking control of the companies involved. By announcing fictitious business ventures and mergers they were able to artificially bump up the share prices, then dump their stock. Tens of thousands of smaller investors lost millions while they creamed off massive profits.'

'And Pitts was housed in the main prison?' asked Blake.

Mullins nodded. He ran a finger along a sheet of paper in Pitts' file. 'He's been with us for three years.'

'And the prison and the HSU are operated completely independently?'

'Absolutely,' said Mullins.

'And there's no way inmates in the two blocks could have any contact with each other?'

'Security in and out of the HSU is incredibly tight, as I'm sure you've seen for yourselves,' said Mullins.

'So if the HSU prisoners couldn't get out and the inmates in the main block couldn't get in, how did Ricky Vaughn manage to take Elias Pitts hostage?'

'That's a very good question.'

FOURTEEN

The thudding clunk of bolts being slid into place heralded Blake's return to incarceration. It was a sound that set his nerves on edge and made him wonder why he'd argued so hard to be allowed back onto the wing. Standing in the middle of his cell, the walls closed in. The block remained on lockdown and the frustrated screams and angry banging from inmates furious at their prolonged imprisonment carried through the thick walls. The window, with bars cemented into the brickwork above the head of the bed, served only to tease him with temptation of the freedom beyond.

He tried to find distractions. Firstly he washed, rinsed his stubbly face and the back of his neck, lathered his hands and rubbed the dirt from his forearms. He really needed a shower and shave but he had to make do. He ran wet fingers through his hair, flattening it where he could feel tufts standing on end, and dried with a thin towel. He hauled himself up to the window, and tried to snatch a glimpse outside but saw only the top of a wall and a patch of cloud-splattered sky. He dropped to the floor and dragged his body through enough press-ups and sit-ups to make his muscles weak, then collapsed on the bed.

The mattress was thicker than the soiled and lumpy makeshift bed in the punishment cell, and smelled clean by comparison. The sheets were unsoiled and the pillow full enough to support his head. He stretched out his legs, kicked off his shoes and lay staring at a patch on the ceiling where the paint was flaking.

They'd bullied Mullins into letting Blake back into the High Security Unit but he'd agreed only to a twenty-four hour window. It was hardly long enough to make headway into Rahimi's death but it was the best deal they could hope for in the circumstances. Mullins had wanted Blake thrown out of the jail immediately, fearful of allowing an MI5 operative into the HSU with the liability of his identity being discovered. If the inmates found out, they'd string him up, he'd warned them, and he wasn't prepared to risk it. But Mortensen had been most persuasive, flirting and flattering to win him over, promising the service would clear Mullins' name with the Home Office and ensure no disciplinary action would follow for the escape of two prisoners under the noses of his guards.

It was late afternoon when the lockdown was finally relaxed and the cell doors unlocked. Blake followed a stream of prisoners filing their way up a flight of stairs and joined the back of a queue for food in the canteen. Blake was pleased to see Sweeney standing behind a stainless steel serving counter, his black, gelled hair glistening under unforgiving lights. He was ladling meat and gravy onto plates from metallic bowls.

'So you're back,' he said to Blake, passing him a plate under a heat lamp.

'For now.'

The canteen was alive with the murmur of insignificant

chatter. Groups of men were sitting around tables eating, talking and laughing, their relief to be out of their cells palpable. No one made eye contact with Blake, so he found an empty table in a corner and tucked into his meal with the relish of a man who'd not eaten for three days.

He glanced up when a tray clattered onto the table and Sweeney swung himself into a seat opposite with lithe energy.

'How is it?' He nodded to a fork that was halfway to Blake's mouth.

'Okay,' said Blake.

'So you missed all the excitement.'

'The break-out?'

'It was a-maz-ing.' Sweeney elongated the word so that it sounded like three. 'Apparently they came in over the wall with a crane. Can you believe it?'

'I saw it, from the interview room. I was meeting my brief.'

'So? What happened?'

Blake gave a blow-by-blow account of the escape. 'You must have heard about it being planned?'

'Uh-uh,' Sweeney shook his head. 'Nothing. Not a peep.'

'Tell me about Vaughn.'

'Not much to tell.' Sweeney shrugged. 'Thinks he's better than the rest of us. Nobody's sad to see him go.'

'What's he in for?'

'Armed robbery. He fancied himself as a player but there's not much going on up here.' Sweeney tapped his forehead with two fingers. His ragged fingernails had been chewed down beyond the tips of his fingers. 'Mind you, they say he took down a few coppers when they caught him, so he can't be all bad, eh?'

Sweeney pushed away his empty plate and dug in his

pocket for a pouch of tobacco. He rolled a skinny cigarette, lit it and exhaled a vapour trail of smoke.

'What about the guy he took hostage?'

'Elias Pitts?'

'Know him?'

'Yeah,' Sweeney said with a knowing grin. 'Some guy from the main wing.'

'So how did Vaughn get to him?'

'Maybe he was already inside the HSU?' Sweeney sat back in his chair, folded an arm across his chest and let Blake puzzle it out.

'But how? The security around here's tighter than Fort Knox.'

'Not for everyone. Not for a librarian, say.'

'I don't understand.'

'Pitts was in charge of the library. We get to visit once a week. Didn't they tell you? It's a very popular service,' Sweeney said with a conspiratorial wink. 'And as the prison librarian he had certain privileges, like being able to move around the different wings to restock their books.'

'So he's the one prisoner from outside who's allowed in?'

'The only one.'

'So what's he like?'

'Don't know. Never met him. None of us are allowed in while he's changing the books. He always supervised and we're always locked out. Supposed to be for his own protection. He's some kind of hotshot banker who got caught with his fingers in the till. Good bloke though.'

'Why'd you say that?'

Sweeney shot a glance over his shoulder and waited for one of the prison officers to pass. 'He was our bagman,' he said, grinning from ear to ear and then breaking out into a chesty laugh when he saw Blake's confused frown.

'A courier?'

'You wanted it, Pitts could get it for you. For a price, you know.'

'He was smuggling stuff in? How?'

Sweeney crushed the remnants of his cigarette under his heel, picked up the butt and dropped it onto his plate. 'We leave requests in the books and a week later the stuff arrives. He leaves it hidden on the shelves.'

'What sort of stuff?'

'Snout mostly but smack if you want.'

'Phones?'

'No problem. He could get you pretty much anything you wanted.' Sweeney leaned across the table. 'And now he's gone which is a complete bummer.'

'But you said he was always supervised. So how did he manage to get the gear in?'

Sweeney shrugged. 'You ask a lot of questions.'

'I'm curious,' said Blake, holding Sweeney's stare. 'That's all.'

'I don't know, mate. As far as I'm concerned he got it, no questions. Reckon one of the screws must have been in on it but, who cares? Right, washing-up duty calls.' Sweeney stood and swept up his tray. He was halfway across the canteen when he turned back to Blake. 'You know, Vaughn's not done us any favours you know,' he said.

After the meal, most of the inmates remained on the upper floor, watching television, playing pool, table tennis or cards. A few of the younger men were lifting weights. Some drifted away to make calls from the payphones mounted on a pillar. Blake sat on his own, observing the others for a while. When he was certain no one was watching, he slipped back to the cells.

The doors were all open but the corridor was deserted.

He walked lightly, carrying his weight on the balls of his feet, counting the cells off on his right. Vaughn's was almost exactly halfway along the corridor. It was a mirror image of his own with the same stainless steel sink, toilet bowl and concrete bed set against the side wall. The sheets had been pulled roughly over the mattress under a woollen blanket while a greasy, brown dent cratered the centre of a pillow at the head of the bed. A vague hint of disinfectant and the odour of another man's sweat hung in the air. One of the fluorescent bulbs flickered and strobed and a stream of burnt amber flooded through the window at the top of the far wall, signalling the departure of the late afternoon sun as it faded beyond an unseen horizon. A toothbrush and paste were lined up on the edge of the sink, next to a bar of soap crusted with dried foam. Against a wall by the door was a square-topped wooden table where a book and an empty mug had been set. The book was a novel by Dostoyevsky, wrapped in a protective, clear plastic cover. On the inside first page, Blake found a faded blue stamp identifying it as belonging to HMP Marshside. The pages had turned brown and stiff like baking paper and gave off a musty smell as Blake flicked through them with his thumb. He turned it over, smiling at Vaughn's choice of reading matter. He wondered if 'Crime and Punishment' was Pitts' idea of a joke. But there was no obvious communication inside, so he set it down and turned his attention to the rest of the cell.

With one hand he lifted the mattress, pulled back the sheets and ripped off the blanket but found nothing. He checked under the bed and shuffled around the room tapping the walls with his knuckles, checking for any hollow sounds that might reveal a cavity.

Next he turned his attention to a number of pages ripped from magazines stuck to the wall above the bed. They were mostly pornographic images of surgically enhanced women pouting at the camera with sultry eyes and arching backs. The centrepiece was the image of a sports car parked in a harvested cornfield in front of a rising sun. Below it, a key fob decorated with a blue and white chequered BMW emblem hung from a lump of blue putty. Blake grabbed it, weighed it in his hand and puzzled at why a prisoner would keep a car key in his cell. It sat comfortably in his palm, beautifully weighted and designed. Typical of German engineers to extend their ergonomic skills to the key fob, he thought. It was about six centimetres long with two silver buttons on one side. Blake turned it over and noticed a catch which seemed to serve no discernible purpose. When he pressed it, a plate opened with a click. He flipped it up with one finger and found the miniature keypad and LCD screen of a cleverly disguised mobile phone. With the nail of his thumb, Blake held down the green call button and the screen flickered to life. A message on the display flashed up: 'Please insert SIM'.

'Bingo,' said Blake to himself, powering the phone down and slipping it into the pocket of his trousers.

He barely registered the sharp blow that caught him at the back of his neck as he was turning to leave. He legs collapsed and his vision blurred as his brain shut down. The last thing he saw was the cold, hard floor rushing up to meet him.

FIFTEEN

A doctor checked his watch, noted the time and snatched a clipboard from the end of the bed. He bit on his lower lip and nodded his satisfaction at the notes. The man lying motionless before him was lucky. Blake appeared to have suffered no lasting damage but was unrecognisable. His face had blown up like a ball, discoloured by a vibrant patchwork of purples, blues and reds. His eyes were swollen closed, his lips split open and there were cuts across his forehead, cheeks and chin. The bruising had spread down his neck onto his chest and arms, leaking from black into all the colours of the rainbow like ink spots spreading through blotting paper. After ten years at the prison hospital, the injuries were familiar to the doctor, the contusions and abrasions consistent with a serious physical beating. Remarkably there were no broken bones or internal organ damage.

Blake's breathing came in rasps, slightly out of time with the metronomic pulse of the machine he was plugged into recording his vital signs. A colourless tube looped into his arm from a bag of fluid suspended above his head. The doctor moved around to the side of the bed and checked

Blake's pupils, peeling open each eye and dazzling him with a penlight torch.

Blake stirred and winced. He tried to shift his weight but his muscles screamed that he'd be better off remaining still. His mouth was dry and his head was pounding. He tried forcing open his eyes but could only see through narrow slits. Everything around him glowed white and, for a confused moment, he wondered if he'd died. Only the throbbing ache that ran from his legs, through his torso and into his arms dissuaded him of the idea. Slowly his vision came into focus and he saw he was in a narrow room painted white. There were no windows or furniture other than the bed in which he lay but the room seemed to be filled with people staring at him.

'You're awake. How're you feeling?' the doctor asked. He had a bald, domed head and a stethoscope draped over the shoulders of his white coat. He was leaning over Blake so closely he could make out pimples on the doctor's cheek and the whites of his eyes tinged yellow against his ebony skin.

'Sore,' Blake whispered, the word rising from the back of his throat. He struggled to remember what had happened to him. He wasn't sure he was still in the prison.

'You're lucky,' said the doctor. 'Nothing broken. I think you'll live.' He smiled and straightened up.

'I don't feel lucky,' said Blake.

'Given the beating you took, I'd say you're very lucky indeed.' Blake remembered being in Vaughn's cell and the mobile phone that looked like a key fob. 'I heard they had to drag them off you.'

'I don't remember...'

'Any nausea? Dizziness?'

'No.'

'That's a positive sign but to be sure I'd like to get an

MRI scan. You've taken a number of blows, possibly kicks to the head.'

'That won't be possible.' Jim Mullins stepped into Blake's line of sight from behind the doctor.

'Governor, there's a high probability...'

'I said that won't be possible,' Mullins raised his voice to cut off the doctor. 'I want this prisoner prepared for transfer as soon as possible.'

'I have to protest. There could be any number of complications we don't know about until we get a scan.'

'In which case, I'll find another doctor and you can start looking for a new job. I want him out of here.'

Mullins and the doctor stood toe-to-toe, facing each other down.

'He needs at least forty-eight hours more bed rest before we even contemplate moving him,' said the doctor.

'He's got twenty-four.'

For a moment it looked like the doctor would protest, then thought better of it. 'Then that's your decision and on your head,' he said as he shepherded the nurse from of the room.

Mullins waited for the door to close before turning to Blake. 'I warned you this would happen. They nearly killed you.'

'Who?'

'Dragoslav's men. Who do you think? You were followed to Vaughn's cell and they found you alone. Fortunately, two of my officers noticed they were missing. Like the doctor said, they had to be dragged off you.'

'I didn't hear them coming. I should have been more careful.'

'Damn right, you're a liability. I knew this would happen if they found out about you.'

'They didn't. It was retribution for what I did to

Dragoslav, I'm sure of it. I promise they have no idea. I humiliated their boss while they stood outside and let it happen. It was their way of evening the score and I was careless. It won't happen again.'

'That's right, because by tonight you're out. I can't put my officers in any more danger. I won't have it on my conscience.' Mullins pulled a phone from his jacket and tossed it onto the bed. 'Call your people and make the arrangements. We'll provide an ambulance but after that you're on your own.'

It was dark when they came. Two porters in short-sleeved shirts arrived just after three in the morning, threw on a light and woke Blake with a start. He'd been in a deep but restless sleep, his head full of nightmarish visions, until an adrenaline shot hot-wired his heart.

'What's going on?' he grumbled, briefly unable to make sense of his surroundings.

'Time to leave, mate,' said one of the porters pushing a wheelchair. He grabbed a linen bag from the seat and threw it at Blake. 'Get dressed.'

The doctor who'd examined Blake followed the porters into the room. His cheeks were shadowed by stubble and there were bags under his eyes. Blake looked for a name badge but saw only red and blue ink stains above a pocket where he'd kept his pens.

'I apologise for the sudden intrusion. Governor's orders,' he said, striding towards the bed. 'Let's get you as comfortable as we can.'

He set down a kidney-shaped dish and picked out a syringe and a vial of clear liquid.

'What is it?' asked Blake, his voice hoarse.

'Something to help with the pain.'

'No more drugs.'

'It's only a little morphine. Honestly, it will make your move a lot more bearable.'

'I said I don't want it.'

The doctor shrugged and dropped the syringe back into the dish. 'Your choice.'

Blake struggled to sit up, gritting his teeth against the agony of movement. He opened the linen bag and found his old clothes laundered and pressed. He swung his legs out of bed, letting his feet drop onto the cold floor. He tried reaching the ties that held his surgical gown in place but his arms were stiff and uncooperative.

It took a twenty minute effort to finish dressing with the porters' help. Then, determined to show some independence, he insisted on making it to the wheelchair unaided. He fell into the seat and waved away a blanket they tried to drape across his legs. It was humiliating enough to be wheeled out without being wrapped up like a geriatric on a day out to the coast. They took him past a nurses' station lit up by the glow of a desk lamp and into a service lift panelled in stainless steel.

They descended two floors into a vehicle bay heavy with diesel fumes where an ambulance was waiting with its engine running. A fresh-faced paramedic stepped forwards, guided Blake into the back of the vehicle and made him lie down on a stretcher.

With a degree of effort, Blake hauled up his legs and lay flat, allowing the paramedic to secure him with two straps across his chest and thighs. He pulled them tight, maybe a little too tightly, so Blake was immobilised. It was all part of the plan, he told himself, fighting the claustrophobia of being able to move only his head, hands and feet. The worst part of it was a sense he had no control over what was happening to him or where he was being taken. The arrangements had been made by his former unit commander and he trusted Harry Patterson with his life. He took a deep breath and reminded himself Patterson had it all under control and there was nothing to worry about.

The paramedic pulled the doors shut and took a jump-seat as the ambulance rolled forwards. It slowed to negotiate a series of security gates and then picked up speed, accelerating away hard from the prison with a siren blaring. Blake exhaled a long breath and let his shoulders relax. He had no regrets about leaving HMP Marshside. His eyes fell closed and he fantasised about taking a warm shower, drying with soft towels, and enjoying a bottle of cold beer with freshly baked pizza. Soon the comforting tendrils of slumber began to wrap themselves around his mind as his conscious thoughts melded into dreams.

He was jolted awake as the ambulance bumped through a tight turn that sent it rolling on its soft suspension and pinned Blake's bruised arms against the straps. He howled in pain but his screams were lost amid the screech of tyres and the whine of the engine being thrashed. The paramedic had braced himself with one hand on the stretcher and another on a cabinet. He was staring out of a window wide-eyed and tense. Blake struggled against the straps biting into his arms as a knot of panic tightened in his stomach. What the hell was going on?

Things progressed from bad to worse in a millisecond. The wheels squealed under the heavy load of braking and the ambulance slewed across the road. Thin rubber tyres burned and shredded, leaving dirty black trails across the asphalt. In the back, packets, boxes and plastic tubes flew into the air, rising like seeds scattered on a gentle breeze and Blake sensed the vehicle listing. It pitched further and further towards its tipping point until there was a moment of weightlessness before the five-ton, out-of-control lump of metal crashed down in a spray of sparks on its side. The paramedic's body was thrown across the cabin, his arms and legs sprawling in all directions. An appalling scraping sound was accompanied by the acrid stench of burning metal.

The ambulance came to rest amid the hiss of ruptured radiator pipes. The siren slurred, faded and stopped. Blake was suspended on his side with his aching muscles bearing the strain of the straps, the pain temporarily dulled by adrenaline. There was carnage below him. The paramedic was lying in an awkward heap, semi-conscious and groaning with a bloody gash across the side of his head. He was covered in detritus dislodged from cupboards and cubbyholes. Blake tried shouting for help but the words choked in his throat. Not that he expected anyone to hear his cries. At that time of the morning it was unlikely to be anyone around.

But he was wrong. He heard the rumble of tyres, the murmur of an engine and heavy footsteps. Two, maybe three people approaching the stricken ambulance.

'Help!' he called. He stopped struggling. Lay still to listen.

Someone tried the handle of the back doors, now horizontal to the ground. They rattled and popped. The sound of someone forcing their way in. Blake's spirits lifted. He arched his neck to see but as the doors creaked open he was blinded by a powerful beam of light.

'Get down! Don't move!' a voice screamed to no one in particular.

Two figures scrambled over the debris of medical equipment behind shafts of white torchlight that tunnelled through a swirling pall of smoke filling the interior. In the gloom Blake saw the unmistakable shape of a Heckler and Koch MP5 sub-machinegun, a torch integrated into the barrel of the weapon and a finger poised over the trigger.

The gunman's face was hidden behind a ski mask. He levelled his weapon at the paramedic's head while a second man approached Blake, slung his weapon over his shoulder and with a flick of his wrists released the straps holding Blake to the stretcher. Blake fell onto the floor that had once been the side of the ambulance, his weight crumpling onto the legs of the paramedic.

'Time to get out of here, sport,' a gruff voice said, his accent muffled through his mask. He hauled Blake up by his collar.

Trust Patterson to send in the boys from the Regiment to add a sense of drama, thought Blake with a smile. A little over the top but a nice touch.

Blake limped his way into the street towards a black Range Rover Sport with tinted windows. Its headlights were blazing and its engine running. Between the two soldiers, he was half-dragged and half-shoved towards the car.

'Get in, quickly!' the first soldier shouted, pushing him through an open rear door.

Blake perched on the middle seat, the cream leather creaking as he settled in. The two troopers joined him on either side. A third man who he realised had been covering the rear of the ambulance hopped in beside the driver. His door had barely closed before they took off to the fanfare of a throaty V6 roar.

They headed away from the crash scene with impolite speed, their seats punching them in their backs. Nobody spoke. The only sound over the road noise was the laboured breathing of the three soldiers rasping through their masks. They sat with their weapons locked and loaded on their laps.

Blake twisted to look out of the rear window. The ambulance was a mangled wreck, lying on its side and straddling the road with its blue lights still pulsing. The carriageway was littered with the shards of metal and plastic wrenched from the vehicle as it had skidded across the road.

'What the hell happened back there?' Blake asked.

The Range Rover slowed as it turned into a back road, assuming a more respectable speed that wouldn't attract attention.

'Your driver was an idiot.' The man behind the wheel caught Blake's eye in the rear-view mirror. 'I thought they were supposed to be professionals?'

'You ran him off the road?' asked Blake.

The two assault troopers in the back with him had pulled off their masks. The man on his left ran a hand through a crop of sweat-soaked black hair. He checked his MP5, unclipped its magazine and handed the weapon and ammunition to the soldier in the front seat to stow in the foot well.

'They were only meant to pull over, not crash the bloody thing,' said the driver, a cold fury in his eyes. Blake understood his anger. He could see it should have been a straightforward job, jeopardised by the ambulance driver's inability to control his vehicle when confronted with a Range Rover trying to force him to stop. Now there was a mess to be cleared up and questions to be answered.

'So where now?' Blake asked. No one replied.

He didn't recognise anything of the network of streets and couldn't tell if they were even heading north or south. Empty offices and shops flashed past. Traffic was light apart from the occasional black cab and the odd early morning delivery van. Eventually they pulled into an ugly housing estate where high-rise tower blocks rose into the amber-tinged night sky. They slowed to a crawl, passing a children's play area behind wrought-iron railings. The driver stopped in a residents-only car park beneath a high-rise block.

And suddenly Blake knew exactly where they were. It was a location he knew well. The car had barely stopped when the rear door was thrown open from outside.

'Hello, Blake,' said a voice he wasn't expecting to hear.

SIXTEEN

'You look terrible,' said Mortensen, giving Blake the once over.

'It's good to see you too,' Blake replied, easing himself out of the car. It was the twilight hour between the dead of night and the start of the new day but Mortensen looked fresh and alert. Her eyes sparkled and her skin had a rosy glow, as if she'd just stepped out of the shower. She thumped the tailgate twice to dismiss the vehicle and marched into a leafy pocket-square with mature oaks and a neat lawn enclosed by a wrought-iron fence. She halted abruptly in the middle of a sweeping path.

'Patterson said to wait here,' she said. 'Don't ask me why we couldn't meet at the office.'

'Because he knows it brings me out in a rash.' Thames House, the headquarters of MI5 since the late 1980s, was an unobtrusive building on the corner of Millbank and Horseferry Road, overlooking Lambeth Bridge on the north bank of the Thames. But Blake refused to step inside. 'It's full of stuffed shirts and Oxbridge toffs,' he said.

'Like me, you mean?' She wrapped her arms around herself and stamped her feet to ward off the chill.

'I'm guessing King's, Cambridge?'

Mortensen gave Blake a wry smile. 'Wrong colours. I'm a dark-blue girl through and through. Lincoln College, actually.'

'As if to prove my point. Come on, this way.' Blake headed for a densely overgrown tangle of shrubs had overrun a nearby flower bed. With his feet sinking into the damp earth, he cleared a path through the branches to reveal a steel door set into a low, concrete building hidden by vegetation. The walls were a dirty algae green and the door defaced by scrawls of faded graffiti. Blake grinned as if he was a magician producing a dove from thin air. The door, as he had expected, was unlocked. The handle was stiff and the hinges rusty but it opened wide enough for them to squeeze through.

'Come on, you don't want everyone to see, do you?'

'What is this place?'

Mortensen stepped into a narrow hallway with a low ceiling. It was illuminated by the flickering light of an ancient fluorescent bulb. The air was stagnant and damp, the grey concrete walls stained by rivulets of water that had accumulated in pools on the floor.

'A nuclear bunker. A legacy of the Cold War. It's rather cool, don't you think?' said Blake.

'It's a bit grim.'

'It was supposed to have been used by Government officials if there was a nuclear strike on London. It would have been a command and control centre but since the thawing of the East they've forgotten it's here. Patterson requisitioned the key from the Ministry of Defence and now it's a useful meeting point away from prying eyes and ears.'

Blake pulled the door closed and headed for a set of steps that spiralled below ground. Harry Patterson was waiting for them in an airless round room. He was pacing up and down with his hands stuffed in his trouser pockets. Metal plates on the heels of his expensive brogues tapped out a rhythm on the hard floor. His mousey hair, receding at the temples, was sleep-ruffled and there were dark bags under his eyes.

'Everything okay?' he asked, watching with only mild concern as Blake hobbled down the stairs, his battered body stiff and his face a patchwork of coloured bruises.

'A few aches and pains. Nothing that won't mend.'

'He was attacked when he returned to the cells,' said Mortensen. 'The Governor reckons he's lucky to be alive, let alone to suffer no lasting damage.'

'I wouldn't worry about him too much, Alex. He has extraordinary powers of recovery.' Patterson had seen Blake put his life and body on the line more times than he could care to recall. 'It'll take more than a few bruises to keep him down. So, what progress?'

'You know about the escape, I presume?' said Blake.

'Alex briefed me and besides, it's all over the news. What's the significance?'

'I think one of the guys who escaped was Rahimi's contact on the inside.' Patterson raised an eyebrow. 'His name's Ricky Vaughn, an armed robber serving multiple life sentences for murder. I searched his cell and found a mobile phone missing a SIM card. My bet is he was using the SIM we found at Rahimi's flat to communicate with the Iranians.'

'Rahimi was smuggling the SIM in and out of the High Security Unit? How?'

'Through the second escapee, a guy called Elias Pitts,' said Blake. 'He was the prison librarian and the only Category A prisoner who had access into the HSU. It gave him a unique opportunity to operate a smuggling racket. Mostly he was dealing in tobacco and cannabis but

I was told he could lay his hands on most items, for a price.'

'So there are two of them involved?'

'Pitts is innocent collateral, a means for Vaughn's escape and an easy hostage. He's a former banker serving time for fraud. I don't suppose he even put up any resistance.'

'So assuming he's dumped Pitts somewhere, what's Vaughn's next move?'

'It depends on the deal he cut with the Iranians. It seems logical to assume that his Iranian contacts organised the logistics of the escape, which means whatever he was offering was worth the trouble.'

'The crane was hired by a bogus building firm, paid for in cash,' said Patterson. 'It was picked up by a guy called Whittaker on a fake driver's licence. We've got a description but to be honest it's so vague it matches a quarter of the population of London. Witnesses say there was a gang of four, including the crane driver. They disappeared in two stolen cars, both found burned out. Forensics are going over them but they don't hold out much hope of pulling anything useful from either vehicle. Whoever it was knew what they were doing and covered their tracks.'

'So what's our next step?' asked Blake. 'What about Vaughn's gym?'

'The Met sent a couple of officers to speak with the owners and we've put surveillance on it but nothing yet,' said Mortensen.

'I'll go in,' said Blake, 'see what I can dig up. I bet there's someone there who knows what's going on.'

'My thoughts exactly,' said Patterson. He pulled a slim paper file from a briefcase and passed it to Blake. It contained a single sheet of paper with an address, brief background notes on the gym and a list of names. Clipped to it were a dozen grainy images shot on a long lens of men walking in and out of the building. 'Some of the characters we suspect have connections with Vaughn,' Patterson explained.

'I'll get up there straightaway, sign myself up,' said Blake, tucking the file under his arm.

'You certainly look the part. Get back to me as soon as you have anything,' said Patterson.

Blake touched his face under his eye where the skin was purple and swollen. He was sporting cuts on his cheek and forehead. At least it would give him credibility at the gym. He turned for the stairs and had taken three steps when Patterson called after him.

'How are you two getting on, by the way?' Blake stopped in his tracks. 'Alex is one of the agency's rising stars, you know. You're lucky to be working with her.'

'I work alone.'

'I need the two of you co-operating. The PM's spitting feathers. It's bad enough it took the Americans to intercept those calls from Marshside. The breakout's added a whole new level of complication. There's real pressure coming from Downing Street. We're all under increased scrutiny. I've promised them we can deliver a result, but the deal is that you have to make it work with Mortensen. Is that clear?'

'I work with people I trust, Harry. You authorised her to have me drugged and arrested at gunpoint.'

'It was in your best interests, Blake,' said Mortensen.

'And Sir Richard personally asked for your involvement,' added Patterson. 'Let's get on with it shall we? You need each other. You bring different sets of skills. Work out a way of getting along, and quickly.'

Patterson unclipped his briefcase and pulled out Blake's Browning Hi-Power nine millimetre with two ammunition clips. Blake begrudgingly stepped back into the room and snatched the gun. He checked the chamber was clear, snapped a clip into the handgrip and loaded a bullet into the breach. The other clip went into the back pocket of his trousers, the Browning into his waistband behind his back.

'I'm serious, Blake. Cut her some slack.' But Blake was already halfway up the stairs.

Mortensen caught up with him as he reached the upper hallway. She followed him through the reinforced steel door, emerging into the park under a lightening sky.

'I thought I was doing the right thing, Blake,' she said.

'You should have talked to me about getting into Marshside.'

'Okay, I get it. I'm sorry. It won't happen again.'

'Damn right it won't. From now on, I work on my own.'

'You heard Patterson; he wants us to work together.' Mortensen was struggling to keep up with Blake's long strides.

'Fine, that's exactly what we'll tell him. Don't worry, I'll give you a glowing report.'

'Don't patronise me, Blake. I know what this is about.' They reached a deserted main road and stopped on the pavement. Blake scanned both ways looking for a taxi.

'Really?'

'Your pathetic masculine ego. I've put a dent in it because you thought I was trying to seduce you. Not used to women saying no, is that it? Can't they usually resist the green eyes and the silky charms?'

'That's what you think this is about?' He spat the words out with venom, staring at Mortensen with narrow eyes and flattened brows.

'Close to the mark, aren't I?'

'You're not even in the arena.'

A black cab trundled towards them, an amber light shimmering on its roof like a beacon. Blake shot out his arm.

'Where are we going?' Mortensen asked, climbing in behind Blake as the car pulled to a halt.

'*We're* not going anywhere. I'm going to Vaughn's gym. You can please yourself.' Blake gave the address to the driver who swung the cab around.

'Come on, Blake, we need to work this out. Can we start over?'

Blake settled into his seat and stared out of the window at the dull grey streets zipping past. Despite everything he enjoyed Mortensen's company. The prospect of spending more time in her company was appealing. His head told him to accept her apology but his heart remained stony. He knew he was acting like a petulant teenager and blamed it on his male pride. He came to a decision, took a deep breath and was about to speak when Mortensen's phone rang. She held a finger up to stop him as she plucked the mobile from her pocket.

She listened for a few minutes and frowned. 'Are you sure?' She checked her watch. 'Okay, we're on our way. We should make it by late morning. Lunchtime at the latest.'

'What is it?' asked Blake as she hung up.

Mortensen held the phone in her lap, staring at it with thin lips. 'That was Patterson. He's just picked up a message from Scottish police. A family was abducted at gunpoint last night. They took the husband, wife and two young kids.'

'What does that have to do with anything?'

'Forget Vaughn's gym, we need to get up there as soon as possible.'

Mortensen leant forwards in her seat. 'Sorry, change of plan, driver. Can you get us to Biggin Hill airport as soon as you can?'

SEVENTEEN

A Cessna Mustang was prepared and waiting when Blake and Mortensen arrived at the airport, its engines idling with a low whine. They buckled into cold, leather seats and watched the pilot going through a pre-flight check-list.

'We have a provisional slot for take-off in five minutes,' he said, turning in his seat. 'The weather's looking fine so we should make Oban in a little over an hour.'

A few minutes later they rolled to the end of the runway and paused momentarily before the engines roared and the aircraft accelerated into a steep take-off. As its nose lifted, Blake's blood drained into his boots and his head swam. Through the narrow portal windows they watched a patchwork of fields and ribbon roads disappearing while weak, auburn rays of light from the early morning sun poured into the cabin. They banked hard right through a veil of low cloud and swiftly reached a cruising altitude of 30,000 feet. Blake stretched out his legs, tilted back his seat and closed his eyes, his body relaxing into the cushioned leather.

He was woken an hour later by Mortensen shaking his arm. They were passing snow-peaked mountains that rose up with ice-crystal caps sparkling like glitter balls. Below, the ink-blue waters of an icy-loch were looming closer as the Cessna descended through wisps of altocumulus. They bumped down on a short airstrip and rolled up to an arrivals hall with a corrugated tin roof adjacent to a rudimentary control tower.

A hire car was waiting for them. Mortensen took the keys and jumped into the driver's seat. She checked her watch, fired up the engine and pulled away, waiting until they were out of sight of the rental agent before flooring the accelerator. They stopped an hour later at a roadside filling station where they grabbed a stale sandwich and metallic-tasting vending-machine coffee. They ate sitting on the bonnet of the car, filling their lungs with the clean Scottish air.

'How much further?' asked Blake.

'We should make Skye by late morning. I spoke to the senior investigating officer while you were asleep and warned him we were on our way.'

'Did he tell you what happened?'

'A neighbour raised the alarm. She saw everything, apparently. Two men arrived in a dark-coloured 4x4 some-time between eight-thirty and nine last night.'

'Two men?' Blake raised an eyebrow.

'That's what he said.'

'Descriptions?'

'Not yet.'

'What about the family?'

'Benjamin and Sophie Pitts.'

'Pitts?'

'Benjamin is Elias' brother. He's three years older. They've got two young children, Ellie and Charlie. The girl's eleven, the boy's eight. They've lived on the island for about six years.'

Blake fixed his gaze on a patch of rock on a distant mountain slope. 'Do they have a theory for the abduction?'

'I had the distinct impression they're completely in the dark. I got all the guff about following a number of lines of inquiry.'

'But they know about Elias escaping from Marshside?'

'They're not convinced the two incidents are connected.'

'Fair enough. So how was the copper you spoke to? Co-operative?'

'He was okay, a detective superintendent they've sent from Inverness. Wasn't too happy about our involvement but what do you expect? I'd be the same if they'd sent someone up from London to trample all over my case.'

'Trample?'

'You know what I mean. Just trying to see it from his perspective.'

'It sounds like the sooner we get there, the better. Let's go. This time I'll drive.'

They found the house off a narrow track in a desolate spot exposed to the elements, overlooking the Sound of Raasay. It was an unremarkable building constructed in a traditional style with white rendered walls and a slate roof surrounded by ragged fir trees and scrubby fields. A steep driveway led into a gravelled courtyard packed with police vehicles and a bustle of activity. A constable with ruddy cheeks posted at the top of the drive stopped them as they approached. Mortensen flashed her identity card. 'We're here to see the SIO,' she said.

'You'll need Detective Superintendent Douglas. He's down there,' the PC pointed in a vague direction towards the house and ushered them through.

Blake parked alongside a mobile incident van where uniformed officers were mingling with white-suited crime scene investigators. From the far side of the courtyard, a scraggy figure in a pinstriped suit and heavy overcoat watched them. He combed his fingers through fine, grey hair and sauntered over as they spilled out of the car.

'Ms Mortensen? We spoke on the phone earlier,' he said with an outstretched hand. Mortensen took it and noted his firm shake. 'Superintendent Torquil Douglas. It's a long way for British Intelligence to travel. What am I missing?'

Mortensen ignored his question with an apologetic smile. 'This is my colleague Blake.' The two men exchanged a cautious nod. 'We need to know what happened last night.'

The detective peered down his aquiline nose as Blake regarded him over Mortensen's shoulder. His face was grey and creased, the skin sagging from under his eyes and cheeks as though the muscle had wasted away and allowed gravity to take hold. It gave him a melancholic countenance. Not a man for many laughs, Blake thought.

'I can't tell you much more.' Blake struggled to tune into his thick brogue. 'The emergency call was made late yesterday evening. The house was empty when the first response team arrived, and the back door was wide open.'

'Any sign of a break-in or a struggle?'

'The door's intact so we think the family let them in willingly. There's nothing to indicate any violence and nothing seems to have been taken from the property either.'

'Other than the family,' said Mortensen.

Douglas gave her a wan smile. 'Of course, other than the family.'

'Who reported the abduction?' asked Blake.

'The woman next door.' Douglas nodded towards a second

house about twenty metres away. It was built in a similar style but closer to the cliff and in a depression in the ground so from the courtyard only the upper floor and roof were visible. 'She saw what we think was a 4x4 pull up at around eight thirty. A short while later two men marched the family out of the house at gunpoint. They were driven off in the car they arrived in.'

'Is she sure? It must be as dark as Hades here at that time of night?'

'Security light.' Douglas pointed above the door at the back of the Pitts' house. 'Lights it up like Christmas.'

'Did she give you a description?'

'They were both white, one taller than the other, both wearing dark clothing. She's helping with a photo-fit but that could take a little while.'

'What about the car?'

'Dark-coloured, possibly blue or black. She didn't get the number plate but she thinks it was a new model.'

'Can we see inside?' asked Mortensen.

Douglas shrugged. He dug his hands into his pockets and trudged towards the house with Blake and Mortensen trailing behind. As they reached the door, they stepped aside for two crime scene investigators carrying clear, sealed plastic bags containing an assortment of objects neither Blake nor Mortensen could make out.

'See for yourself, no sign of a forced entry.' Douglas indicated to the doorframe as they passed through.

'You think they knew their attackers?' said Mortensen.

'You mean was it Benjamin's brother? I don't know. This is a quiet island. Crime is low and folks don't tend to keep their doors locked. The intruders could have let themselves in. We're keeping an open mind.'

The entrance led into a kitchen where the worktops were cluttered with plates, pans and cooking utensils, as though someone had been in the middle of preparing a meal. Blake was struck by the bitter stench of burnt food.

'The pans had boiled dry and whatever was in the oven was burned to a crisp,' said Douglas.

In a room that led from the kitchen, an oblong table was set for two and a bottle of wine had been opened. On the other side of the room were two faded sofas, a television on a grey stand and toys strewn across a patterned rug in front of a wood burning stove, a few embers still glowing faintly through the carbon-stained glass. A staircase coiled up behind the chimney breast and light flooded in through a window overlooking the cliffs and the bay beyond. A mantelpiece was crowded with ornaments and an assortment of photographs in frames. In one, a smiling couple peered into the room with faces fixed in wedding-day grins. Others showed the children at various ages, from birth to school.

The image that caught Blake's attention was a group shot. He stepped over dolls, toy cars and assorted coloured plastic bands, to look more closely. It was framed in dark wood behind a sheet of glass smudged with finger marks. The family was posing in front of a sandstone-cottage with pale blue shutters. A woman, who he assumed was Sophie Pitts, was sitting with a young boy on her lap. Her hair was cut in a boyish bob and her eyes sparkled. The boy was little more than a toddler, grabbing his mother's chin in a pudgy hand oblivious to the camera. An older girl was standing at the woman's side, her arms crossed and she was pouting coquettishly. Her free flowing blonde locks tumbled over her shoulders. Behind them and leaning into the lens was the man Blake took to be Benjamin Pitts. He was peering through a pair of glasses that would have been fashionable five years earlier. It was a portrait of a perfect family. Happy, relaxed and without a care in the world.

'What do you think happened to them?' Blake asked, holding up the photograph.

'Best guess? They were the victims of a robbery that went wrong.'

'But you said nothing was taken.'

'They've not ransacked the house, which is unusual but it's possible they came looking for something in particular, something they thought was in the house. The fact is, we don't know.'

'So why abduct the family?' asked Mortensen.

'If we knew that, we'd be closer to catching them. There's also the possibility of extortion or blackmail. We're checking the Pitts' financial records and we've frozen their accounts for good measure.'

Blake shot Mortensen a look that Douglas missed. 'How much was in their accounts?' he asked.

'Not a fortune. Enough for a rainy day,' said Douglas.

'And what do you know about Benjamin's brother?'

'Elias? I know he was doing time for fraud and that he escaped from prison a few days ago but there's not much evidence he and Benjamin had had any contact in recent years, which is why I'm not jumping to any assumptions.'

'Elias was a successful banker who lost everything in the global financial crash,' said Mortensen. 'He wasn't only made redundant but lost millions as his personal invest-ments nosedived. He was involved in a complex fraud conning thousands of people out of their savings. We don't think he planned his own escape. He was an unwitting victim of a hostage situation but now he's free we think he might be trying to lay his hands on some easy money. His brother might have been his best option. But if Benjamin was unwilling to help, maybe Elias was desperate enough to try to force him to hand over his savings?'

'The woman next door is sure two men were involved.'

'In which case, he could still be with the man he escaped with,' said Mortensen, glancing at Blake.

'His name's Ricky Vaughn. He's an armed robber who was serving his sentence for multiple murders in Marshside's high security unit. He's extremely dangerous. Your officers need to know he should be approached with extreme caution. He won't think twice about shooting if he's cornered.'

'I see,' said Douglas, rubbing a finger across his bottom lip. 'And nobody thought to mention this earlier?'

'We're mentioning it to you now,' said Mortensen.

EIGHTEEN

The woman who answered the door of the adjacent house wasn't elderly at all. She appeared to be no more than in her early thirties although she had the demeanour of someone older.

'Yes?' she asked, in a tone that suggested she was surprised to see strangers on the doorstep.

'Mrs Aitchison?' Mortensen asked.

'No. Who are you?' Her hair was scraped back severely in a bun. Her eyes were hawkishly sharp.

Mortensen produced her identity card, held it at head height for a second and snapped it shut. 'British Intelligence. We're investigating a prison break we believe is connected to the abduction. We need to speak with Mrs Aitchison about what she saw last night. Are you a family member?'

'Family liaison officer.' The woman stepped to one side. 'She's in the living room. I'll put the kettle on.'

The old woman was sitting in a threadbare armchair by a window overlooking the cliffs. Her translucent skin barely concealed a network of thread-like veins and her hands were so badly deformed that her fingers were clawed under her palms.

'More questions?' she asked with weary resignation.

'Mrs Aitchison, we understand you had a clear view of what happened last night?' asked Mortensen, leading the questioning without any introductions.

The woman settled back in her seat and tugged her cardigan tightly around her shoulders. 'Like I explained already, I saw headlights in the yard and thought it was a bit strange for visitors at that time of night,' she said, as if she'd rehearsed the line. 'I've been through this several times.'

The sound of a kettle boiling and cups being rattled floated through from the kitchen. 'Just one more time please, Mrs Aitchison. If we're going to find your neighbours we need as much information as you can give us. Now what time did the car arrive?'

'Well, I was upstairs fetching my hot water bottle after my programme had finished, so it must have been after 8.30. There were two men. They came in a fancy car, one of those off-road types.'

'Did you get a clear look at them?'

'Oh yes, they set off the light at the back of the house. They were an odd pair, shifty-looking. You wouldn't have put them together.'

'What do you mean?'

'One was like a boxer, tall with a flat nose and no neck. His head looked like it came straight out of his shoulders. He looked arrogant to me, something in the way he walked.'

Mortensen gave her an encouraging smile. 'And the other man?'

'He was shorter, with scruffy hair that looked like it needed a cut. I don't remember much else about him.'

The family liaison officer carried a tray with mugs and a

pot of tea into the room. She set it down on a low table. 'Shout if you need anything. I'll be in the kitchen.'

'And how did they act?'

'They seemed to know exactly what they were doing. They went straight to Ben and Sophie's so I thought they must be friends of theirs.'

'And they went straight in?'

'I don't know, I can't see the back door from my window. I heard raised voices which was odd because I don't usually hear anything from the house, only sometimes if the children are playing outside.'

'Could you hear what was being said?'

The old woman's wet eyes looked off into the distance. She wiped the end of her nose with a crumpled tissue she had clutched in a misshapen hand. 'Not really. It was just voices shouting. Then there was a scream. Sophie, I think, not one of the children but I couldn't be sure, I'm sorry.'

Mortensen rested a hand on the woman's arm. 'Don't worry, every detail you remember could help.'

'I didn't like to go outside but I saw one of them had the children. They were dragging them out of the house and into the car. I could tell they didn't want to go. Ellie was crying. She tripped over on the gravel and one of them raised his hand to hit her.'

'What about Ben and Sophie?'

'They came out behind the children. The tall one was at the back with a gun.'

'Are you sure?'

'I think so.'

'What sort of gun? A handgun?' asked Blake, speaking for the first time, his interest piqued.

The old woman nodded. 'They made Sophie and the children get in the back of the car with the shorter man. Ben sat in the front next to the driver and then they were gone. That's it, that's all I saw.'

'Think carefully, Rhona,' said Mortensen. 'You definitely didn't recognise either of those men?'

'I'm sure I've never seen them before.'

'What about the Pitts family? Do they have relatives nearby?'

'Sophie has a sister who lives abroad, in Canada. Ben mentioned having a brother but I don't think they're close.'

'Friends?'

'They're friendly enough but they keep themselves to themselves on the whole.'

'And they both work?'

'Sophie's a teacher at the local school. Charlie still goes there but Ellie's moved up to the high school. Ben works for a laboratory in Glen Brittle. He did try to explain what he did once but it went over my head. Something to do with testing vaccines. Developing a flu vaccine I think. I'm sure that's what it was.'

Blake set his mug of tea on the tray, his eyes narrowing. 'He's a scientist?'

'He didn't really talk about his work.'

'What about the name of the company?'

'I don't remember. Sorry, is it important?'

'It might be. How far is the laboratory?' Blake asked, retrieving his mobile phone from his jacket.

'I don't know where it is for sure,' the old woman said,' but Glen Brittle is on the other side of the island. It's no more than an hour's drive.'

Blake was staring at his phone. He raised it to head height and when he couldn't find a signal, lifted it higher. 'Is there any mobile signal around here?'

'It's supposed to be bad on this side of the island,' said

Mrs Aitchison. 'But I don't know, I don't have one of those phones.'

Blake stood, towering over the diminutive woman hunched in her armchair. 'I'll try outside,' he said. 'Thank you for your time, you've been most helpful.'

He tramped out of the house, leaving Mortensen behind. His face was set in dogged determination as he crunched across the courtyard and up the drive, his eyes never leaving the screen of his phone. He finally picked up a signal as he reached the lane. The connection was slow but it was better than nothing. His thumb flicked across the screen, tapping at a keyboard but the results of his search left him puzzled.

'That was a quick exit. What's up?' said Mortensen as she joined him on a patch of unkempt grass overlooking the two houses.

'I don't know, yet.'

'From her description, that's got to be Vaughn and Pitts.'

'Almost certainly,' said Blake, distracted by his phone.

'So what next? A trip to Glen Brittle? Must be worth a poke around at this laboratory?'

'There might be a problem with that.'

'Why?'

Blake handed her his phone. 'Look at this.'

'What is it?'

'I've been trying to find any labs listed at Glen Brittle. There aren't any. So I widened the search to the Isle of Skye, and guess what?'

'You didn't find anything?'

'There's nothing like that listed on the island at all. It's like it doesn't exist.'

'Meaning what?' asked Mortensen.

Blake switched off his phone. Below them a dozen

131

police officers were milling around like worker ants toiling for crumbs. He watched them for a moment, thinking.

'Blake?' Mortensen prompted.

'There're two possibilities as I see it,' he said. 'Either Rhona Aitchison is lying or that laboratory is supposed to be off the grid.'

'But why?'

'I don't know. Let's find out.'

NINETEEN

First came the broiling black clouds that stole the day of light, then the thick globules of rain exploding on the windscreen in watery splatters warning of an impending downpour. Mortensen flicked on the headlights and wipers without taking her eyes off the road ahead. She was concentrating on the bumpy track with her foot hard on the accelerator and gripping the wheel tightly as the uneven camber threatened to rip it from her grasp. Blake was rocking around in the passenger seat trying to navigate from a map on his mobile phone. Around them a black mountain loomed like a silent giant, its sharp peaks needling the sky.

'Slow down, the turning should be on the left,' he said, looking up into the near distance.

Mortensen lifted her foot a fraction. A kidney-shaped building concealed within a mature woodland at the foot of Cuillin mountain was Blake's best guess for the location of the laboratory. It had stood out among the pixelated green and brown squares of a low resolution satellite image, its unnatural colour and shape a curiosity among the trees. It looked to have been constructed in a clearing at the end of a spindly track and flanked on two sides by what appeared to be a small car park. Blake found it after a little more than fifteen minutes poring over images from the western side of the island. He'd painstakingly scanned section by section, hampered by a painfully slow mobile signal. As they drew near, they shared a sense of anticipation that the net was closing on Vaughn and Pitts.

'There,' said Blake, pointing ahead to a slim gap between the rows of firs.

Mortensen jumped on the brakes. They skidded to a halt on a patch of loose gravel, overshooting the turning into an unmarked driveway barely wide enough for a car. She backed up and rolled the vehicle into the forest where the trees closed in overhead.

'Take it slowly and kill the lights,' said Blake.

'Are you sure this is it?'

'Not really. Let's see where it goes.'

The asphalt drive had been built long and straight, cutting through the forest for a quarter of a mile before opening out into a wide glade. A stark, modern building with white walls and banks of tinted glass rose from the ground behind an eight-foot chain-link fence. The roof was cluttered with metal boxes of ducting and vents. It was an alien blot on the landscape, in marked contrast to its natural surroundings.

'Someone must've had good connections with the council to get that through planning,' said Mortensen.

'Or a very good case for it to be hidden away up here.'

The heavens finally opened as they pulled up in front of padlocked double gates. The deluge beat down on the roof like a hundred tiny hammers. The windscreen wipers, running at double speed, struggled to keep up with the volume of rain that was falling. Mortensen left the engine running and turned up the heating to full blast to clear the fog clouding the glass.

The building appeared to be deserted. The car park was empty and there were only a few perfunctory lights on inside. A dozen 'Keep Out' signs in vibrant yellow were attached to the fence. More warned of CCTV and 24-hour security patrols. Blake counted no less than eight cameras, probably only the ones intended to be noticed, put up as much as a deterrent as for surveillance, like the empty alarm boxes people attached to the front of their houses to discourage burglars. He wondered how many more hidden cameras had recorded their arrival.

A board with a company name printed in blue on a white background alongside a triangular logo was mounted on two metal poles. Skyevax Sciences Laboratories.

'Ever heard of them?' Blake asked.

'No. Is there anything on the internet about them?'

Blake tried his phone but it had lost the weak signal he'd picked up earlier. He slipped it back in his pocket with a shake of his head. As the worst of the cloud-burst passed over, he zipped his jacket up to his chin.

'Time for a closer look,' he said, letting himself out of the car.

Outside the rain hissed noisily through the trees, almost drowning out the sound of the idling engine. Ignoring the rivulets running from his brow into his eyes, Blake stood silently scanning the site. Mortensen appeared at his side gripping a Glock 23 nine millimetre. She'd thrown on a cream raincoat over her suit.

'Looks like someone's been here before us,' she said, nodding at the padlocked chain. It had been cut through leaving two ends hanging loose. A crude attempt had been made to conceal the break-in by pulling the gates closed. They opened with a gentle push and clattered against two concrete posts, disturbing a crow which took off from a nearby tree with a loud cack-aw.

To the right of the entrance was a gatehouse. Blake put his hands to the glass of a window and peered in. The blank screen of a computer monitor sat on a desk alongside a clipboard, assorted pens and a copy of a tabloid newspaper.

'Let's check the main building,' he said, drawing his Browning from the small of his back. He ejected the magazine, cracked it back into place and chambered a round. The gun sat snugly in his palm, its weight reassuring. It was like being reacquainted with an old friend.

They padded across the puddled asphalt to a glazed, semi-circular vestibule with curved sliding doors. Beyond it was a second glazed door that led into a double-height atrium in semi-darkness that housed a sweeping reception desk surrounded by leafy pot plants.

'I guess no one works at the weekend,' whispered Blake. 'Wait here, I'll check around the back.'

It took him precisely ninety seconds to scout around the outside of the building and conclude there was no other way in. There were no windows on the ground level and a fire exit at the back was locked from the inside. He found Mortensen where he'd left her, with rain dripping from the end of her nose, her hair flattened to her scalp and mascara running down her cheeks.

'Nothing,' said Blake. 'If Vaughn and Pitts got inside it was with Benjamin's help.'

'The security's pretty sophisticated.' Mortensen ran a hand over the glass of the outer sliding doors. 'This one's opened by a basic electronic swipe card but beyond that it looks like there's a retina scanner to access an airlock entry pod.'

A metallic box with a dark screen was mounted on a pillar at head height inside the first door.

'Both doors leading from the reception area have some kind of electronic entry system too. It looks like a number pad with a fingerprint scanner,' Mortensen added. 'If Vaughn and Pitts wanted to get in here, I don't think they could have done it without Benjamin's co-operation.'

'Conclusions?'

'It's the pharmaceutical industry. Standard precautions,' she shrugged. 'The sector's worth billions, so whatever they're working on in there is bound to be commercially sensitive. They're sensible measures to protect their investments.'

'So it's feasible that Benjamin was working on some kind of new drug?'

'In which case, what's Vaughn's interest?'

'Money?'

'I'm not so sure,' said Mortensen. 'It's a bit sophisticated for an armed robber.'

'You're right, this doesn't stack up. And there's something else. If Vaughn and Pitts came to steal pharmaceutical secrets, then Elias' escape from Marshside was no coincidence. He wasn't picked out by Vaughn randomly, he was the key to getting to Benjamin,' Blake said, looking up to the sky as the rain finally stopped.

'Which begs the question, what does this all have to do with Rahimi?'

'Or the Iranians?'

'Maybe nothing at all, in which case we've been chasing a blind lead,' said Mortensen. She holstered her gun under her suit jacket and stepped back to study the building, as if seeing it as a whole might present a solution to the conundrum. 'You know it's entirely possible the breakout was unconnected with Rahimi. The only link to Vaughn so far is a mobile phone missing its SIM.'

Blake's face clouded. It was a long way to have travelled on a wild goose chase. If Mortensen was right, they were back at square one. 'We need to find Benjamin.'

'If he's still alive.'

'My gut instinct says he is and twenty quid says they're all still on the island.'

'But we don't have the remotest idea where to start looking.'

A trickle of rainwater rolled down the back of Blake's neck and inside the collar of his shirt. But he didn't notice. His eyes had fallen on a security camera over the main entrance, trained on them like a beady eye. He turned to another attached to the wall of the gatehouse and two more facing in different directions on a pole secured to the security fence.

Blake jogged back to the gatehouse and tried the handle of the door. It swung open easily. That surprised him. He'd expected to find it locked. What kind of security guard signs off duty and doesn't secure the gatehouse? Come to think of it, if security was so tight on site, why wasn't there a guard posted twenty-four hours a day? It didn't seem right. Nor did the smell that hit him. The rank and pungent odour of death. He stepped inside, his weapon raised. He saw the feet first. Boots attached to a pair of legs emerging from under the desk. Dark, heavy-duty trousers. Blake dropped to his knees and dragged the crumpled body of the security guard out into the middle of the floor. A bloodied hole in his chest revealed where he'd been shot. His eyes were open, bulging and staring blankly at the ceiling.

Mortensen appeared in the doorway and shrieked.

'Is he dead?'

Blake felt for a pulse under the man's chin but knew he'd long gone. He closed the guard's eyes with his fingers. 'For some time,' he said. 'There's nothing we can do for him. Help me move the body.'

Blake stepped around the lifeless corpse and slid his hands under his arms. Mortensen reluctantly grabbed his ankles and between them, they shifted him to the opposite side of the room.

Blake wiped his hands on the back of his legs and pulled up a chair to the desk. The computer was attached to a dated-looking keyboard made grubby from dirty fingers. He hit a random key and a monitor sparked into life revealing a chequer-board of grainy, monochrome video images.

'What are you doing?' asked Mortensen.

'Looking for unexpected visitors.'

There were feeds from every conceivable angle around the exterior of the building. More cameras covered the inside showing empty offices, gloomy corridors and sterile cloakrooms where white overalls hung from pegs. Blake navigated to the desktop page using a plastic mouse so clogged with dirt that the on-screen pointer jumped and jerked erratically.

He found a document that contained seven sub-folders labelled with the days of the week and clicked on a file from the previous day. It brought up another set of video images. Twenty feeds, five by four across the screen. The locations were identical to the live feed but the light was different.

'Let's start from nine o'clock last night,' said Blake, tapping in a series of numbers on the keyboard that jumped the videos forwards by twenty-one hours.

The feeds went blank momentarily and reappeared showing a handful of people variously around the labora-tory. A cleaner was running a vacuum around one of the offices. Another camera picked up a couple of indistinct figures leaving through the main entrance and walking to cars. No doubt late night workers making their way home.

'Can you speed up the action?' asked Mortensen.

Blake hit another key and they watched in as the cleaner finished her rounds in double-quick time. She left after an hour, driving off in an ancient Ford.

By a little after ten, the security guard, who they'd found dead, was the only person left on site. He fastened the gates with the chain after the cleaner had driven off, and retired to the gatehouse.

When the counter at the bottom of the screen hit midnight, the feeds stopped playing and Blake had to load a new file. It started at a second past midnight with the familiar shots of the empty building.

The timecode was approaching two in the morning when they spotted the glare of headlights illuminate the entrance gates. Blake slowed the footage to real time as the bonnet of a dark-coloured car materialised. It drew to a halt and the driver hopped out. He was a man of medium build in jeans and a leather jacket whose movements were quick and precise. He disappeared behind the vehicle and reappeared with a pair of bolt cutters. In less than half a minute he had cut through the chain.

'Vaughn?' asked Mortensen.

'I'd say so.'

A second figure appeared in shot. The guard emerging from his booth to investigate the disturbance. He was unsteady on his feet as if he'd been woken unexpectedly. Vaughn looked up, pulled a gun from his belt and pointed it at the guard's chest. A second later the guard collapsed, sprawled out on the floor. On the grainy camera footage, a dark, grey patch spread across his front where the bullet had pierced his chest.

Vaughn hauled the body back into the guardhouse, shut the door and returned to opening the gates for the car. A Volkswagen 4X4 rolled into view and pulled up outside the entrance of the laboratory.

Vaughn was first out. He straightened his jacket and looked around as if he was checking they weren't being observed. Blake froze the image and zoomed in on Vaughn's face revealing eyes that were hard and unforgiving. His nose was distinctively misshapen and one side of his mouth was scarred and twisted, giving him a perverse, permanent sneer.

A second man appeared from the passenger side. He was shorter and stockier with lighter coloured hair that fell limply over his ears and collar. His shoulders were rounded and his stomach ballooned with a paunch that looked as though it had been earned from a lifetime of good living. He looked around nervously, scratching the back of his hand.

'Elias Pitts?' said Mortensen, her eyes flicking between the feeds that showed him from various angles.

Vaughn used his gun to persuade a third man from the back seat. Even on the black and white shot, Benjamin Pitts' face was etched with terror, his tired eyes no more than narrow slits behind thick-rimmed glasses. He was as tall as Vaughn but seemed to shrink in his presence. Vaughn shoved him roughly towards the entrance and he fumbled in his pocket for a credit-card sized plastic fob that he used to open the sliding doors. He disappeared inside the vestibule and the doors slid shut.

'Why aren't they following him?' asked Blake.

'They can't get in. Benjamin's about to go through the airlock entry pod which I'm guessing is fitted with an air pressure sensor and probably weight pads too. It's designed so only one person can pass through at a time. If the air displacement's too great, the door won't open. They've got no choice but to trust him. But of course, that's why they've got his wife and kids. Nothing like a little family leverage.'

A camera fixed high above the reception desk in the atrium showed Benjamin turn left towards a solid door, punched a code into a keypad and placed his thumb on a scanner. After passing through the door he disappeared for a brief second, caught between cameras. Mortensen finally spotted him as a distant speck at the far end of a lens in a room filled with rows of desks cluttered with computer monitors, paperwork and phones.

He was wringing his hands, his head jerking to the left and right as if he was looking for something important. He rushed to a desk, snatched up a phone but almost immediately slammed the handset back in its cradle.

'They cut the phone lines,' said Blake. 'It was a fair assumption that he'd try to call for help as soon as he was inside, I guess.'

Benjamin stood by the desk with his head slumped on his chest and his hands hanging by his sides. His shoulders shook and he collapsed to the floor, sobbing.

'Poor guy,' said Mortensen under her breath.

But the tears didn't last long. With one finger he pushed the bridge of his glasses up his nose and lifted his chin. He stood up, spun around and scanned the room as if searching for something he'd lost. His eyes fell on the camera. He stepped closer, staring at the lens. His eyes were wide and focused, his fingers stroking his bushy beard. As he moved closer, the fisheye lens distorted his features, drawing his face into a thin oval.

'What's he doing?' asked Mortensen.

'I don't know.'

Benjamin jumped up and down, waving his arms frantically. His mouth yawned open wide and clamped shut.

'He's trying to call for help,' said Mortensen. 'Except nobody's watching. Until now.' She bit on her finger. Blake touched her arm. They both feared they were watching the final desperate moments of a dead man.

Benjamin kept up his energetic jig for nearly a minute. His chest heaved with the exertion and he squinted at the lens as if trying to work out whether he'd been seen.

Finally, with a dispassionate calm that belied his state of

stress, he performed one simple act that would save his life. When Blake and Mortensen realised what he was doing, they looked at each other and grinned like clowns.

'You clever old stick, Benjamin,' said Mortensen, clapping Blake on his shoulder and grabbing a pen and scrap of paper from the desk.

TWENTY

The corridors blurred as Benjamin Pitts flew through the guts of the building. His heart was racing and beads of sweat pearled on his brow despite the air-conditioned chill. He wasn't sure whether it was from the exertion or his fear. He skidded to a halt at the top of a metal staircase, wiped his forehead with his sleeve and checked his watch. Eight minutes gone already. He'd promised to be out in thirty. Make it twenty, said the thug with the broken nose and the twisted grin who'd leered at Sophie with a lascivious glint in his eye. He couldn't risk over-running while his wife and kids were being held hostage. So why had he wasted precious minutes gambling on trying to raise the alarm? As if anyone would be monitoring the security camera feeds at that time of night. He cursed his stupidity.

A short flight of steps took him into a square hallway and he slammed his palm on a button on the wall.

'Come on, come on,' he urged under his breath, rocking impatiently from foot to foot as he waited for the lift.

The doors sighed open sluggishly and an iris scanner took the best part of a minute to confirm his credentials before he was dropped two floors into the concrete-encased bowels of the building where the laboratories were concealed. Running into a storeroom he snatched a set of navy-coloured scrubs, stiff from the laundry, and in an adjacent changing room ripped off his jumper and faded Rolling Stones t-shirt. He kicked off his shoes and jeans and dumped everything in a heap on a bench as he pulled on the cotton top and trousers that were rough against his skin. Not comfortable like cotton should be.

Eleven minutes gone.

The suit room was through two heavy steel doors. Inside, coils of red hoses snaked from the ceiling like giant springs and a row of orange protective suits hung limply from metal hooks. Benjamin grabbed the nearest suit and slid his legs in easily. He found the left arm on the third attempt, twisting to reach behind him and wiggling his fingers into a glove pre-attached to the sleeve. After easing the bucket-hood over his head he grasped a hose from the ceiling and attached it to an umbilical cord at his waist. Two brass connectors clicked together and triggered a noisy hiss of compressed air. He zipped himself in and chose a pair of plastic boots, all the while trying to steady his raging pulse.

'Calm down, Benjamin', he told himself, slowing his breathing as the hazardous materials suit inflated.

A hot flush prickled his face and neck despite the flow of compressed air. A dribble of sweat stung his eyes. He blinked his vision clear and focused on the red light on the door ahead, beckoning to him. Part of his brain screamed for him to leave. He could walk out and tell them he couldn't do it. Be a man. Call their bluff. Without him there was no way into the laboratory and soon enough someone was going to notice they were missing. Or maybe they wouldn't. It was the early hours of Saturday morning. Neither of them were due back to work until Monday morning. Probably the first time anyone would suspect something was wrong. And that was still thirty hours away. Plenty of time for Elias' friend to inflict any manner of suffering on his wife and children to ensure his compliance.

He closed his eyes and, with a grudging acceptance, realised he'd come too far to turn back. He pictured Sophie cradling the children, trying to calm them with soothing words, her wrist shackled to an old gas pipe and her face streaked with tears. And in that moment he hated his brother more than he'd ever done in his life.

Drawing air tainted with the odour of mechanical processes through his nostrils, he punched in a code on a keypad on the door, overriding the lock usually controlled by the lab director. It opened smoothly on oiled hinges and closed behind him with a muted thud. The container he'd come for was on the top shelf of a large refrigerator. No bigger than the jewellery box on his wife's dressing table and unremarkable other than for a white label fixed to the silver lid printed with the identifying code 'HR2T-v'. Five innocuous characters that veiled the true horror of what lay within.

He carried it in two hands, overcompensating for the thick gloves by gripping it too tightly. He set it down in the centre of a glass bio-hazard cabinet cluttered with rows of test-tubes, a stand of pipettes and plastic trays in vivid colours. With trembling fingers he eased open the lid and stared six glass tubes. A Pandora's Box filled with enough deadly virus to wipe out six large cities. A super-strain of bird flu mutated and engineered to pass from human to human as easily as winter flu.

Benjamin steadied his hand as he leaned forwards to pinch one of the test-tubes between his thumb and forefinger, careful not to squeeze too hard. The virus was suspended in an inch of clear liquid that slopped lazily around the bottom of the tube. Ten millilitres of lethal fluid, viscous like a shot of vodka that coated the glass with a thin layer of translucent residue. He placed it in a plastic rack, took a second tube and placed it next to the first.

Elias had been clear. He wanted the lab's entire stock. But that wasn't going to happen. It would be Benjamin's gesture of defiance. Without at least one of the samples it would be impossible to produce a vaccine. Using a pipette he drew off half the liquid from each of the two vials and divided it equally between two empty test-tubes. A small step towards redemption. The loss would set the lab back several months but at least there would be some virus left to continue their work.

Benjamin struggled to screw caps onto each of the test-tubes. His hands were clammy and the hair on the back of his head was soaked through with sweat. He bit his lip as he concentrated, and when he was done threw a glance at the clock on the wall to his left. Five minutes to make it back outside. It was going to be tight but he was banking on them waiting for him.

'Damn it!' he said, realising he needed a case for the tubes. There was one on the other side of the room. Benjamin sprang from the chair and made it across the lab in three strides.

He felt the tug at his waist too late. The connectors attaching the air supply to his suit flew apart. The hiss of air in his ears fell silent and a loud crack of smashing glass echoed around the lab. He turned, fearing the worst, to find the air supply hose had snagged on his seat and was swinging wildly, its brass end bobbing up and down from the ceiling. His eyes flashed to the bio-hazard cabinet. The protective glass screen over the working area was crazed with a thousand cracks. Shattered but intact. He let out an involuntary gasp as his suit began to deflate.

The four tubes he'd lined up in a rack were undamaged.

Of the two original glass tubes, one was missing its screw cap. It was also shorter by a centimetre or two. A hairline crack ran down its length. The hose connector had taken the top clean off. It was a miracle it hadn't knocked the case over or spilled any of the liquid.

He found the missing top behind a pipette stand and reached into the cabinet to retrieve it.

'Shit!' he whistled as a sharp edge sliced through his glove and nicked the end of his finger.

He flinched at the shock. A short incision across the pad of his index finger, seeping blood, was visible through a tear in the glove. He stared at it for a second or two, the horror of his own stupidity sinking in. In his panic he was rushing, forgetting the precautions. And now this. Maybe it was rough justice. Bad karma, Sophie would have said. Chances were he'd been infected. Nothing he could do now but to hope.

He grabbed the four test-tubes from the cabinet and packed them into the tight polystyrene lining of a transportation case. He snapped the lid shut, tucked it under his arm and, with a last look back at the mess he'd left, stepped out of the lab and into a decontamination chamber.

TWENTY-ONE

The road to Carbost was a narrow and rutted sliver of asphalt that cut through a barren heath of greens, greys and browns. The landscape pitched and rolled for as far as the eye could see, an unspoiled wilderness where trees struggled for a foothold and only the hardiest grasses flourished. Not that Blake took much notice. He was in the passenger seat clutching his mobile phone while Mortensen, back behind the wheel of the rented Ford, was fixed on the winding route ahead. Blake was looking for a decent signal but didn't find one until the threatening waters of Loch Harport, dark and unforgiving, opened up before them.

'I've found it,' he said finally. He scrolled down the screen, flicking through the internet search returns with one finger.

'Care to enlighten me?'

The words Benjamin had held up to the security camera had been unequivocal. He'd scrawled 'Loch Cill Chriosd' across a blank sheet of paper in a thick felt pen, in capitals, big and bold.

Blake's brow furrowed as he read. 'It's not a loch at all. It's the ruins of an old church.'

Mortensen shot Blake a look, taking her eyes off the road for a split second. 'What?'

'It's a former parish church, although it looks nothing more than rubble and a few walls to me,' he said.

'Do you think that's where they're being held?'

'It doesn't seem right,' said Blake. 'It's like a local landmark and right on the side of the road. Why would they take them there?'

'Maybe it's the closest point of reference Benjamin had? How far is it?'

'About twelve miles as the crow flies but by road more like thirty. It'll take us at least an hour.'

'I'll have us there in forty,' said Mortensen with a devilish grin. She floored the accelerator as they flew around a blind bend.

'Preferably in one piece,' said Blake, gripping the dashboard with his free hand.

They made it in a little over thirty five minutes, Blake thankful the roads were deserted. Mortensen only slowed when he pointed out the salt and pepper stone remains of a church on a mound approaching on their right. It was a long, roofless building enclosed by a moss-ridden stone wall encircling a graveyard with lichen-covered headstones jutting out of the ground at oblique angles. They pulled up onto a grass verge opposite.

'What now?' Mortensen asked.

Blake peered up at the skeletal ruins of the church, grey and sinister under wide skies heavy with the remnants of the passing storm. 'Drive on slowly but keep your eyes peeled. We're looking for a building, maybe a farmhouse or a disused barn.'

Mortensen drove on for a hundred and fifty metres before they spotted mud on the road. Indistinct trails partially washed away by the rain had stained the asphalt brown. The trails led from a grass track that ran away from the carriageway towards an inland loch.

'Worth checking out?' asked Mortensen.

'Sure.'

The car struggled for traction where the grass had been cut up by the wheels of another vehicle. Their tyres slid and spun, spitting out clods of mud, and after their high-speed flight across the island, their progress was became painfully slow.

A croft house appeared over the crest of a rise, a simple, single-storey building to the south of a copse of dark green firs in the shadow of a black mountain. Bleached beams were exposed through wide holes in its roof where sections of tiles were missing. Along its back wall, two square windows were cut into the stonework.

Mortensen cranked on the handbrake.

'It looks derelict but someone's obviously been here,' said Blake.

Mortensen killed the engine. 'I'm going to take a look,' she said, stepping out and closing the door quietly.

Blake pondered the wide tranches of tyre tracks that led to the building for a moment. They looped around in messy circles where a car had been driven back and forth.

'Wait,' he called, jumping out of the vehicle and jogging the short distance Mortensen had covered. They approached the house in silence together, eyes wide and ears tuned for any sound.

The entrance to the house overlooked the loch. Blake drew his Browning, thumbed off the safety and nodded to Mortensen to approach from the left while he circled the perimeter, stopping only to snatch glimpses through the windows at the rear. The panes were smashed and the frames rotten. Inside was in darkness. The interior comprised of a single room bare and forlorn. Spots of light shafted through the holes in the roof illuminating patches of stone floor where rubble and debris had collected in piles. Too much of the room was in deep shadow to be certain whether there was anyone inside.

Mortensen was waiting for Blake at a paint-flecked wooden door hanging from rusted hinges. On either side, two windows had been sealed with old boards grey with age. Tufts of spiky grass had been trampled into the mud by what looked to be several pairs of feet. Blake urged himself not to jump to conclusions. Maybe local teenagers had hung out here for a smoke or it had been used as a refuge by fishermen caught in a storm. He put his finger to his lips and they listened. But there was only the rush of wind through the branches of the nearby trees and the lap of water on the loch.

An uneasy feeling swelled in Blake's stomach and his hand tightened on his nine millimetre. The croft measured no more than six metres by four, a tight space for a gun fight if Vaughn and Pitts were holed up inside. He already knew how it would play out. Loud and fast. The dizzying disorientation of muzzle flashes lighting up the room and the splintering cracks of gunfire. Blake and Mortensen would hold the initial advantage of surprise but they'd be silhouetted in the door-frame. At best could count on two or three seconds before Vaughn and Pitts grabbed their weapons – the same length of time it would take for their own eyes to adjust to the gloom. But calculations like that were immaterial. It would be madness to storm the croft with guns blazing and four hostages inside. Not unless they fancied a body count on their consciences. Blake preferred the odds to be stacked higher in his favour. A belt-full of stun grenades would have helped that but there was no time to think about the what-ifs.

He stepped back and regarded the grey walls one last time but there was no alternative way in.

'Ready?' he whispered to Mortensen.

She nodded and her long, thin fingers flexed around her Glock. Her breathing was slow and assured.

Blake forced his shoulders to relax and released a violent kicked at the door close to the handle. It crashed open, the desiccated wood fracturing with a loud snap. He rushed inside with Mortensen at his back, sweeping his gun into the darkest recesses of the room. As his pupils adjusted to the murk, he hunted out tell-tale signs of movement. But there were no screams of surprise, nor volleys of gunfire. Just thick motes of dust cannoning into the beams of light shining through exposed rafters.

Mortensen saw them first. Four crumpled figures slumped on the floor and huddled so closely together that at first it was impossible to tell how many there were. Benjamin, recognisable from the security footage at the Skyevax laboratories, was at the back, his eyes dark and tired behind the lenses of his glasses. A woman half-lying in front of him held up her head. Her hair was bedraggled and a wisp of fringe that fell over her face. She possessed a rugged boyishness and a spirit of defiance. She held an arm around two children crouching between her legs, their bare arms trembling with cold.

Mortensen slipped her gun into a holster under her arm. One of the children whimpered.

'It's over,' said Mortensen. 'It's all over,' she repeated softly.

The woman kept her eyes fixed on Blake's gun. He remained standing inside the door, his feet planted and his aim levelled at the family.

'Where's Elias?' he barked.

'Gone,' said Benjamin, squinting.

'And Vaughn?'

'The other guy? He went too. They've not been here for hours.'

'Where did they go?' Benjamin stared back at Blake blankly. 'Where?' Blake repeated, raising his voice.

'I don't know.'

'Blake, for God's sake,' said Mortensen. 'Let's get them out of here first, okay?'

'Who are you?' The woman's voice was calm and measured.

'We're the good guys. Are you hurt?' asked Mortensen.

A spot of blood had congealed below the woman's left nostril and a purple bruise was rising on her cheek. She shook her head.

'And the children?'

The woman tried to speak but the words caught in her throat. Tears welled in her eyes as she shook her head again.

'It's Sophie, isn't it? Let's get you out of here.' Mortensen draped her coat over the children, noticing the chains that bound their wrists to a pipe running along the wall. She turned to Blake with eyebrows raised. 'Any ideas?'

Blake lowered his gun.

'Hang on,' he said, turning and running out of the house.

He returned with a scissor jack he'd found cocooned inside a spare tyre in the boot of their hire car. He wedged it between the wall and pipe. It took six turns of the crank to wrench the pipe from its fixings that had been weakened by age and rust.

'Get them into the car to warm up,' said Blake. 'And call an ambulance. We should let Douglas know too, put him out of his misery.'

Mortensen helped Sophie and the children to their feet.

They rubbed their wrists and stretched, their hollow eyes full of fear.

'The car's just outside. We'll have you home in no time.'

Mortensen ushered them towards the door and they shuffled through the dust and debris, blinking as they emerged into the daylight.

Benjamin tried to follow but Blake stepped across his path. 'Not you,' he said.

They stood eye-to-eye, Blake a little taller, a little broader across the shoulders. A flicker of fear clouded Benjamin's face as he massaged blood back into his arm where the chains had cut off the circulation to his hand. His eyes flitted to the gun at Blake's side.

'We need to talk.' There was no warmth in Blake's voice. His eyes were emotionless orbs.

'I just want to get home...' Benjamin stuttered. He tried to sidestep Blake but was prevented by a muscular arm across his chest.

'Not until I get some answers.'

'How did you find us?' asked Benjamin.

'We saw your message on the Skyevax cameras.'

'Really?' Benjamin's tired face lit up.

'We also saw you leave the laboratories with a silver case which you gave to your brother and his accomplice. Both known criminals, and both currently at large from prison.'

Benjamin's delight vanished in a second. He hung his head and shuffled his feet.

'I need to know where Vaughn and your brother are right now.'

'I told you. I don't know,' said Benjamin.

'I don't believe you.'

'You think I'm involved in this?'

'Are you?'

'Of course not. They had my family. What was I supposed to do? What would you have done?'

Blake's expression was impassive. He wanted to believe Benjamin was an unwitting victim, coerced into breaking into the Skyevax building by threats to his wife and young children. But he needed some convincing.

'Who are you anyway?'

'My name's Blake. I work for the Government. That's all you need to know. I'm here to help but this isn't looking good for you right now. You need to start talking.' He slipped his gun into the waistband of his jeans.

'The Government? Jesus, what a mess.' Benjamin ran his hands through his hair, slipped off his glasses and rubbed his eyes. 'You don't have any idea what I've done.'

Blake clamped Benjamin on the shoulder. 'I need to know the truth. I can't help you otherwise,' he said, his tone softening. 'We saw you disappear into a lift. Wherever you went wasn't covered by cameras, and when you reappeared you had a case which you gave to Elias and Vaughn. What was in it?'

'I'm so sorry. I didn't have a choice...' Benjamin began to sob, his pent up emotions finding a release.

'Benjamin, tell me,' said Blake, removing his hand from the scientist's shoulder but leaving it hovering behind the back of his head. Benjamin looked up, his eyes red and puffy.

Blake heard the distant sound of a car door slamming shut. Sophie and the children. By now Mortensen would be on the phone to Douglas. He'd be on his way within minutes accompanied by a fleet of wailing squad cars and crime scene investigators. There would be ambulances and paramedics, psychologists and smiling liaison officers to look after the children. Blake's time with Benjamin was running short.

'Turn around,' he ordered, spinning the scientist through ninety degrees and using his boot to kick his feet together so his ankles smashed together. 'Now look at me.'

When Benjamin looked up, he found a hand in front of his face hovering above his eye line, drawing his focus away from Blake's wide-eyed stare. His brow furrowed but his bewilderment lasted only a second as Blake tapped him lightly on the forehead.

'Sleep,' said Blake.

Benjamin's body crumpled. His eyes fell closed and his legs gave way as if someone had flicked an off-switch on his back. Blake caught him under his arms and eased him onto the ground, intoning soothing words into his ear. Benjamin lay still with his arms at his side and his eyes shut.

'You're safe here now,' said Blake, taking a seat on the floor with his back resting against a wall. 'You're in a deep state of relaxation. In a moment I'm going to ask you some questions. I want you to answer truthfully and honestly. Do you understand?'

'Yes,' said Benjamin.

'I want your mind to return to the last time you were at the Skyevax laboratories. Your brother, Elias and a man called Vaughn took you there and asked you to fetch something for them. Do you remember?'

'Yes.'

'You gave them a case.'

'Yes.'

'I need to know what was in it.'

There was a flicker behind Benjamin eyelids and the lines on his forehead tightened. He took a deep breath and started to talk.

TWENTY-TWO

The way Blake viewed it, the procurement of information from someone unwilling to give it up was an art. And like any art form true proficiency took years of practice. He'd found traditional interrogation methods cumbersome and slow; barbiturate truth serums unpredictable and the use of torture not only morally dubious but highly unreliable when it came to weeding out lies and half-truths. But hypnosis guaranteed a hotline to the brain that could bypass any conscious reluctance someone might have to talk.

His first encounter with the possibilities hypnosis could offer had come from a vulgar performance at a party. He'd watched mesmerised as a stage comedian put a handful of willing participants into a trance with a snap of his fingers. Some obligingly grunted around on their hands and knees when told to behave like pigs in a sty, young women were convinced that cleaning mops were handsome young men at a dance and others were persuaded they were standing naked on stage.

They were cheap gimmicks but Blake was fascinated by the apparent ease with which the hypnotist had been able to induce total control over a random selection of people. It was the start of his journey towards the development of rapid hypnotic induction, and the manipulation of someone's mind to reveal secrets they ordinarily wouldn't divulge.

He experimented with its use in his role as chief interrogator with the black-ops Special Forces counter-terrorism unit, Echo 17. And it produced spectacular results. His first success had been with an Al Qaeda commander snatched from a compound on the Afghanistan border with Pakistan after a six day covert stakeout. The Afghan went out like a light and coughed up detailed plans of an imminent attack being planned on an American base. Even Blake had been surprised at how easily he'd reeled off the information. It was like chatting to his grandmother about the weather.

But that was a long time ago. In a different lifetime.

Benjamin's chest rose and fell, his face implacable. Rainwater was dripping from the broken roof and puddling in pools while the wind howled down two chimney stacks that opened up into soot-blackened fireplaces at either end of the room. Blake shifted on the stone floor to make himself more comfortable but it was cold, damp and covered in the dirt from a generation. He stretched his legs and examined mud that had accumulated on the toecaps of his boots.

'Tell me about the laboratory,' he said. 'Why all the security?'

'We're developing a vaccine for a human variant of avian flu.' Benjamin's body was in stasis, his muscles loose.

'I don't understand. What interest would Elias have in a vaccine for bird flu?'

'He doesn't. He wanted the Armageddon Virus.'

'The Armageddon Virus?'

'It's a super virus we engineered so we could develop the vaccine, a strain of avian flu that's just as potent but much more infectious to humans.'

'How infectious exactly?'

'One infected person could spark a global pandemic in a few days. It's passed on by coughing or sneezing. Just like winter flu. You could contract it in exactly the same way.'

'And you've grown this virus in a lab?'

'It's in a secure state-of-the-art bio-hazard unit so it's impossible for it to escape into the environment.'

'Unless someone deliberately removes it from the building, of course. But why the need for a vaccine for a virus that's only manufactured in a laboratory?'

'Because the avian flu virus will eventually mutate in nature and if we don't have a vaccine ready tens of millions of people could die.'

'That's a bit melodramatic, isn't it?'

'Not at all. Winter flu claims around half a million lives a year, mostly old, young and chronically-ill victims. But avian flu is different. It's highly pathogenic and constantly evolving.'

'You mean there's a possibility of it mutating into a virus that could behave like winter flu?'

'It's not a possibility. It's a certainty. The only doubt is when. We've already had a strain of avian flu that had limited ability to be contracted by humans. And in the late 1990s it wiped out millions of birds.'

'The H5N1 virus, right?' Blake remembered it dominating news bulletins and swathes of newspaper column inches after the first cases of the human strain were reported. The media had become hysterical about the threat, warning of a global catastrophe before it slipped from their consciousness and their attentions switched to the next calamity waiting to befall humanity. 'I thought that had all gone away,' he said.

'The danger is greater than ever. At the moment the avian flu virus is still difficult for humans to contract but the concern is that sixty per cent of those who have, have developed severe symptoms and died.'

'And if avian flu was as easy to catch as winter flu, it would be catastrophic?'

'We've calculated the numbers would be on a massive scale.'

'My God, it could trigger widespread global panic.'

'Our models suggest international borders would close, healthcare systems would be overrun and eventually economies would collapse.'

'But that's just a model, right? Those things are designed to predict the worst case scenario.'

'In 1918 the Spanish Flu killed fifty million people. That was before you could fly around the world in a matter of hours on a jumbo jet. And already the latest mutation, H7N9, is showing signs of being able to transmit between human carriers,' said Benjamin.

Somewhere above an eagle screeched. Blake saw the silhouette through a gaping hole in the roof, a magnificent bird with wings outstretched, soaring on the currents. It was the picture of effortless grace and beauty. Hard to imagine a species so magnificent threatening the existence of mankind.

'So let me get this correct, you've artificially manipulated bird flu to make it behave like winter flu so you can work on a vaccine to protect the world?'

'There's much opposition in the scientific community to what we're doing because people fear the Armageddon Virus. That's why there's so much secrecy around our work.'

'What are the symptoms?'

'Of catching the Armageddon Virus? Much like winter flu at first but death would almost certainly follow, especially for the fit and healthy.'

'But I thought you said flu mostly affects the old, the young and the chronically-ill?'

'Avian flu is different. It causes your immune system to generate killer cells that attack healthy lung tissue and makes the blood vessels leak.'

'So you'd end up drowning in your own blood?' said Blake.

'If you don't suffer any complications like pneumonia or multiple organ failure.'

'In which case the healthier you are, the worse it could be.' Blake sucked in breath through his teeth. 'How long before the vaccine's ready?'

'There were still a few months of testing.' Benjamin hesitated for a beat. 'The loss of some of the control virus will set us back.'

'So, how did Elias find out about the virus, given all the secrecy surrounding the laboratory?'

'I told him,' said Benjamin, without a hint of remorse. People were often detached from their emotions under hypnosis.

'Why would you do that?'

Benjamin didn't have a response to the question so Blake tried another tack. 'Tell me about your relationship with Elias. Are you close?'

'I hate him.'

'Why do you hate him, Ben?'

'He was always the favourite. I was the disappointing sibling with a pointless low-paid job in scientific research.'

'Your parents favoured him because he was more successful? Is that it?'

'He was an A-grade student who went to Cambridge and earned a massive salary working for an investment bank in the City.'

'Who ended up in jail for fraud,' said Blake.

'Only after my parents died. They never knew.'

'So you told him about the virus to prove you were a success too? When did you tell him?'

'After he was convicted.'

'Tell me how it happened. Did you visit him in prison?'

'I despised him for how he'd always treated me but Sophie wanted me to try for a reconciliation after he was convicted. She said it would be good for my peace of mind.'

'I see.'

'I put it off for a long time.'

'What persuaded you to go in the end?'

'I wanted to see him behind bars.'

'As a common convict? How was he?'

Benjamin flinched. 'More arrogant than I'd known. It was as if he was proud of being in that jail.'

'How did that make you feel?'

'Angry.'

'So you told him about the virus?'

'After he made fun of me. He laughed and said no one should have to wear a white coat and fill test-tubes for a living. So I told him about the laboratory. I knew I wasn't supposed to but I couldn't help it.'

'What exactly did you say?'

'That I'd been risking my life every day working on a super virus that could wipe out humanity.'

'Did he take you seriously?'

'Yes, I think so. He asked lots of questions.'

'What sort of questions?'

'He wanted to know where the laboratory was and what sort of security we had on site.'

'And you told him?'

'Yes.'

'Didn't you think about the consequences?'

'He'd never been interested in my work before and the

more questions he asked, the more carried away I became talking about it.'

'Oh, Benjamin. What have you done?' In the distance, Blake caught the wail of sirens. In a few minutes the house and surrounding area would be swarming with police. There wasn't much time. 'Did you know he'd escaped from Marshside?'

'No.'

'Tell me what happened when he turned up at the house.'

'He was with another man who was in charge. They pushed their way in, barged past Sophie. The other man was waving a gun, and started shouting and screaming, ordering us all to get down on our knees.'

'And Elias?'

'He was there too. He kept saying we should do as we were told if we didn't want to get hurt.'

'And they asked you to fetch the virus?'

'They wanted to know how to get into the laboratory.'

'But you told them it wasn't possible because the security systems couldn't be overridden?'

'Yes.'

'So they threatened Sophie and the children?'

'The one in charge kept telling me how pretty Sophie and Ellie were and he could have some fun with them. He held a gun to Sophie's head and told me I had to steal the virus for them if I wanted to see her alive again.'

'How much did you give them?'

'Twenty millilitres.'

'And in real terms, how many people could that infect?'

'Hundreds. You'd only need the smallest dose to develop the virus.'

'And of course it would rapidly spread. Did they tell you what they planned to do with it?'

Benjamin hesitated as though his brain was scanning a bank of memory chips for information. 'No,' he said finally.

Blake sighed, eased himself to his feet and brushed dust from his trousers. The sirens were louder now. It was hard to tell how many there were. Their tones merged into one dulled through the thick stone walls. Blake stepped towards the windows at the rear of the room. Through a cracked pane he counted four police cars forming a lazy semi-circle around the croft house. Two more appeared as he watched, mounting the crest where their rented car was parked.

'Time's nearly up, Benjamin. One last question. Think very carefully. Did you hear either Elias or Vaughn talk about what they were going to do with the virus?'

Benjamin thought about the question for a few moments. Policemen in thick coats emerged from their cars, pulled on gloves and caps and moved in a line towards the building scanning the ground as they walked.

'There was a phone call,' said Benjamin. 'Elias took the call while the other one chained me up. They were talking in loud voices.'

'Arguing?'

'Yes, I think so.'

'About what? Do you have any idea?'

'I don't know.'

'Think, Benjamin. It's really important. Remember your wrist chained to the pipework, Sophie and the children with you. Think about the cold stone floor, the sound of the wind through the loose tiles. Put yourself back in that moment.'

Benjamin screwed his eyes tight. His breathing became laboured. Outside an unmarked gunmetal grey Volvo bounced over the track and slid to a halt.

'Remember Elias' phone ringing, watching him disappear outside and Vaughn following. Did they leave the door open?'

'Yes,' said Benjamin.

'So you could hear their voices. They started arguing. Remember their words, Benjamin. Dig deep into your memory.'

'I can't,' he said.

'Think. Hear the sound of their voices again.'

Benjamin's lips began to move, like he was mouthing the words in his mind. 'It was where they had to make a rendezvous,' he said, his voice husky. 'I think they were being told where to take the case. The one with the gun didn't want to go. Elias said he had to if he wanted the money.'

'Benjamin, that's great. Stay with the voices and think hard. Did they say where the rendezvous was taking place?'

Benjamin opened his mouth to speak but his words were lost in the sound of the croft house door crashing open. Detective Superintendent Douglas stood framed in the opening. He combed a grey fringe away from his eyes with his fingers.

'What's going on?' he asked, nodding at Benjamin laying on the ground.

Blake knelt at Benjamin's side, whispered in his ear and helped him to sit up. 'We were just chatting,' said Blake. 'Come on, Ben. Time to get up.'

Benjamin stood slowly, blinking. He looked around the room as if struggling to make sense of his surroundings. A post-hypnosis disorientation clouded his face. It always happened when they came around. Usually lasted no more than a few minutes before they were back to their full consciousness. Blake put an arm around Benjamin's shoulder and guided him out of the door, brushing past Douglas without a second look.

TWENTY-THREE

The delay was out of his control but it didn't make Stijn Bogaert any less anxious. He was paid good money not to ask questions but there was also an expectation he'd keep to schedule. An unspoken part of the deal. Like making sure the plane was fuelled and serviceable. He based his reputation on it and it kept the work coming his way. With an ex-wife and two kids to support, God knows he needed the money. He wiped his palms on the thighs of his jeans, his eyes behind the mirrored aviator sunglasses fixed on the horizon ahead. Visibility was good and the wind was light. He checked the rows of dials on the instrument panel and settled into his seat. The Cessna C340A dipped and rose as it caught a thermal. Bogaert steadied the wings with a slight adjustment on the control wheel and tried to relax. The plane was flying beautifully. Everything was fine. He should still make the pick-up within the hour.

His instructions had been straightforward. Pick up two passengers from an airfield on a place called Skye, a Scottish island he'd never heard of but it fitted his expectations. No doubt a tiny airstrip used predominantly by hobbyist fliers, one of thousands of quiet airfields dotted around Europe that could be dropped into without attracting the attention of border control or customs. Minimal time on the ground. Land, pick-up and take-off. Same as always. There'd be no time to refuel, so he'd taken off with full tanks. The Cessna, with its bulbous wing-tip fuel tanks, could easily cover a thousand miles, more with a favourable wind. Plus its manoeuvrability made it perfect for nipping in and out of even the shortest airstrips. There was comfortably space for five passengers and it could cruise happily at 200mph.

The only departure from his previous assignments was the parcel he'd been asked to stow in the hold. Delivered by courier to his house two days earlier and wrapped in brown paper, sealed with parcel tape. Slightly larger than a shoebox and considerably heavier. No label and no return details. They said it was needed by his passengers when they arrived at their destination in Norway. Bogaert knew better than to be curious about its contents. Curiosity only found you a whole heap of trouble. So he'd tucked it next to the briefcase he always took with him on business trips. Thought nothing more about it.

He checked his charts, then his watch. Opened the throttle a little further, comfortable he could afford to burn more fuel to cut the journey time. It irritated him that he'd allowed plenty of time for the journey and yet he was still going to be late. But really, it wasn't his fault. He could never have predicted the problems at the airfield in Belgium. He'd been manoeuvring towards the end of the airstrip when the voice from the control tower crackled in his headphones, advising him to hold his position. He'd had no choice. An incident with a pilot experiencing medical issues who had to make an emergency landing. Ten minutes passed. Fifteen. Twenty. Finally, after half an hour, a flimsy two-seater popped through the low cloud like a dragonfly on the breeze, bobbing and pitching in the crosswinds. It hit the runway with a bounce that sent its tail sliding one way and then the other. It buzzed past Bogaert with a mosquito-like whine and drew to a halt fifty metres further along the runway. Another twenty minutes passed while the pilot was attended by medical staff in his cockpit. Nearly an hour wasted. But he had no way of warning his passengers. They'd have to wait.

Two paramedics were fussing over Sophie and the children when Blake returned to the hire car with Benjamin. Mortensen was standing a few feet away with two police officers hovering in the background. She pulled a forced smile at Blake and watched Benjamin smother his family with hugs and kisses as they were reunited.

She walked with them back to the road where two ambulances were parked while Blake struggled to reverse the car along the track. He caught up with her the family were being ushered into the back of one of the vehicles.

'We've got to go,' he shouted through an open window.

She jumped into the passenger seat and Blake navigated around a fleet of emergency vehicles scattered across the road, doubting whether the island had ever seen so many cop cars.

'Did Benjamin tell you anything useful?'

Blake gave Mortensen an abridged version of the events Benjamin had set out. 'There are four vials in the case we saw Benjamin remove from the laboratory, each with enough virus to start a chain reaction that could sweep the globe in a matter of days,' he said. 'We're talking deaths in their tens of millions.'

'So where is it now?'

'We have to assume it's with Vaughn and Pitts and they've made it off the island.'

'The police have put up a roadblock on the bridge so I think it's doubtful they escaped by car.'

'Agreed. So that realistically narrows it down to boat or aircraft. Check your phone. Are there any landing strips nearby?'

Mortensen plucked her phone from her pocket. 'You think aircraft rather than boat?'

'It's what I'd do. They need to get somewhere fast now they have the virus. They can't risk being caught with the test-tubes and I doubt they'd waste time going to sea.'

'Not even on a speedboat?'

'I wouldn't have thought so. A plane or helicopter would be the faster option.'

'Okay, say we narrow it down to an aircraft, what then? We have no idea where they're going.'

'Benjamin overheard Vaughn and Pitts arguing about a rendezvous.'

'With the Iranians? Did he overhear where?'

'He heard a name but wasn't sure. Ever heard of a place called "Stoit"?'

Mortensen's brow knitted. She looked up from her phone and stared at the road ahead without really seeing it. 'It sounds familiar but I'm not sure.'

'It means nothing to me but see what you can find online.'

'Hang on, I think I might know where it is,' she said, diving back into her phone. Her fingers darted across the screen but an intermittent mobile signal meant the results of her search were slow coming. She tapped the dashboard with her fingernails as she waited.

'What are you thinking?' asked Blake.

'I think it's in Norway,' she said. 'Yes, I'm right. It's actually Stord but it's pronounced "Stoit".'

'How did you know that?'

Mortensen shrugged. 'What can I say? Must be something in my Scandinavian blood. I have a vague recollection of it from somewhere.'

'Where is it?'

'South of Bergen. About 450 miles due north east from here, straight out over the North Sea.'

Blake slowed at a junction. 'What's there?' He looked both ways and on a whim turned right, as much as anything to keep driving. While they were moving it seemed like they were making progress.

'It's a municipality and an island. I can't imagine why they'd choose it as a rendezvous though.'

'Something we're not seeing perhaps. What about an airstrip? Anything on Skye?'

'Give me a minute,' said Mortensen as she continued to tap away at her phone. 'There's an airstrip at Broadford. It's less than seven miles from the ruined church.'

She looked up at the road, glanced left and right and back at her phone again. 'We're on the right road. It's up here on the left.'

TWENTY-FOUR

Bogaert began his descent through a woolly blanket of grey cloud. It rushed past his windshield cloaking the wings in droplets of dew. He could see neither land nor sea but an altimeter dial rolled backwards to remind him how rapidly they were racing to meet him. He was never entirely comfortable putting his faith in instruments but accepted it as a necessary evil as he dived through the thick Scottish stratus. The fuselage popped and creaked with each lurch of rising current and swiping side-wind. He felt every bump and jolt of turbulence through his hands resting lightly on the control wheel.

A twinge in his back reminded him how much he longed to stretch his legs and uncurl his spine but he was running late and his instructions had been quite specific. A quick pick up and get airborne as soon as possible. There would be no downtime. Good job he didn't have a weak bladder.

At just under two thousand feet, the Cessna broke through the cloud and Bogaert was relieved to see he was lined up perfectly with a distant airstrip. It was as if a giant ruler had been dropped from a great height and had landed in the middle of a field, abnormally straight like nothing nature could have produced, an anomaly in its craggy surroundings. In the distance dark mountains framed the horizon and beneath him were a dark blue sea ragged with rolling whitecaps and the foaming bow waves of tiny fishing boats.

The airfield had been built on a small peninsula alongside a sliver of golden sand and a narrow lagoon, which meant any approach had to be from over the water and away from the dwellings that peppered that side of the island. Bogaert peered over the centre console and tried to estimate its length. It looked short. Very short. At best it was a little over two thousand feet. The maths was simple. He could bring the Cessna down in eight hundred at a push but that didn't leave much room for error. He wondered why he hadn't checked the detail before he'd left.

With a flick of a switch and a mechanical groan, the landing gear unwound itself and locked into position. Bogaert checked his airspeed and adjusted the flaps. He reminded himself there was no room for error, his stomach tightening. Not that the landing was weighing particularly on his mind, rather the anticipation of the job ahead. There was only one sort of passenger who required the kind of taxi service he was able to provide. The sort you'd go out of your way to avoid under any other circumstance. But they were paying handsomely for his services and that was all he needed to know. He eased the throttle back a fraction and wiped his hands dry.

The white centre lines loomed large and then he was on top of them, over them, drifting downwards, counting off the distance in his head, careful not to let the nose drop despite his urgency to land. He let the wheels touch down with a gentle bump, pulled back on the throttle and stamped on the brakes, only vaguely aware of fields and fences flashing by as the plane ate up the ground, hurtling towards the end of the runway. He stared at the speed on a dial, urging the aircraft to slow, trying to judge whether he'd overshot. Had he nailed it? If not, he had about two seconds to reapply the power and hope there was enough concrete left to make it back to take-off speed, which in the Cessna's case was precisely 91 knots.

Then directly ahead he saw a car. It had been nothing more than a dark speck before. Now he realised it was 4x4 with its front doors wide open, pointed down the runway, and he was bearing down on it at startling speed. He applied more pressure to the brakes until his calves ached but it was like stopping an oil tanker. The plane was slowing but not quickly enough.

Ricky Vaughn brushed crumbs from his clothes and reached for a pack of Marlborough on the dashboard. He lit one with a plastic lighter he'd picked up with packets of sandwiches and cans of soft drink when they'd stopped at an all-night garage. The tobacco crackled as he inhaled.

'Do you have to smoke in the car?' said Pitts, throwing open his door. They'd been sitting in the stolen VW parked at the end of the runway for the best part of two hours. A rusting steel corrugated hangar had initially provided them with a hiding place but they'd moved, as much for the change of view as to allow them to see their plane arrive. Vaughn took a slow, deliberate drag, turned and blew the smoke in Pitts' face.

'For Christ's sake!' Pitts exploded. 'What the hell's wrong with you?'

'Relax will you?'

'How can I relax? We're sitting in a knocked-off car waiting for a plane that might never turn up on an island that's probably swarming with police.' Elias scratched at a patch of flaky skin on the back of his hand with nails bitten down to the tips.

'It'll be here.'

'You sure?'

'Yes, I'm sure.'

'I wish I had your confidence.'

Vaughn put his cigarette between his lips and snatched the silver case from Pitts' lap. 'Let's check on the booty while we wait shall we?'

Pitts lunged for the case and grabbed it back with both hands. 'They were due an hour ago.'

'You worry too much.'

'You do know there's no other way off the island? Unless you fancy swimming? If that plane doesn't turn up we're stuck here.'

Vaughn shrugged. 'Worse case scenario? We steal a boat. Look they're happy to pay twenty-five million for the contents of that case. That makes them eager beavers. The plane will be here. You ever seen twenty-five million before?'

Elias didn't reply. He knew what twenty-five million pounds looked like. On a computer screen at least. Never in cash. He imagined bundles of notes stacked in a brief-case or loosely thrown into a holdall. Like he'd seen in the films.

'If they're that eager, they're not going to stand us up are they? Have patience,' said Vaughn

'And hope the cops don't turn up first?'

Vaughn flicked the remnants of the smouldering cigarette out of the window and reached into a pocket in the car door. He wrapped his hand around a nine millimetre Berretta. Pulled it out slowly. He made a big deal of ejecting the magazine, checking the exposed parabellum, rolling it with his thumb. 'I wouldn't worry too much about that,' he said.

'Easy for you to say.'

Vaughn twisted in his seat and swung the Berretta into Pitts' face. He pressed the barrel into the gap between his eyes and watched the blood drain from his face. 'Shut up with your moaning will you? I've got the virus thanks to your brother and now I'm struggling to remember why you're still here. No reason why I shouldn't put a bullet in your skull and save myself your share of the fee.'

Pitts swallowed hard. The urge to itch his forearm, where his eczema was red and inflamed, was overwhelming. But a sudden movement to scratch wasn't going to end well.

'We're a team, right?' Pitts mumbled. 'Without me there would be no virus and you'd still be doing sixteen hour stints behind bars in Marshside. You owe me.'

'I don't owe you nothing. Remember who got you out in the first place.'

'All I'm saying is that we need each other.'

'Wrong. I don't need you,' said Vaughn. His finger played over the trigger.

'Listen, you just got really lucky. Twelve million pounds lucky to be precise. Easiest payday you've ever had I reckon, so don't blow it. I could have asked anyone in that prison for help but I asked you. Do you know why? Because I trusted you. Because I recognised you had principles. Maybe you are some hotshot gangster but I heard you were loyal. And honourable. A rare quality among thieves.'

'Don't think you know nothing about me. You're just some rich kid who got caught with his hand in the till. Right now I'm standing in line for twelve million. But I'm not stupid. If I kill you here and now, I take it all. You think anyone will give a shit?'

'It's your conscience,' said Pitts as his attention was

caught by a movement in the sky. His eyes darted to the left for a split second. He looked again, longer this time. 'It's here,' he said, quietly.

Vaughn turned while keeping the gun pressed into Pitts' flesh. In the distance he saw the outline of an aircraft drop out of the cloud. It might have been a sea bird other than for the bright landing light mounted in its nose piercing the gloom of the day.

'Now what did I tell you?' said Vaughn, breaking into a grin and lowering the Berretta. 'Looks like our lift's arrived.' He threw open his door and stepped out into the chill air.

The aircraft grew larger, floating towards the concrete runway where tufts of grass poked through wide cracks. To their left a ragged old air sock flapped noisily against a metal post, a relic of when the airport had supported a commercial operation. All that had gone.

Pitts eased himself out of the passenger seat and stood leaning against the door while the Cessna bobbed and dived towards them with its wings dipping and rising as the pilot battled to keep them level. The buzz of its twin engines carried across the emptiness. It took less than two minutes for it to reach the runway where it seemed to hover, suspended in flight over the crumbling concrete. And then it dropped the final few metres, landing with a skittish bounce. Behind the windshield, they saw the outline of the pilot, his expression fixed in concentration. As he hit the brakes and cut the throttle, the nose of the aircraft dipped and its tail rose up, like the exotic bird bowing to a mate Pitts had seen once on a wildlife documentary. But it continued to race towards the VW on a collision course, fast at first but slowing. Slowly.

Pitts shot a concerned look over the top of the VW at Vaughn. 'It's not going to stop,' he said, shuffling away from the vehicle, eyes wide.

Vaughn said nothing. He squinted as he watched but stood still.

The buzz of the twin props became a roar and the dizzying aroma of aviation fuel hit them. The draft of the propellers ruffled their hair but Vaughn remained impassive. Pitts turned and ran, diving for cover, clutching the silver case. He visualised their car being mangled, the thin panels of aluminium ripped and sawn apart.

At the last moment the plane swung away, arcing in a wide loop to their right, missing the car by a clear two metres. Vaughn didn't even blink.

TWENTY-FIVE

The road to the airport was an unobtrusive single track off the main A87. It was signposted 'Raon-Adhair' with a helpful image of an aircraft for motorists without an understanding of Gaelic. The entrance was over a cattle grid and through a metal gate which opened up into a wide apron adjacent to a concrete airstrip. There was a distinct lack of facilities. Blake noted a large hangar and two deserted single-storey buildings, like mobile homes set back on the edge of a gravel car park. They looked as if they might be used as office space or a clubhouse for a local flying club. The runway lay on an east to west axis, poorly maintained with tufts of grass growing through cracks in the surface that from a distance looked like green veins. Its eastern approach was obscured by a bank covered by a crop of scrubby vegetation. To the west was the village of Broadford. A narrow ribbon of land beyond the airstrip gave way to icy-looking loch waters and the distant dark mountains of Scalpay which rose up like primordial sleeping giants.

'We should check the hangar,' Mortensen said. 'If they're here, it's the only place you could hide a vehicle.'

Blake nodded, eased his foot off the brake and let the

car grind forwards in first gear. The hangar was an ugly structure, constructed around a curved frame with a skin of corrugated steel the elements had turned rusty amber. Where daylight penetrated a wide opening Blake saw sections of aircraft; tail fins, propeller blades and wings. Mortensen was right. There was probably plenty of room to hide a car. He dropped the clutch and let the car freewheel.

The low hum of an idling aircraft engine was quiet at first but grew louder. It was being carried on the breeze. Distinct and familiar, resonating through the air almost in a whisper. It wasn't coming from the hangar, rather from somewhere behind them. Blake hit the brakes throwing Mortensen forwards in her seat. He ignored her scowl. Cocked his head to listen.

He realised he'd been wrong. It wasn't a single engine. It was a twin-prop, the double stuttering ticker of one propeller fused with another and minutely out of sync. He wound down his window and was hit by a cold blast of air. The engine murmur grew louder.

'Listen,' said Blake.

'Maybe we're not too late,' said Mortensen, loosening the seatbelt and turning to look over her shoulder through the rear windshield but seeing nothing beyond the bank which obscured the far end of the airfield.

The murmur wound into a grunt which evolved into a high-pitched whine.

'Whatever it is, it's taking off,' said Blake. He slammed his foot hard on the accelerator but the hired Ford was old and tired. It had been thrashed too often by too many careless drivers. The engine was loose and suffocated with carbon. The best it could offer was a wheezy gasp that set the tyres spinning and squealing. Blake shifted the gear lever, dropping into second and letting the revs jump into the red zone. The worn rubber tyres finally found some traction and the Ford bumped onto the runway.

Like a mirage the Cessna came into view, shimmering in the heat haze from two 300-horsepower Continental engines mounted beneath its wings. It was lined up for take-off with its propellers a blur.

'There's the VW,' said Mortensen pointing to a dark-coloured 4x4 parked behind the plane, the vehicle they recognised from the Skyevax security footage.

'In which case, time to get introduced to Mr Vaughn and Mr Pitts,' said Blake.

With a free hand he yanked on the handbrake, forcing the Ford's back end to slide out so the car ended up facing the Cessna. He crashed into third gear and let the revs build through the asthmatic rasp coming from under the bonnet. Their speed rose slowly. Thirty. Forty. Fifty miles an hour. Not exactly race car acceleration but the best he was going to achieve with four-cylinders of naturally aspirated engineering.

The windscreen was covered in a film of filth but through a clean arc cut by the wipers, he saw the Cessna roll forwards. Slowly at first but quickly building pace. Blake heard the gutsy grunt of the Cessna's props reaching maximum power and pictured the pilot with one hand on the throttle, concentrating on keeping the plane on the centreline. If Blake wasn't able to force the plane off the runway, it would be like hitting a brick wall. But mutually assured destruction wasn't in his game plan. He rammed the gear stick into fifth and placed both hands on the steering wheel, eyes narrowed, focused on the Cessna, watching it grow bigger, the distance between them shortening.

'What the hell are you doing?' Mortensen screamed. She had braced herself against the dashboard. Her body was stiff with tension. Fight or flight responses. Except she had no choice in either. There was nothing to do but watch events play out.

'Rolling the dice,' said Blake.

His father had been no great gambler but was fond of telling Blake nothing worthwhile had ever been achieved without someone having taken a chance. Right now Blake was gambling the pilot would lose his nerve first. A lethal game of chicken. Except the plane continued to accelerate towards them and was showing no sign of giving up the runway.

Blake saw the outline of the pilot's head, his eyes obscured behind a pair of sunglasses, a headset clamped over his ears. He didn't look at all concerned that there was one-and-a-half tons of metal, plastic and rubber racing towards him.

'It's going to hit us!' Mortensen shouted.

Doubt crept into Blake's mind. If anything, the pilot was still accelerating, holding an unwavering line down the middle of the runway. The engine noise was deafening as the whirling propellers grew closer, giant steel blades that could slice through the Ford's fragile aluminium bodywork like a band-saw through plywood. Blake tried not to think what they could do to flesh and bone.

The plane was almost on top of them, about to reach the point of no return. Blake swore under his breath, jumped on the brakes and pulled the steering wheel hard to the right. The front wheels seized and, as he fought with all his upper body strength to keep the car from spinning, the plane shot past within a hair's width.

Blake's attention was entirely on keeping the car in a straight line but he no longer felt in control. The vehicle screeched off the runway and hit rough ground with a heavy thud. Wheels dug into soft earth and bounced over rocks and divots, the chassis buckling and the suspension coils struggling to keep the car in contact with the ground. Inside their necks snapped and their bodies rolled.

They came to a sudden halt when the car hit an immoveable pile of rock dumped from an earlier construction project. Airbags inflated with a loud bang and the front end of the Ford crumpled like a wet cardboard box. A radiator pipe ruptured in a hiss of steam and the bonnet sprang up over the cracked windscreen.

Blake's brain processed the scene in double quick time. He saw in slow motion the white bags inflate to cushion his head and the drawn out sound of cracking glass and splintering metal. The dashboard shifted towards his knees as the engine block shifted backwards.

And somewhere behind him he heard the buzz of the Cessna.

TWENTY-SIX

Stijn Bogaert gripped the throttle levers tightly, feeling the rotors throbbing through his hand and up his arm.

'Do not abort this take-off!' the guy called Vaughn with the ugly grin and the broken nose had shouted when he saw the car racing towards them. The sour stench of his breath filled the cockpit. 'I want this plane in the air now.'

As if to reinforce his words he'd unbuckled his seatbelt, risen from his seat and produced a handgun. He'd jammed the barrel into the base of the pilot's skull.

'But he's heading right for us,' said Bogaert.

Vaughn cut off his protestations with a sharp prod of cold steel.

'I don't care. Shut up and fly!' he yelled over the roar of the engines.

Bogaert planted his feet on the rudder pedals, applying the brakes, his eyes fixed on the Ford. It had appeared from nowhere and was bearing down on them like an Exocet missile, spewing a dirty cloud of exhaust in its wake.

'We'll all die,' said Bogaert, his voice strangulated. 'There's not enough room. We'll hit him before we make fifty knots.' Beads of sweat pearled under his shirt and over his scalp. He wandered about feigning a mechanical fault but dismissed the thought as quickly as it had entered his head.

'Tell me, can you fly without the use of your legs?' said Vaughn. He slid the gun from Bogaert's neck, caressed the pilot's arm and hip and let it come to rest pressed against his thigh. 'I guess you probably can, if you don't pass out with the pain. I'm only going to ask nicely one more time and then I start shooting. First a bullet through your right femur. Then one through the left. I doubt you'll walk again but we can stem the blood flow enough to keep you alive. Isn't that right, Elias?' There was no response from the man at the back of the cabin. 'I want this plane off the ground!' Vaughn's voice rose to a shrill crescendo.

'You're crazy,' said Bogaert, lifting his feet from the pedals.

The Cessna rolled forwards, bumping along the airstrip, slowly at first but rapidly gaining speed. Bogaert's eyes zipped between a dial showing their speed and the view of the advancing car.

'Let's see how good you are,' said Vaughn.

'We're not going to make it. You're going to get us all killed.'

A wide grin spread over Vaughn's face. 'Don't be so dramatic. He'll pull over. You'll see.'

Bogaert wasn't so sure.

They were already up to 45 knots but the car was so close he could see two figures inside. A man was driving and a woman was in the passenger seat, hugging the white centreline and showing no sign of backing down. Bogeart was numb. It was the first time in all his years' flying he hadn't enjoyed the excitement of a take-off. He loved the controlled power of the dual Continental engines pulsating through the fuselage, the kick in the back of the seat and the heady aroma of aviation fuel. But not today. Today he was convinced he was going to die.

Vaughn moved his gun back to Bogaert's head. The Cessna made it to 55 knots and was still accelerating, but not quickly enough.

Ten metres.

Bogaert pictured the ball of flame that would engulf them. He wondered whether he'd feel pain.

Five metres.

At the moment before impact, Bogaert snapped his eyes shut, stamped on one of the rudder pedals and pulled both throttles back. The aircraft veered off the runway and onto the grass verge, narrowly missing the car as it pulled away in the opposite direction. Vaughn fell backwards, catching his shoulder against the back of one of the seats and cracking his head against the fuselage with a satisfying thud. Bogaert was too busy wrestling for control of the plane to pay much attention. The Cessna shook and rattled uncontrollably as it clattered along the scrub. It wasn't designed to run on anything more rugged than rough concrete. Bogaert gritted his teeth, trying not to think of the damage he might have done. Or how much it might cost to put right. At least he was alive. For the moment.

Vaughn hauled himself to his feet as Bogaert brought the aircraft to a standstill and killed the engines.

'You stupid idiot!' he roared, rubbing the back of his head. 'What do you think you're doing?'

Bogaert twisted in his seat. 'I'm sorry. Are you okay?' he asked with genuine concern.

He didn't see Vaughn's punch coming. It caught him squarely in the mouth sending his aviators flying. It cracked two teeth and split his lip. 'I told you to get this plane in the air. Now look what you've done.' Vaughn's eyes burned with rage.

The colour had drained from Bogaert's face and he was trembling from the shock of the unexpected blow. He was used to the company of uncompromising men. It was a peril of the job. But none had ever hit him. Or held a gun to his head as he was trying to fly a plane. He dabbed his nose with the back of his hand and discovered he was bleeding.

'Get yourself cleaned up, get this plane back on the runaway and be ready for take-off in three minutes,' said Vaughn, turning into the cabin.

Pitts was slumped in one of the executive leather seats with his legs crossed. He was scratching at dry skin on the back of his hand, still gripping the silver case. Vaughn followed his gaze out of one of the windows. The Ford had come to rest embedded in a mound of earth with steam rising from its crushed front end.

'Any idea who that was?' asked Pitts. He glanced up briefly at Vaughn and back out of the window.

'Time to find out,' said Vaughn. He grabbed a sports bag from under one of the seats, unzipped it with stubby fingers and pulled out a MAC-10 sub-machine gun. A pray and spray weapon for close quarter combat and a rival to its more famous cousin, the Uzi. It had limited range and dubious accuracy. But none of that was a concern for Vaughn. Not at the distance he planned to use it.

He grabbed two magazines from a side pocket. Long, rectangular boxes filled with thirty two rounds of nine millimetre cartridges. He clipped one into the MAC's grip handle and stowed the other in his back pocket.

'Do what you've got to do but hurry up,' said Pitts. 'Let's get off this miserable island.'

Vaughn glared at him, reached for the door handle and jumped out. He landed heavily on the grass, found his balance and headed directly towards the crashed Ford with the gun swinging in one hand at his side.

Bogaert watched him from the cockpit, nursing his bleeding nose with a handkerchief. Vaughn was taking loping strides, walking with his shoulders square, his head held high. A man with one purpose in life.

He was less than five metres from the car when he swung the gun level and pulled the trigger. It purred as it spewed its deadly load, cutting a ragged line of thumb-sized holes along the length of the driver's side. He unleashed another burst into the boot. Stopped, switched magazines and emptied another round into the passenger door. As the echoes of the gunfire died away, Vaughn reached for the door and pulled it open with his weapon raised, squinting into the interior, ready to finish off the job.

Blake and Mortensen were lying face up with their backs pressed into the soft ground. Mortensen's breathing was hard and laboured in Blake's ear. She had a smear of blood across her cheek and a wild, terrified look in her eye. She was trembling, whether from the cold, the shock of the crash or fear, Blake wasn't sure. A burst of gunfire crackled somewhere behind them on the far side of the mound where they were hidden. Mortensen tensed and drew a sharp intake of breath. Blake squeezed her hand.

He'd had to half-drag her from the car, up the steep bank and down the other side. The first salvo of bullets had made them both jump. Blake put his finger to his lips and Mortensen nodded her understanding. They waited for the firing to stop, praying Vaughn wouldn't come looking for them. As silence settled across the airfield, a car door opened and slammed shut. And then another.

Blake rolled onto his stomach and up onto his elbows. The earth was wet and slippery so he had to dig his toes in to stop himself sliding. He flicked off the safety on his

Browning and grimaced at the sound, fearful it had carried. He hauled himself up the bank using his elbows like pick-axes and peered over the top. The wild grass had been crushed flat when they'd scrambled over but it still provided enough cover to hide his face.

He saw Vaughn prowling around the car and kicking at the spent brass cartridges that littered the ground. It was the first time Blake had seen him face-to-face since Marshside, a bruiser with a pumped out chest and arms that swung at his side like an ape. He'd only caught a brief glimpse of Vaughn's face before but his flattened nose and the unnatural curl of his lip that gave him a permanent sneer had stayed with him. His weapon hung loosely from his hand.

The Cessna had come to rest a hundred metres behind Vaughn. Its engines had either stalled or been killed. A figure hung out from a door, and although it was too far to make out his features, Blake was in no doubt who it was. Elias Pitts shouted something Blake didn't catch. Vaughn yelled back.

'I'll be there in a minute. Make yourself useful and get that plane back on the runway.'

Pitts didn't reply. He ducked inside and a moment later the engines coughed and spluttered. With one last despairing appraisal of the car, Vaughn backed away, turned and jogged to the plane.

Blake supported his Browning in two hands and lined up Vaughn in his sights, a laterally shifting target disappearing quickly out of range. He had one shot to make it count, one shot that would give away their position to a man carrying a gun that could unleash a magazine of nine millimetre shells in a split second.

Blake sensed movement at his elbow. Mortensen had clambered up the bank to join him. He took his finger from the trigger and relaxed his grip.

'They're going. We've got to stop them,' she said.

'We're outgunned but if we can draw Vaughn's fire there might be a way to stop them. He's already wasted an entire magazine ripping up our car and I heard him change clips. At best he has sixteen rounds left, assuming he's out of ammo clips. He needs some encouragement to waste the rest of them before we take our chance.'

'How do you know he doesn't have another magazine?'

'Educated guess.'

'Great,' said Mortensen. 'So what do we do?'

'He's furious we disappeared. He was hoping to have vented his anger by pumping us full of lead, so I don't think it will take much to draw his fire. We'll give our position away and his trigger finger should do the rest.'

'That's your plan?'

'Given that we have less than a minute before he makes it back to that aircraft, do you have any better ideas?'

'I just thought you might have come up with something less suicidal than starting a firefight with a guy holding a sub-machine gun.'

'It'll be okay if we can stack the odds in our favour.'

'And how do we do that?'

'There're two of us for a start. But we don't have much time.' Vaughn was already half way back to the Cessna. 'You attract his attention and I'll find an alternative line of sight.'

'How?'

'I'll whistle a signal when I'm in place and you start firing. You won't hit him from this range but make sure he sees you.'

'Oh, terrific.'

Blake scrambled down the bank and scuttled away to the right. He kept his head low, running in a half crouch. Vaughn still had his back to him but the Cessna's engines were running at full throttle and the plane was rolling forwards. It bounced over the soft grass, turning back onto the runway. Blake took his chance and broke cover. He sprinted hard across the verge and fell flat on his stomach on the edge of the runway, halfway between the wreck of their car and the plane.

Vaughn was carrying the MAC-10 in his right hand, so Blake figured it was his dominant side. The odds were he'd spin to his right when he heard Mortensen's shots and hopefully would be so distracted by the fire he wouldn't notice Blake.

Mortensen had climbed to the top of the mound, her hands wrapped around her Glock and her elbows locked out. She was aiming at Vaughn with her head slightly cocked. Blake double-checked Vaughn's position. Thirty metres from the plane, putting Mortensen outside of the effective range of the MAC. Close up it was a nasty gun. Good for gangsters sorting out turf wars. Particularly effective in drive-by shootings. His old unit used them from time to time. But he wasn't a fan. At a distance it was good for nothing. Unless it was fitted with a suppresser which you could use to control the kick-back. Otherwise it was a one-handed weapon with a powerful recoil. At best it would manage seventy metres. No way Vaughn would be able to pick off Mortensen. He'd have to turn, close the gap and walk straight into Blake's line of fire.

Blake pursed his lips and whistled a birdsong trill. Mortensen opened fire with four rapid shots over Vaughn's head. Vaughn ducked and spun around, moving to his right as Blake had predicted.

Mortensen made sure she was seen before cracking off three more shots that echoed along the length of the airfield. Vaughn drew himself to his full height and smirked. He levelled his gun but didn't fire. He stepped forwards, his eyes focused on Mortensen's slight frame silhouetted on top of the mound. She didn't move. He started to march purposefully towards her. He covered ten metres. Fifteen. Twenty. But he held his fire.

'Come on,' Blake urged under his breath. He lifted the Browning, taking its weight through his forearms and pivoting on his elbows. He sized up Vaughn through the sights with one eye squinted closed. He had a reasonable shot but didn't fancy the risk of missing. If the MAC was still loaded, Vaughn could cut him down like mincemeat from that distance.

Blake checked over his shoulder, saw Mortensen raise her gun and squeeze the trigger twice more. Two more harmless shots. And then she stood up, her arms by her side, legs slightly apart, her gun hanging loosely from her hand. A defiant stance like she was willing Vaughn to take a shot. Yanking on his male ego.

Vaughn couldn't resist. His trigger finger twitched and the MAC purred. A short burst of shots. Less than a second. Spent cartridges tinkled onto the concrete. Mortensen stood still. She tossed back her head, the picture of calm serenity. Another angry burst of fire. A half dozen more spent shells hit the ground.

The Cessna bumped onto the runway away to Blake's left, its door wide open and its engines idling on quarter power. Blake was vaguely aware of it moving onto the concrete in a lazy loop behind him as it prepared for a second take-off attempt but he doubted it would leave without Vaughn.

Blake stretched out the tension in his fingers and clasped them around the Browning's grip. He slipped his index finger through the trigger guard and applied a little pressure, took a deep breath and let it go, letting his body sink into the ground as his lungs deflated. His focus was fixed on Vaughn but in his peripheral vision he saw Mortensen raise her gun and take aim for a third time. Vaughn responded with another burst of fire. The bullets whistled through the air and landed harmlessly, buried in the earth mound. Mortensen collapsed, hit the ground and rolled down the bank while Blake concentrated on keeping Vaughn's head in his sights. He hoped she'd not been hit but forced the thought from his mind.

Vaughn's submachine gun fell silent. He tilted the weapon on its side to check the chamber, as if a rogue shell might have blocked the breach. Only Blake seemed to have realised he'd just spent the last of his ammo.

Blake sensed the Cessna drawing closer, tiny vibrations through the concrete and the murmur of the engines becoming louder. He let the tension out of his shoulders and lined up his shot. Vaughn glanced at the approaching plane and saw Blake. His eyes widened and his sneer grew more grotesque.

Blake braced himself and fired.

TWENTY-SEVEN

The bullet left Blake's gun at close to four hundred metres a second, hitting Vaughn in the beat of a hummingbird's wings. Vaughn predicted the shot and tried to dive to his right, not quick enough to dodge a bullet but fast enough to save his life. The round caught him in the shoulder in an explosion of red mist that knocked him off his feet.

Blake scrambled across the uneven concrete and stood over Vaughn, his Browning aimed between the injured man's eyes. A pool of blood was puddling under Vaughn's shoulder, his useless MAC-10 lying out of reach. Vaughn rolled onto his back and grinned at Blake, his eyes cold and emotionless. He showed no fear and in any other circumstance, Blake would have been impressed. His finger found the trigger and started to squeeze.

'Blake!' Mortensen's shout of alarm caused him to glance over his shoulder. The Cessna was barely a few metres away, its whirling propellers moments from ripping into his flesh.

Blake tumbled onto the grass, rolling on his shoulder under the wing tip and planted himself flat on the floor.

The turbulence of the propellers buffeted his back and the noise of the engines left his ears ringing.

Mortensen ran towards him, her clothes streaked with mud and her hair loose, tight curls bobbing around her face. Blake was relieved to see no sign of a gunshot wound.

'Are you okay?' he shouted.

'I'm fine. What happened to Vaughn?' Mortensen asked.

'I shot him.'

'Is he dead?'

'Only a flesh wound sadly,' said Blake sitting up.

From under her belly of the Cessna they saw the movement of shadows. No doubt Vaughn being helped back on board by Pitts. The plane turned in a sharp arc to line-up on the runway again, the engines roaring.

'What now?' Mortensen yelled over the noise. The Cessna was already accelerating along the airstrip, rumbling over the rough concrete.

'We have to stop it taking off. Aim for the engine housings or the landing gear.'

Mortensen didn't need to be told twice. She broke into a sprint alongside Blake with her Glock in her hand. Blake emptied what was left in his ammo clip more in frustration than in any realistic hope of hitting a vital area of mechanics as the Cessna pulled away. It hurtled along the concrete airstrip, building speed until its nose pitched up and it climbed sharply into the air.

Blake pulled up with his lungs burning and his heart racing. There was nothing he could do but watch the aircraft disappear into the low cloud. Mortensen jogged up to him a second or two later. Her breathing was hard and heavy.

'They've gone,' she said, unnecessarily.

'At least we know where they're going. We need to get a

flight,' said Blake, retrieving his phone from the front pocket of his jeans. He called up one of the few numbers he stored in a contacts file and waited for a connection.

Harry Patterson answered his mobile after two rings. 'Blake?'

'We've lost them.'

Patterson's voice on the other end of the line was muffled, as if he was juggling the handset between his jaw and shoulder. 'Where?'

'We're still on the Isle of Skye. I presume by now you know about Elias's brother, Benjamin, and his work at a secret laboratory on the island?'

Patterson hesitated. 'Yes, I've been briefed. He was working on a Government-funded project to stop the spread of avian flu.'

'Harry, he was involved in the creation of a modified super virus.'

'Yes,' said Patterson, matter-of-factly. 'Did Vaughn and Pitts manage to acquire any samples?'

'Four test-tubes, about twenty millilitres. We tracked them to an airport on the island but we weren't able to stop them escaping. They were picked up by a light aircraft. Vaughn's injured but they both escaped I'm afraid.'

'And the Pitts' family?'

'Being looked after by the local emergency services. We think Vaughn and Pitts are heading for a rendezvous in Norway, possibly to meet with their contact. If we can get there we might be able to stop them. Can you track the plane?'

'Give me the details.'

Blake reeled off the registration number of the Cessna that he recalled had been stencilled along the side of its fuselage. 'We think it's heading for a place called Stord.' He pronounced it "Stoit" but spelled it for Patterson. 'It's near Bergen.'

'I'll get our boys onto it.' Blake could hear the rustle of paper as he wrote down everything Blake had told him.

'It's not too late to stop this thing, Harry, but you've got to get us off this island. We're still at the airfield at Broadford. The airstrip's a bit on the short side but it's not in bad condition. If you can get us an aircraft as soon as possible we can pursue.'

'I'll do what I can. Stand-by.'

Twenty minutes later, a police car screamed to a halt in front of the aircraft hangar at Broadford airport and a young-looking constable jumped out of the passenger seat.

'Major Blake?'

Blake nodded. He despised anyone addressing him by his former rank since he'd been discharged from the Army but he let it go.

'We were told you needed a pilot in a hurry.'

The officer opened a rear door. A middle-aged man with a grey beard and glasses appeared with a smile that lacked assurance.

'Meeson Heath,' he said, extending a hand. 'They told me you need a plane?'

'We thought a plane was being sent for us,' said Mortensen as Heath headed off in the direction of the hangar. She traded Blake a puzzled look.

'Oh, I see.' Heath stopped in his tracks. 'I was told there was an emergency. They asked if I could help out,' he said, indicating to the police officer who remained standing by the car. 'He said you needed to get off the island as a matter of urgency? Government business?' He whispered the last sentence as if he'd been made privy to some kind of conspiracy. 'I wasn't doing much so I thought, what the hell. Now give me a minute or two and I'll get our ride sorted.'

The pilot disappeared inside the hangar while Blake and Mortensen waited on the apron.

'They've sent you to fly us?' Mortensen called after him.

Heath reappeared with an oily rag in his hands. 'I'm sorry, I assumed you were expecting me?'

'Not exactly,' said Blake, reaching for his phone again. He jabbed at the screen with his index finger, found Patterson's number and redialled. It only rang once.

'Harry, what's going on? I said arrange a flight off the island, not send a weekend pilot from the local flying club.'

'It's the best we could do at short notice,' said Patterson. 'Try to show some appreciation. Now, the good news is the Navy are tracking the Cessna and just as you said it looks like the plane's en route for Scandinavia. There's a destroyer on exercise in the North Atlantic not far from where you are. They have a radar locked on it.'

'Are they going to bring it down?'

Patterson sighed. A drawn-out breath. 'Blake, we're not contemplating shooting it down. That would be...' he struggled for the right word, '...inappropriate at this stage.'

'Inappropriate? You understand what happens if they make that rendezvous?'

'It's complicated.'

'They're over international waters. Shoot down the Goddamn plane before it's too late. Make it look like an accident.'

Blake watched Heath haul a single-prop Piper Arrow onto the apron, duck under its short wings and begin a series of pre-flight checks around the exterior of the aircraft.

'And when crash investigators find the wreckage and piece together that the plane was taken out by a British missile? What then? How's that going to look?'

'A whole lot better than when they find out that the British military had a chance to stop the virus being sold to terrorists and they did nothing.'

'It's not as simple as that. The aircraft's registered in Belgium, for a start. They'll want their own investigation.'

'Then tell them the truth. The pilot's unavoidable collateral.'

'It's not an option,' said Patterson firmly. 'And besides, there's no guarantee the virus would be destroyed.'

'A high altitude explosion over the North Atlantic? I think the odds would be pretty good.'

'It's not going to happen.'

'Why? I don't get it.'

Meeson Heath sprung up onto one of the Piper's wings with the energy of a younger man and jumped into the cockpit to continue his preparations.

'Look, if you're right and the rendezvous with the Iranians is at this place in Norway, then there's still a chance to intercept them,' said Patterson.

'Sounds to me like you're trying to cover up the theft.'

'I've made arrangements for you to be flown to Inverness airport where you can pick up a direct flight to Bergen,' Patterson continued.

'The question is why. Who's arse are you trying to cover?'

'We're not trying to cover anyone's arse. We're trying to locate a virus before it falls into the wrong hands.'

'Of course, if the virus was illegally manufactured in the face of an international ban, that would explain everything. Certainly it would account for the secrecy surrounding the Skyelab laboratories.'

'The Norwegian authorities have been alerted. We've asked for them to provide surveillance on Vaughn and Pitts but not to intervene until we get there. They seem happy to co-operate and will allow us to make the arrests.'

'You told them about the virus?'

'Of course not. No sense in causing them to panic. A senior team from the Norwegian Police Service will pick you up when you get to Bergen. The rest is up to you. Good luck.'

Heath was finishing up when Blake ended the call.

'Hop in,' he said, opening a door over the wing.

Mortensen climbed into the back, settling into a well-worn leather seat. Blake took his place in the front next to the pilot and strapped himself in as the plane rolled onto the runway, past the bullet-ridden hire car that remained embedded in a bank. Heath stared at the wreck but said nothing.

They came to rest at the end of the airstrip while Heath conducted a brief conversation with air traffic control.

'Ready?' asked Heath.

When Blake nodded, they pitched forwards, accelerating along the bumpy concrete with the engine racing. Before they knew it they were levelling out over the top of a thin layer of stratus and into bright sunshine and blue skies.

The vibration of his phone ringing in his pocket surprised Blake. He hadn't anticipated he'd pick up a signal while they were airborne. Heath shot him a look.

'You can't use that up here,' his voice crackled in Blake's ears. 'It'll interfere with the navigation systems.'

'It's urgent. I won't be long,' said Blake, knocking his headset from one ear to answer the call. He'd recognised Harry Patterson's number.

Patterson's voice was distant and distorted. It dropped in and out as they reached the limit of a signal that wasn't designed to be picked up in the skies.

'Harry, we should make Inverness in less than half an hour. What's up?'

'Bad news, I'm afraid. The Navy say they've lost the Cessna.'

'What? How did they manage to lose it?'

'I mean it's vanished. One minute it was there, the next it was gone. I've just had word. We're trying to find out exactly what happened but it looks as though there was a mid-air explosion. It seems they've been blown clean out of the sky.'

TWENTY-EIGHT

A dwarfish grey Westland Lynx helicopter with pumped-up muscular lines was waiting for them at Inverness. Its navigator was a tall, lean airman with perfect teeth. He met Blake and Mortensen in a pre-fabricated hut that passed as a heliport lounge, tucked away behind the main airport terminal building. He introduced himself as Lieutenant Peter Hawkes.

'Major Blake?' he said, approaching them with a chipped flight helmet tucked under his arm. Blake shook his hand and introduced Mortensen. 'We're planning to fly you straight to the crash site if that's okay?'

'I thought Patterson was arranging a direct flight to Norway?' said Mortensen.

'That's fine,' said Blake. 'We need to find out what happened to that plane and whether the virus survived. Has the Coastguard been notified?'

'Yes, Sir,' said Hawkes. 'Their rescue chopper was scrambled from Shetland.'

'As eyes only?'

'They're under strict instructions to keep out of the

water. We've also imposed a five mile exclusion zone. Fishing vessels in the area have been told to keep clear.'

Hawkes had them pull on olive-coloured flight suits and handed them tough black boots made of cracked leather.

'The chopper's ready to go when you are,' he said, then waited patiently as they pulled on lifejackets and stuffed foam noise defenders into their ears. 'Hopefully we can eyeball the wreck site before returning to HMS Dashing.'

They fastened on helmets and the airman led them from the building, around the back of an enormous hangar and onto a helipad where the Lynx was waiting. They were struck by the potent fumes of hot exhaust gases and aviation fuel, the bone-rattling noise of the engines and the rhythmic beat of its rotor blades.

The Lynx was one of the Royal Navy's favoured aircraft, a jack-of-all trades that could be fitted with air-to-surface missiles, torpedoes and submarine-busting depth charges but was also compact enough to operate from a fleet of frigates and destroyers. Blake and Mortensen took seats in the rear bay on opposite sides of a central canvas bench. Strapped themselves in and plugged communication cables into their helmets

The pilot, his face obscured by a mirrored visor, turned in his seat and gave them the thumbs-up. The aircraft shuddered violently as he opened the rotor throttle and a moment later they were lifting off, rotating through ninety degrees as the pilot concentrated on working the collective control and foot pedals. He swung to a north-easterly direction and zipped across the airport runway. A blue and white passenger aircraft was stationary at one end, its take-off held up by their departure.

They flew low and fast, the land quickly giving way to a sea of dark and uninviting waters with white caps whipped up on the surface by the turbulence of the rotors. Ahead the cloud hung over the horizon as a thick, grey soup making it difficult to determine where the sky ended and the sea began.

'We should be over the wreck site within fifty minutes,' Hawkes' voice hissed over the intercom system.

Blake closed his eyes. The noise and vibration helped him to fall asleep almost instantly, his mind drifting into an oblivion of emptiness he was so tired.

He woke to the sound of Hawkes' distorted voice almost an hour later. 'The Coastguard helo has found some debris. They've sent us co-ordinates. We should be there in a few minutes,' he said.

Blake sat upright and leaned forwards to peer out at the sea below. Mortensen shuffled in her seat behind him.

The darkness of the early evening was drawing in but there was no mistaking the remains of the aircraft scattered in the rolling waters. It was as though someone had torn a sheet of paper into a thousand shards and thrown them to the wind. Some unidentifiable scraps of metal were still burning. Others bobbed aimlessly on the swell. It was hard to believe that all the fragments had once fitted together to form an aircraft.

'Can you give us a wide sweep of the area?' Blake asked the pilot.

The helicopter banked sharply upwards until they had a panoramic view of the site. On the horizon, Blake spotted flashing red and white lights he presumed was the Coastguard.

'There's the tail,' said Blake. A large section of metal that had largely retained its shape was semi-submerged in the dark seas. Nearby a chunk of white aluminium with ragged edges rolled on the current. Two letters in dark paint were clearly visible. They matched a section of the registration number Blake had noted earlier on the fuselage of the Cessna.

'That's definitely our plane,' he said to no one in particular. 'Has the Coastguard identified any survivors?'

'Negative,' said Hawkes. 'It's unlikely anyone survived. The best we can hope for is bodies but there's not going to be much left to find if the plane disintegrated in mid-air.'

'Is it possible the plane was damaged before it took off?' asked Mortensen.

'If we'd managed a lucky shot in Skye, the plane wouldn't have taken off, let alone have travelled half-way across the North Atlantic,' said Blake. 'And I doubt that a nine millimetre round could have done this much damage anyway.'

'So what then?'

'I don't know. It's one for the crash investigators. Let's worry about what happened to Vaughn and Pitts? If they're dead, I want proof.'

'And the virus?'

'Let's hope it was obliterated.'

'I'm afraid we're going to need to return to the ship shortly, Sir,' said Hawkes. 'We're running low on fuel.'

'That's fine. I've seen enough from up here. I need to take a closer look anyway.'

The helicopter banked away from the flotsam and set a heading directly north, skimming low over the waves. After fifteen minutes the shape of a warship loomed on the horizon. It had a sleek silhouette with steep angular lines conceived to generate a low radar signature. HMS Dashing was one of the Royal Navy's newest Type-45 destroyers, a modern generation of stealth ships that wasn't pretty but was effective at hiding from the enemy. It was crammed with technology, most of it in the ugly one hundred foot tower and domed radar unit perched above the bridge and which allowed it to track more than a thousand targets from up to 250 miles away – good enough to single-handedly defend London from an aerial attack.

The helicopter landed with a gentle bump on a narrow deck. Blake and Mortensen jumped out and were escorted into an aircraft hangar busy with mechanics and hardware where they were greeted by a young lieutenant commander with a wide smile and a warm welcome.

'If you'd like to follow me I'll take you to your quarters to freshen up,' he said.

'I need to visit the crash site before we lose the last of the light. Can you find me a boat?' Blake asked. He wasn't keen on waiting until the morning when the seas would have had a chance to disperse the wreckage far and wide.

The officer hesitated for a moment. 'Yes, of course,' he said with a forced smile.

'I'll stay,' said Mortensen. 'I'd like to talk to the team who were tracking the plane.'

'We can arrange that.' The officer summoned a rating who led her inside the vessel, and then shouted orders for a rigid inflatable boat to be made ready for immediate departure.

The only way onto the RIB was by clambering down a cargo net attached to the side of the ship and jumping on board as it rose and fell several metres under a heavy swell. Half a dozen men wearing blue overalls, helmets and serious expressions were waiting for Blake. He landed heavily, losing his footing as the boat rocked on a rising wave he hadn't seen coming. He grabbed the back of a seat to keep himself from falling.

The bosun didn't wait for Blake to compose himself. He backed the RIB away from the warship and, as soon as there was clear water between them, threw the throttles forwards, the Yanmar engine responding with a powerful urgency.

. . .

The boat rode the waves like a marlin chasing a school of fish, jumping from the water on every rising swell and crashing back down on its belly with a jarring thud when gravity regained its grip. As they approached the crash zone, the gloom of the night sky was already descending, making the job of finding anything significant in the debris even more difficult.

'We're looking for bodies and a silver case,' Blake shouted over the din of the engine and the crashing bow-wave. 'But don't touch anything. If you see something, shout. Is that clear?'

There was a general muttering from the grim-faced sailors. None seemed particularly pleased to have been volunteered for an unplanned early evening trip. The bosun cut the power as they approached and evidence of the wrecked plane soon became apparent. High-powered searchlights penetrated the murk, sending bright beams of white light reflecting over the surface of the water. As they drifted through scraps of plastic, foam and wood, Blake clambered into the bow and flattened himself on the rubber tubing. Others took up positions to create a 360-degree lookout.

With the engine idling, Blake was struck by the eerie silence of the North Atlantic. The wind had unexpectedly dropped and the sea quelled. There was hardly any sound over the men's breathing other than the slap of waves against the hull. They picked their way through the flotsam, identifying nylon straps, cardboard, insulating fleece and twisted fragments of metal from the fuselage, but nothing that remotely resembled the silver case containing the four test-tubes.

After forty minutes the crew became restless. It was

cold and almost dark. Blake was thinking about calling off the search for the night when the RIB brushed against a long shard of aluminium the size of a scaffold plank. It looked as though it was probably from a wing. Its edges were torn and ragged. In places the paint was blackened and chipped. Blake reached over the hull and grabbed one end. It struck him as odd that it was sitting so high in the water. It lifted easily and when Blake saw what had been propping it up, he tossed it to one side.

An organic mass bobbed to the surface. A human body lying face down in the water with a mop of black hair spread out around its skull in an almost perfect circle. One arm was twisted from the elbow at an unnatural angle. The other was missing, torn from its shoulder socket. It took three of them to pull the corpse on board and as they lifted it from the water they saw its legs were missing too. Both limbs had been cleanly amputated above the knee leaving fleshy stumps of muscle and bone.

The corpse thudded into the bottom of the boat and the crew crowded around. Someone shone a torch over Blake's shoulder lighting up an unfamiliar face. Most of the man's forehead and one of his eye sockets was missing. In its place was an ugly star-shaped wound where flesh and bone had been blown away.

TWENTY-NINE

Mortensen was sitting at a table in the officers' mess with the ship's commander when Blake returned. He stooped through a low entrance hatch, reminding himself why the Royal Navy had never been a career option for someone of his height. All the low beams and watertight hatches would have meant a lifetime of bumped heads and mild concussion.

The officer jumped from his seat. He was a small man with a shock of black hair tinged with grey and two gold epaulettes on the shoulders of his black sweater.

'Commander John Saxby,' he said, gripping Blake's hand firmly. Blake caught the aroma of strong aftershave, an old-fashioned scent that reminded him of his grandfather. The commander ushered him to a seat next to Mortensen and beckoned to a steward to bring them coffee.

Mortensen had stripped out of her flying overalls but still wore the heavy black boots with her business suit. 'Did you find anything?' she asked, as Blake slumped into a chair.

'A body but no sign of the case.'

'Pitts?'

Blake shook his head. The steward approached their

table with a silver pot and thick white cups and saucers balanced on a tray. He laid them out with a jug of cream and a pot of brown sugar rocks.

'It's the pilot,' Blake said when the steward retreated. 'Shot before the crash and with half his face missing.'

Mortensen was about to take a sip of coffee. Her hand stopped half way to her mouth. 'Shot?'

'A bullet in the back of the head. Not much of an entry wound, so probably fired at close range.'

'An execution? But why shoot the pilot?'

Blake had no answer. He took a mouthful of coffee. It was strong and hot.

'At least that explains the crash,' Mortensen continued. 'They had an argument, killed the pilot and the Cessna ditched into the sea.'

'It doesn't explain the explosion though. And who in their right mind shoots the pilot of a plane mid-way across the North Atlantic, argument or not?'

'Maybe the pilot was threatening to blackmail them? Or was demanding more money? What about the case? Any sign of it?'

Blake shook his head. Saxby had been listening with interest. He leaned forwards with his arms on the table juddering from the power of the two 25-megawatt gas turbine engines in the belly of the warship.

'Could you kindly explain what's going? I was given orders to track a light aircraft from Scotland supposedly because it was carrying two escaped British prisoners. Why the interest from MI5?'

Blake set his cup down on a saucer. 'It's a sensitive issue,' he said.

'And I signed the Official Secrets Act too,' said Saxby.

'There were two escaped prisoners on that plane.' Blake lowered his voice. He was conscious the mess hatch was open and there was a constant flow of people passing. 'Our interest is in an experimental virus they stole from a laboratory on the Isle of Skye. It was developed by British scientists researching a vaccine for a bird flu mutation. If it's released into the environment it has the potential to infect millions of people. The men who stole it were on their way to trade it with an Iranian terrorist.'

'I see,' said Saxby. 'And the virus was on the plane?'

Blake nodded. 'So you can understand our urgency to search the crash site as soon as possible.'

'And what were you hoping to find? This virus couldn't possibly have survived an explosion.'

'Ideally? A couple of bodies and a silver case containing four test-tubes. So far we have the body of the pilot and a hell of a mess. The best outcome is our escapees have been killed and the virus vaporised, but I'd like some proof.'

'And if you can't find it?'

Blake shrugged. 'I guess we keep looking.'

'The Coastguard has been using thermal imaging to look for any survivors. If your prisoners haven't been found by now then it's safe to assume they're dead but you may never recover their bodies. The ocean is a cruel mistress. As for the case, it's more than likely on the seabed. That's about two thousand metres below us, about the safest place it could be. No one's going to find it down there.'

'I hope you're right,' said Mortensen.

Saxby's eyes drifted to the door. Blake subconsciously followed his gaze and saw another officer waiting patiently to attract the captain's attention.

Saxby beckoned him in. 'Ms Mortensen, I think you've met our principal warfare officer, Lieutenant Commander Hughes?'

'He kindly talked me through the radar operations and

how you tracked the Cessna before it disappeared,' she said with a smile in his direction.

'I'm sorry to interrupt, Sir, but there's something I thought you should know,' he said, stepping across the room and hovering by the table. 'I've had the operators review the radar imagery in case there was something we missed.' He turned his attention to Blake and Mortensen. 'Advanced technology means our systems can store a large amount of radar images that we constantly record from a 250-mile radius around the ship. It's all kept on a hard drive. It's a lot of data and sometimes things get overlooked,' he explained.

'And?' said Saxby.

'We concentrated specifically on the immediate crash zone and rolled back to an hour before we lost contact with the plane. There was a boat, Sir, within half a mile of where the wreckage was found. It had been anchored in the same location for several hours.'

'A fishing boat?'

'I don't think so. The signature was all wrong and, besides, fishing boats don't tend to weigh anchor in the middle of the North Atlantic.'

'What are you trying to say?' asked Blake.

'Well, within minutes of the plane disappearing the boat was gone. The radar imaging shows it set off at high speed on a north-easterly bearing.'

'Are you still tracking it?' asked Blake.

'Of course,' said Hughes. 'It appears to be making a direct course for the Norwegian coast.'

THIRTY

The Princess V56 was skimming across the ocean in excess of thirty knots. Rolling and pitching, its fibreglass hull thudding through the swell. Below deck, a nauseous wave rose from the pit of Ricky Vaughn's stomach. His face flushed and a hot sweat broke over his brow. Closing his eyes only made it worse. He'd remembered from somewhere that focusing on a single point was a good way of overcoming sea sickness. He tried fixing on a light fitting in the galley opposite and inhaled lungfuls of air through his nose. It didn't make any difference. His head was thick and fuzzy and he had to concentrate hard on keeping the contents of his stomach down. And every time the vessel crashed over the top of a wave, a dagger of pain exploded down his arm and across his chest. A handful of pills had taken the edge off but he wasn't going to get better with a bullet lodged in his shoulder. The crew had done their best to patch him up. They'd cleaned and bandaged the wound and hung his arm in a sling around his neck. But he needed a surgeon, anaesthetic and a few weeks' recovery. None of which was an imminent prospect. Still, there'd be plenty of time to worry about his health when they'd delivered the virus.

It was all right for Pitts. As soon as they'd been hauled on board he'd found a cabin below deck and fallen into a deep slumber on one of the king-size beds below deck. The thunderous reverberation of his snoring reminded Vaughn that he was suffering no ill-effects from the journey.

A judder from the engines was the first sign of a problem. It was as though they were running low on diesel or there was dirt in the fuel lines. Vaughn knew he should have been concerned. They were in the middle of the ocean and a good two hours away from the coast. But as the powerboat slowed he was relieved. His nausea eased a little as the pitching and rolling subsided. Eventually the engines died completely and the vessel was left bobbing gently on the rolling swell.

One of the Norwegian crew members stuck his blond head through a hatch.

'Small mechanical problem. Engine is overheating. Soon have it fixed,' he said.

Vaughn heard footsteps clattering over the deck. He raised his good arm, gave a thumbs-up and the Norwegian disappeared. He struggled to sit upright, dragged his feet together and felt the hard edge of the silver case he'd stowed on the floor. He reached for it, set it on the table and flicked open its metal catches. Inside four glass test-tubes sealed with orange plastic caps were lined up in their tight-fitting polystyrene lining. He plucked one out between a thumb and forefinger, rolled it on its side and watched the viscous liquid flow lazily along the glass.

'What are you doing?'

He hadn't heard Pitts emerge from his cabin. His lank hair looked even more unkempt than usual. His eyes were bleary with sleep.

'I was curious to know what twenty five million pounds looks like,' said Vaughn.

Pitts shrugged. He knew exactly what twenty five million pounds looked like. It looked like green numbers flashing on a computer screen. In the good old days. Before the crash. 'Put it back,' he said.

'What?'

'I said put it back.'

'Screw you.'

'I'm not joking. You don't know what you're doing.'

Vaughn's eyes burned. 'Don't tell me what to do.'

'Smash that tube and you sign our death warrants. Weren't you listening to Benjamin? A couple of drops and we'll both be infected. Then it's an inevitable, slow death. Like the sound of that? Now put it back.'

'I don't like your tone,' said Vaughn, setting the vial on the table. It rolled across the polished surface. Pitts held his breath as it came to rest with a gentle chink on a raised lip. 'Speak to me like that again and I'll blow your brains out, you jumped-up public-school prick.'

Vaughn had reached for his handgun. He aimed for the centre of Pitts' forehead, right between his piggy eyes. He stared at Pitts' face, puffy and bloated, feeling something between pity and revulsion. Even incarcerated within the confines of a maximum security prison he'd kept to a strict exercise regime that maintained his muscle tone. Pitts' body was a corpulent disgrace. He had a physique that had grown fat on a lifestyle of riches. His skin was pasty and his stomach bloated.

'Ricky, come on,' Pitts said softly. 'We're partners aren't we?'

When Pitts started scratching the back of his hand, Vaughn felt his trigger-finger twitch. 'Partners in crime? Don't make me laugh you fat freak. I don't need you any more.'

The test-tube rolled across the table. Pitts' eyes darted

between the gun and the virus. His pupils were full and black.

'Not looking good for you right now, is it?' Vaughn was enjoying Pitts' obvious discomfort.

'You need me.'

'I don't need you.'

'It's my deal.'

'Correction. It *was* your deal.'

'My plan. My deal. My virus.'

'Not any more, sunshine. It was a good plan but we all have to adapt to survive. Didn't they teach you that at university?'

It was true. It was a decent plan that had largely worked out, apart from the incident at the airport in Skye. But a flesh wound to Vaughn's shoulder was a small price to pay for a twenty five million pound jackpot. And they were almost home and dry. It had been easy to persuade the lily-livered pilot to reduce the Cessna's cruising speed and altitude as they headed out into the Atlantic. A nudge in the back of his neck with the cold steel of Vaughn's nine millimetre Sig Sauer had done the trick. He'd put up little resistance when they'd demanded he depressurised the cabin. That was Pitts' idea. No good killing the pilot and finding the air pressure had sealed the door closed. Vaughn had made him switch on the auto-pilot and then shot him. The bullet barely left a mark in the back of his skull. It made a mess of the dashboard though. A pebble dash of blood, bone and brains that splattered the dials and peppered the windscreen.

The Norwegian powerboat crew were waiting exactly where they said they'd be. Two giant men with forearms like girders had dragged Vaughn and Pitts on board after they'd parachuted into the sea. The captain of the vessel had put himself in charge of detonating the bomb, using a mobile phone to trigger a device hidden in the parcel that Bogaert had unwittingly stowed in the hold.

'You want more money? Is that it?' asked Pitts.

'I don't want more money. I'm taking *all* the money.'

'You know I could have asked anyone in that stinking jail to get me out. But I chose you. I trusted you. I offered you a fair deal, half the money for helping me get the virus and deliver it safely.'

'Maybe you're a bad judge of character. The thing is you needed my help but now I don't need you. I have the virus and you have nothing,' said Vaughn.

'Think you're smarter than me? So go ahead, shoot me. Let's finish it here and now.'

Pitts lifted his chin and threw up his arms. Vaughn's finger twitched again. The knuckles on his gun-hand were white.

'But first let me ask one question.' Vaughn let the barrel of his gun drop a fraction. 'Where is the rendezvous with Khan? I assume you must know if you feel confident enough to kill me? I mean you might have the virus but do you have the contacts to sell it?'

Vaughn's twisted mouth turned up in an ugly smile. 'You already told me, you fool. It's a place called "Stort".'

'The island or somewhere in the municipality?'

Vaughn's grin fell from his face.

'The fact is you have no idea and without knowing where the rendezvous is that virus is worthless. No deal, no cash.'

'Tell me,' demanded Vaughn.

'And if I do? What then? You'll shoot me. Not much of an incentive. And don't think the crew have any idea either. They're under instructions to deliver us into harbour and that's it.'

Vaughn lowered his gun. 'I could make this very painful for you. Are you a Tarantino fan?'

'What?'

'Quentin Tarantino? Reservoir Dogs? I love that film. Remember how it starts with Mr Orange shot in the stomach and bleeding, a lot, after a robbery's that's gone tits up? He knows he's dying but Mr White tells him that although it's painful to be hit in the stomach, it's not as painful as being shot in the knee.'

Pitts' eyes followed the barrel of Vaughn's gun as it came to rest aimed at his legs.

'It's called kneecapping. It's supposed to be the most painful place to be shot without killing someone. Something to do with the bone and cartilage and muscle fibres or something. But mostly it's about the bone. So, where's the rendezvous?'

A defiant smile crept over Pitts' lips. 'Screw you.'

'Problem?' said a voice.

The captain had appeared from the deck above, an MP5 slung over his shoulder. He ran a hand through the thick black beard that covered most of his face.

Vaughn glanced over his shoulder without lowering his weapon. 'No problem,' he said, as the engines coughed and growled back into life.

'Problem's been fixed,' said the captain. 'We're about to get going again.'

Vaughn saw his eyes were focused on the silver case lying open with the tops of the test-tubes exposed. Vaughn dropped his gun in his lap and snatched the loose tube from the table. He slipped it back into its slot in the polystyrene.

'Thank you,' he said, as the bow of the vessel rose up under the power of the twin 900hp engines and a spasm made an unwelcome return in his stomach.

THIRTY-ONE

The ship was alive with the quiet efficiency of a crew who knew intuitively what they were doing, a slick operation produced from years of training. Blake was standing alongside Commander Saxby on the bridge watching a radar screen glowing green. The white blip that interested them was on the far edge of the circle, moving at speed towards the Norwegian coast. The vessel had stopped briefly, for some unknown reason, but was back at full velocity.

'I think it's unlikely we'll be able to head her off,' said Saxby, frowning as he glanced up from the screen to peer out into the void of darkness beyond the Dashing's bow. Her Rolls Royce gas turbines had her cutting through the water like a dagger through silk, a foamy trail churned up in her wake. 'They're managing at least 30 knots. We don't have much more than that and we're running at full speed.'

Blake moved away from the radar and stepped between a gap in a bank of screens that stretched across the front of the bridge. An officer at each position was focusing on their various displays. Blake grabbed a pair of binoculars and directed them at a point he guessed was the horizon, searching for lights or a sign of the boat they were pursuing. Mortensen came up behind him.

'We're not to going make it,' she said. 'Time to start thinking about a Plan B.'

'I'm not sure I had much to offer in the way of a Plan A,' said Blake, chewing his lip.

'We still have time to cut them off before they make it to Stord. Could we intercept them by helicopter?'

'Sir, we're approaching the two mile mark,' one of the officers sitting near Saxby called out.

Saxby acknowledged the information and issued a quietly-spoken order. 'Hard on starboard on my command,' he said. 'Standby for my mark.'

'What are you doing? You're calling off the chase?' said Blake.

'We're on the limit of Norwegian territorial waters. We can't go any further.'

'We're NATO allies. We have an agreement to operate in each other's waters.'

'Yes, and I'm sure our Norwegian friends would be very happy to see us. But we can't just drop in unannounced. They'll want to know why. Do you want to tell them?'

Blake stared at the commander, who met his eye and held it.

'No,' said Blake at last.

'I thought not.'

'So what now?' said Mortensen. 'We can't just give up.'

Blake mulled over the possibilities. There was no way the commander was going to allow his ship to cross into Norwegian waters and any other visible encroachment was going to require an explanation they didn't want to give.

'We'll sneak in,' said Blake.

'How?'

'Commander, how would you feel about lending us your RIB again?'

The ride was cold and wet. Blake sat on the floor in the bow next to Mortensen, resting his back against the engine housing and clinging to a rope that looped around the boat's rubber hull. Behind them a grim-faced helmsman perched on the edge of his seat gripping a chrome steering wheel in both hands. Two Royal Marines Saxby had insisted on sending had taken up positions aft with SA80 rifles resting in their laps.

They made quick time crashing over the lumpy sea and soon the hull of the warship faded into the inky night. The Pacific 22 rigid inflatable was designed for speed and manoeuvrability, not for protecting its passengers from the elements. Blake was soon drenched by a shower of salty spray. Ahead a dark outcrop took shape jutting into the water where the coast loomed. Beyond the headland twinkling lights of towns and villages appeared.

They sped into a wide inlet cut into a shadowy landscape shaped by steep cliffs and illuminated by the ghostly light of a half-moon. The helmsman kept them close to the shore, avoiding the shipping channels but where razor-sharp rocks peaked dangerously out of the water. When he shouted to Blake his words were inaudible over the buzz of the engine. Blake stood and leaned closer.

'It looks like the boat's made harbour,' the helmsman said, easing back the throttles. The RIB slowed to swimming pace. He tapped a screen that was taking a direct feed from HMS Dashing's radar. A white dot blipped in the centre of a series of contracting circles.

'How quickly can we get there?'

'In no time at all.'

The harbour turned out to be a natural cove, an almost perfectly symmetrical horseshoe at the foot of a hill peppered with houses. Red and grey roofs of traditional Norwegian homes were visible in tiers among the vegetation. Two short piers came into view as they drifted around a peninsula. A small fleet of pleasure craft and fishing boats was moored up. One vessel stood out among the others. The Princess motor cruiser was tied up alongside the nearest pier. It was four times the size of the next biggest vessel, all sleek lines, sharp curves and tinted windows. Its hull had been finished in pearl white and trimmed with sparkling chrome handrails.

'I guess that's it,' Blake whispered to Mortensen, fearful the sound of his voice would carry.

'They're certainly not skimping on style.'

The sweet pungency of pine fused with the salt of the sea floated on the breeze. Blake drew a deep breath and listened hard. Every sound registered loudly, from the slap of the current against the hull to the cry of a nocturnal creature from the woodland in the hills. A familiar tension tightened the muscles of his stomach. A reaction to the fear of the unknown. He drew his gun and directed the helmsman to take them closer.

They approached the stern of the Princess where a teak-decked platform protruded like a jutting bottom lip. It was either a low-level terrace for swimming or a landing stage for smaller craft. Or maybe both. Whatever its purpose it provided quick and easy access from the sea, which suited Blake perfectly. A light was on in an area Blake imagined was the main living quarters but there was no other sign of life on board. He stood in the bow of the RIB with one foot on the inflatable hull.

One of the Marines grabbed a mooring post on the pier and they came to rest within a couple of metres of the boat.

Blake readied himself. He rocked on one leg, trying to judge the distance of his leap. He was about to jump when a sliding door opened on a deck above. A bearded man sloped out into the open and palmed a cigarette between his lips with a nonchalant cool.

Blake froze with his Browning levelled. He was close enough to put a bullet between the man's eyes. A match flared loud and bright in the silent darkness, lighting up a craggy face lined by age and exposure to the sun. The man drew hard on the tobacco and blew out the flame with a lungful of smoke. His shoulders relaxed with the hit of nicotine. He flicked the spent match over the side.

He stared into the distance, his attention on nothing in particular. A lazy disinterest in the village built into the hill. His gaze shifted to the pier and the fishing boats bobbing on the current. Which was when he saw an arm clinging to a mooring post and found it attached to the body of a Royal Marine with a rifle cocked in his direction. Four more faces were staring at him. For a split second nobody reacted.

Then everything happened at once.

First came the man's shout of alarm. A cry somewhere between an exclamation of surprise and a hollered order. In the same instant he snatched at an MP5 sub-machine gun hidden in the folds of his coat. He swung it in a fluid arc from a strap over his shoulder, firing a rapid volley of shots that somehow missed the RIB and hissed into the water. Muzzle flashes lit up the night. Blake stumbled backwards, knocking Mortensen off her feet.

The helmsman had seen the danger, threw the throttles into reverse and a surge from the two hundred horsepower engine pulled them out of the line of fire. A staccato crack of rifles opened up over Blake's head but the shots flew harmlessly into the air as the Marines were thrown off balance by the sudden acceleration.

Someone fired up the Princess' engines. They snarled with a resonant gurgle like the rumbling digestive system of a giant sea monster. Blake raised his head over the RIB's hull and saw a broiling froth emerge from under the teak platform. The shadow of a figure ran the length of a lower deck freeing the mooring lines and the boat heaved forwards. Its bow rose up and the vessel leapt forwards, charging for open water and spewing a foaming trail in its wake.

'Don't let them get away!' Blake shouted.

The helmsman reversed the thrust and after a brief moment where they seemed to tread water, the RIB shot forwards. It hit the Princess' choppy wake with a thud. The motor cruiser had already made some distance and was pulling away around a headland.

'Can we catch her?' Blake yelled over the din of the engines.

'We can make 27 knots, maybe more with a far wind but she'll be able to max out nearer 35. Best I can do is try to keep her in sight,' said the helmsman.

A quick calculation in Blake's head suggested that in less than seven minutes the crew of the Princess would be able to pull out a lead of around a mile. Unless by some miracle she developed a mechanical problem. Blake tucked himself low into the bow. He squinted at the vanishing Princess. There had to be a way to stop her. He rose into a crouch and shuffled to the rear of the RIB. His progress was hampered by the instability of the vessel. He grabbed the sleeve of one of the Marines as the RIB was pitched sideways threatening to knock him off his feet.

'What's the effective range of your rifle?' Blake shouted in the Marine's ear.

'Around three hundred meters. Why?'

'How good's your shooting?'

The Marine had comic-book heroic features. A square jaw and steely, grey eyes. Clean cut and with a trace of acne that suggested he was barely out of his teens. Not that Blake underestimated his abilities. He knew the type. A man who knew no fear. A professional who'd stop at nothing to get his job done.

'If you're going to ask for a clean shot at that boat while we're bouncing around in this RIB, that's a tough challenge.'

'You have to try.' Blake stumbled as they hit a rogue wave at an oblique angle. 'It's the only way of stopping her. She's outrunning us by five to seven knots.'

'I'll give it my best,' he said but the look in his eye suggested he thought his chances were slim.

'Aim for the stern, above the waterline. Her engines are probably well protected within the hull but there's a chance you could hit a fuel line.'

The Marine crabbed past Blake with his green beret pulled low over his brow and took up a position on one knee with his rifle jammed into his shoulder. He squinted through an optic sight and wrapped a finger around the trigger. But every time he steadied himself for a shot his rifle was thrown askew by a jolt of the hull catching the heavy swell. So he opted to lay down a barrage of rapid fire, banking on the law of chance that at least one of the rounds might find its mark. He emptied his magazine, lowered his rifle and peered across the fjord. In the gloom it was impossible to tell whether the Princess had been hit. She certainly showed no sign of any ballistics damage.

The Marine turned to Blake with an apologetic look. 'I can't be sure I even came close,' he said.

The spluttering cough of one of the engines juddered through the hull.

'We're losing speed,' said a dark-haired Norwegian sitting at the helm.

The captain's eyes narrowed. They were almost out of sight of the chasing RIB. A few more minutes and they'd be clean away. It was poor timing. They should have concentrated on fixing the mechanical problem as soon as they made land. But then they hadn't anticipated this.

'Arnesen, go and fix it,' he said to a third man who nodded and disappeared down a flight of steps.

Jonas Lanvik turned up the collar of his coat against the cold and slotted a new magazine into his MP5. He had no idea who their pursuers were and he wasn't planning on waiting to find out. They'd made their intentions clear and if he'd not happened to step outside for a cigarette as they were preparing to board the Princess, they might all now be in custody. Whether it was a police or military patrol didn't really matter. The fact was they'd been discovered and his priority was to vanish. He'd make some enquiries later about how they'd been rumbled. It was no random patrol. Whoever was in the RIB had been acting on intelligence.

Arnesen reappeared out of breath, cleaning his hands on an oil-stained rag. 'It's the same engine, running too hot. A problem with the water filter or the impeller. Nothing I can fix while we're in the water. We'll have to make do on one engine.'

'Go look at it again,' said Lanvik. 'We'll be dead before we get to a dry dock. Find a way.'

Arnesen rolled his eyes and dropped back below deck. The high-pitched engine hum of the RIB sounded a way off, behind them and slightly to their port side. Then an explosive starburst caught Lanvik's eye followed a fraction of a second later by a loud pop. Three long bursts of rifle fire followed but not a single round came remotely close. It was a desperate act. Lanvik fished in a pocket for a packet of cigarettes. He lit one and exhaled slowly.

'Look,' shouted Mortensen, 'I think we're gaining on them.' Her hair was crusted with salt and her cheeks vibrant with a ruddy glow.

Blake grabbed a pair of binoculars from the helmsman. Mortensen was right. Even from a distance, and through the darkness of the fjord, he could see the Princess's bow was riding lower in the water. She wasn't limping but someone had definitely cut her speed.

'Something's wrong,' said Blake.

'Did we hit her?'

'I can't see any damage but it's difficult to be sure.'

He had a good view of her broadside. One man was at the helm on an exposed fly bridge. He never once looked back. Kept his eyes on the way ahead. The window in the deck below was smoked for privacy and offered no view inside. It was more like a mirror than a window, reflecting the boat's foaming bow wave. Blake swept the binoculars along the vessel's sleek lines and found the bearded figure they'd surprised in the cove. He was standing with an arm gripping a gun and the other looped around a metal rail. A reminder that even if they were able to close the distance to the Princess they remained horribly exposed in the inflatable. The boat was quick and agile but its rubber tubing that kept them afloat was susceptible to bullet holes. Blake knew an attempt to draw alongside the Princess with its crew armed with sub-machine guns was nothing short of suicidal.

Mortensen tapped him on the elbow. 'Blake, look,' she said, pointing away to their left. Both boats were heading for a rocky mass that loomed out of the water. A row of flashing lights snaked their way in a long line across the horizon high above the land. At first Blake wondered if they might be the landing lights from planes. But they were static. Too low and too close together.

Through the binoculars he focused on one of the nearest lights. Indistinct against the night sky he saw the top of a towering concrete column. It was easily a hundred metres tall supporting a thick cable looping from the top and falling into the blackness below.

A bridge. Or more accurately a series of bridges.

They weren't heading towards a single land mass at all but a collection of islands spanning the fjord.

A buzz of machine gun fire crackled through the chill air. The bearded man in the stern of the Princess had opened fire as the RIB drew close. The star-shaped muzzle blasts briefly illuminated his upper body and revealed a face set with a determined grimace. The helmsman yanked hard on the wheel and flipped the RIB onto its port side veering clear of the deadly hail of bullets.

'Keep us just out of range of that gun but don't lose her whatever you do,' Blake shouted.

The helmsman nodded and manoeuvred the RIB. A third man appeared on the Princess and took up position on the bow deck with his arms over the silver railings and a weapon aimed in their direction.

'Stalemate,' said Mortensen.

'Not quite,' said Blake. 'Hold your position and whatever you do don't deviate from this course,' he said to the helmsman as the seed of a plan formed in his mind. Mortensen was right. They'd reached a stand-off. Unless they could regain the element of surprise.

An arrowhead of rock rose out of the water directly in their path. A peninsula that divided the fjord in two. On their current bearing, the RIB was heading for a passage to the east of the island. The Princess was steaming towards a channel on the opposite side and within minutes would disappear from view.

'Give it full throttle, everything you've got,' said Blake.

'We're going to lose them,' said Mortensen. She glanced at the approaching land mass.

'Let them see us racing ahead.'

The helmsman pushed the throttles to their stops and the RIB surged forwards past the first outcrop of rock. A moment later they lost sight of the Princess as it veered away to the west of the island.

'Now kill the engines and bring us around slowly,' said Blake.

The helmsman obeyed the instruction without question. He closed the throttles and the RIB slowed. He threw the wheel hard to the right and tickled the engine to bring the boat around to face the way they'd come.

'Follow the shoreline but don't break cover of the rock,' said Blake.

'Are you insane?' said Mortensen. 'We're losing them.'

'They're expecting us to appear on the other side of the island.'

'Where we can intercept them if we can get ahead.'

'And then what? They'll gun us down. Besides it's what they'll expect us to do. They can't outrun us so their best hope is to slip away in the darkness. If it was me, I'd wait until I was out of sight behind the island, turn around and head back. Hopefully I'd be able to find a sheltered cove to hide.'

'And if you're wrong?'

Blake moved behind the helmsman and tapped the radar screen on his console. 'Which one's the Princess?' The helmsman pointed to a bright white pixel. 'You mean the one that's turning and reversing course?' he said, looking at Mortensen with a triumphant smile.

'So you were right. We're still out-gunned.'

'But now we have the element of surprise.'

They heard the roar of an engine first. Then a flash of white emerged from the other side of a spine of rocks they were hidden behind, racing back along the channel in the direction of the cove where they had found the Princess moored.

'After her!' yelled Blake.

The helmsman had already opened the throttles and they shot into open water, hitting the Princess' wake with a thud that rolled them from one side to the other. Blake was grateful to see the bearded gunman had moved from the stern. There were now three figures standing together on the fly bridge with their backs to the RIB.

Blake waited in the bow with his foot on the hull urging the inflatable on. If they could make it to within a few metres of the motor cruiser he was confident he could leap onto the low stern deck. The helmsman was using all his years of experience to hold the inflatable steady against the turbulent, choppy water. Blake was coiled to spring when the Princess veered sharply away. At the same instant he was startled by a sharp crack of gunfire fired over his head by one of the Marines. The RIB broke to the right. Blake was thrown sideways and grabbed a handful of rope to stop himself falling overboard. Then the night lit up with a burst of automatic fire from the bridge of the Princess.

'Turn around and get back after them,' Blake shouted to the helmsman.

They'd lost their element of surprise. Time to throw caution to the wind. The RIB turned in a tight arc heading back towards the motor cruiser.

'Ride in her wake and get as close as you can.' The two Marines had their rifles primed, jammed into their shoulders and levelled at the Princess. 'Put down some covering fire.'

The RIB dropped back into the Princess' wake and quickly closed the distance. Blake settled himself in the bow with the wind in his hair and sea spray stinging his eyes. He concentrated on the teak-decked platform riding low over the waves, looking for a handhold to grab when he pounced. In the periphery of his vision he saw movement on the bridge. One of the Marines fired a controlled burst of three rounds and the Princess turned sharply off course, heading for the shore.

'I think I zapped one, Sir,' said the Marine with steely grey eyes. 'Target at the wheel went down.'

The Princess had been put on a collision course with a stony beach less than half a kilometre away. And kept going. No one on the boat reacted. It kept hurtling onwards, arcing gently to the left, eating up the water towards the shore. It hit the beach hard and flew straight out of the water. Her hull hissed through the wet shingle and came to an abrupt halt with her functioning propeller revolving at full speed, digging a hole in the ground and spitting stones and coarse sand into the air.

THIRTY-TWO

Two men were sprawled in ugly contortions across the fly bridge. Blake wondered for a moment if they were both dead. Certainly the blond giant slumped over the wheel with the side of his head missing was showing no signs of life. His body was twisted and limp, thrown out of his chair onto a console of dials and screens. A second man was in a heap on the floor. The dark-haired captain, Jonas Lanvik, was lying face down with his coat crumpled around his body and the barrel of his MP5 protruding from under his arm.

Lanvik stirred as Blake approached. A groan slipped from somewhere at the back of his throat. Alive but unconscious. The bridge was covered with blood and brain matter. A viscous coating clung and dripped from the seats, deck and navigating console. But Blake was pretty sure the man on the floor hadn't been hit. More likely he'd been thrown off his feet when the Princess veered and been knocked unconscious as he fell.

Blake found a key still in the ignition lock and killed the engine. He wiped blood-sticky fingers on the back of his legs, failed to find a pulse on the man hanging over the steering wheel and turned his attention to Lanvik. He leant over him with his Browning aimed under his chin and pulled the MP5 clear of his body. The muzzle was still hot and the magazine spent. He tossed to one of the Marines who'd followed him on board.

'Nice shot,' said Blake, nodding to the dead blond at the wheel.

'He stood up and put his head in my sights,' the Marine explained, as if justifying why he'd removed part of the man's skull.

'Good job.'

'What about him?' The Marine kicked Lanvik's feet with his boot.

'Concussed. Looks like he caught his head on the table on his way down but I think he'll be fine.'

Blake swept a patch of hair away from Lanvik's face looking for a head wound. He found nothing. He was about to search the captain's pockets for identity papers when his body twitched and Lanvik rolled groggily onto his back. His eyes sprung open and his expression twisted into a mixture of horror and surprise. He opened his mouth to speak but thought better of it when he saw the Browning in his face.

'Easy does it, sunshine. Now sit up, slowly.' Blake waved the gun in an upwards motion.

Lanvik's eyes fell on the Marine and the SA80 lined up with his chest as he eased himself into a sitting position.

'What's your name?' asked Blake.

Dark, resolute pupils stared back at him. The man's skin was like leather, tanned and lined from a life lived outdoors. Puffy bags sagged under his eyes but his beard was lustrously black and lacking any sign of grey.

Either he didn't understand the question or, as Blake suspected, he was being obdurate.

'Name?' Blake repeated.

242

The man jutted out his chin but kept his mouth shut.

'Let's not waste time with petty pleasantries then.' Blake raised his gun under Lanvik's nose. He didn't have time to play games. 'The two men you picked up earlier this afternoon, where are they?'

Lanvik's eyes flickered upwards for a fraction of a second. An involuntary tell that he'd just visualised the moment. 'I don't know what you're talking about,' he said.

'Don't lie. I need to know where Vaughn and Pitts are.'

No response.

'They had a small case with them. Did you see it?'

Another involuntary glance over Blake's shoulder.

'You took them to the harbour where we found you moored.' Blake said it more as a statement than a question. 'Where were they going?' Blake raised his voice.

No response.

'You want to do this the hard way?' Blake said lowering his Browning. He snatched Lanvik's wrist. He tugged it from his lap and forced it palm flat against the deck, pinning it down with the barrel of his gun. 'Where are Vaughn and Pitts?'

Lanvik drew a deep breath through his nose. His lips pursed tightly closed and his eyes widened.

'Blake!' Mortensen's voice echoed through the boat from the deck below. 'Blake, you need to see this.'

'I'll be right there,' he shouted back. He turned to the Marine standing with his rifle at his hip. 'Go and check she's all right.'

Blake watched him go, listening to his heavy footsteps before continuing. 'Just you and me now. Do you understand? Let's try a different approach.' His tone was softer. Calming.

He grabbed the man by his shoulders, swung him through ninety degrees and tapped his forehead with two fingers. 'Sleep,' he said, and instantly Lenvik's eyes fell closed and his body went limp. Blake intoned soothing words into his ear until he was satisfied Lanvik was completely under. He laid the flaccid body on the deck and crossed the captain's hands over his stomach.

'Blake? You need to come see this.' Mortensen's head peeked through the stairwell. 'What are you doing?'

'Finding out where Vaughn and Pitts are.'

'Blake, this really can't wait.'

'I'll be there in a minute,' he said. Mortensen caught the sharpness in his tone. 'What's your name?' he asked the soporific Norwegian.

'Jonas Lenvik.'

'And you're the skipper?'

'Yes.'

'Do you know the two Englishmen Ricky Vaughn and Elias Pitts?'

'We picked them up after they jumped from their plane.'

'Why did they jump?'

'To make it look like they'd been killed, in case the British authorities were following them.'

'So they blew up their own plane to cover their tracks? How?'

'A bomb in the hold that was detonated by a mobile phone call.'

Blake glanced at Mortensen who was standing motionless halfway up the stairs. 'And you did that from the boat?'

'Yes,' said Lenvik.

'Did Vaughn and Pitts have a silver case with them?'

'Yes.'

'Do you know what was in it?'

'They said it was important and they needed to deliver it to Khan.'

'Who's Khan?'

'The contact they're meeting.'

'Our Iranian agent,' said Blake, raising his eyes at Mortensen. 'Did you see what was in the case?'

'Four test-tubes. The two Englishmen were arguing about them.'

'What did they say?'

'The man called Vaughn was threatening to kill the other one.'

'Where's the meeting with Khan?'

'A house at Mortjorna.'

'Where's that?'

'By a fjord, a few miles inland.'

'When's it happening?' Blake glanced at his watch.

'I don't know.'

'You must know. Think hard.'

'No one told me anything about the meeting.'

Blake stood. 'Okay, sleep deeply, Mr Lenvik.' He stepped over the captain's body and followed Mortensen to the lower deck.

'What's the urgency?'

'There's a body,' she said.

She led him through a sliding door into an opulent lounge fitted out with polished dark wood surfaces, cream carpet and leather sofas. One of the Marines was standing with his rifle aimed at a crewman slumped on a sofa. His hands were bound behind his back. Shoulder-length straw-coloured hair fell over his eyes. Mortensen ignored them both, striding into a sleek galley with marble worktops and shiny stainless-steel fittings. She led Blake down a set of steps into a wood-panelled lobby. She pushed at a door and stood to one side.

Blake squeezed past and saw the body on the bed, its feet on the floor and arms stretched out wide. A head lolled to one side. Rivulets of blood dribbled from the mouth, nose and ears. An engorged tongue protruded from between blue lips and bulbous eyes stared lifelessly from their sockets at the ceiling. Blake walked around the bed. A dark, red ring encircled the neck.

'He's been garrotted,' said Blake. He put a hand on the side of the pale face. It was cold to the touch. 'He's been dead for at least a couple of hours. Any sign of the case?'

Mortensen shook her head and let her eyes fall on the twisted smile that was fixed on the man's face. A loose bandage wrapped around one of his shoulders had leaked onto the bed and stained it crimson.

'I don't understand,' she said. 'Why did they kill Ricky Vaughn?'

THIRTY-THREE

They returned to the horseshoe cove and moored alongside a pier on the far side of the harbour. It was deserted. Blake had been worried the noise of gunfire from the Princess may have woken the village. But they had either dismissed the noise or decided to keep their heads down. Either way it suited Blake. The last thing he needed was a neighbourhood of overly-curious locals asking awkward questions.

The pier extended into the bay from a shingle beach of blue-grey flat stones. There were no houses nearby and the only building was a red tin-roofed boathouse set back from the water's edge. Blake helped Mortensen out of the RIB and onto the pier.

'Persuade you boys to join us?' said Blake.

'Would love to but the Commander was quite clear. We're not allowed to step foot on Norwegian soil. Can't go starting a diplomatic incident. We'll have to leave you to it, I'm afraid,' said the young Marine with the grey eyes.

'Shame,' said Blake. 'We'd have been grateful for the help.'

The helmsman reversed the RIB away from the pier.

He gave a one-handed wave and sped away into the shadows of the night leaving Blake and Mortensen alone.

'Next stop, Mortjorna. Any ideas?' said Blake. He stepped off the pier onto a worn patch of ground where the earth had been scrubbed away by hundreds of pairs of feet.

'I could hitch up my skirt and try to flag down the next passing vehicle.'

'You're not wearing a skirt.'

'I think you're missing the point,' she said. 'Or we could find a car to hotwire.'

'They teach you that at spook school?'

'They teach us lots of things,' Mortensen said with a sly grin. 'So which is it to be?'

'I think I prefer plan B given the lack of traffic at this time in the morning.'

'Good choice,' she said Mortensen setting off along a dusty track that ran up through a hillside of pines. It was the only way in or out of the cove and climbed steeply for several hundred metres before flattening out where the first houses appeared. The car they found was an old four-wheel drive Toyota pick-up parked on the side of the road. A vehicle favoured by African rebel gangs and Middle-Eastern jihadists, minus a heavy machine-gun mounted in the flatbed. Its paintwork was faded and covered in a film of dirt. Mortensen let out a triumphant squeak when the handle of the driver's door clicked open in her hand.

'Your carriage awaits,' she said with a victorious glint in her eye.

The fabric of the driver's seat was badly worn. In places yellow foam was visible through it. Mortensen ducked under the dashboard while Blake leaned against the back of the truck trying to look casual. He surveyed the road left and right. A small crescent of houses had been built into the hillside ahead on their left but there were no lights on in any of the homes. The owner of the truck was unlikely to miss it for several hours.

'Did they leave the keys?' Blake asked in a loud whisper.

'No such luck.'

The click of a starter motor was followed by the sound of the engine spluttering, coughing and finally turning over. It belched a plume of black diesel smoke.

'Get in,' said Mortensen, leaning out of the door.

Blake jumped to attention and hopped into the passenger seat. 'That's an impressive skill,' he said. A bundle of wires like multi-coloured spaghetti hung from under the dash by Mortensen's knee where she'd disembow-elled the ignition's electrics. He watched her tickle the accelerator, trying to counter the cold engine stutter.

'A little trick my dad taught me.'

'What was he, a mechanic?'

'No, a car thief.' She turned to see Blake's reaction. 'I'm kidding. Never mind. See if you can find Mortjorna on your phone.'

Blake held up his mobile between a finger and thumb. 'Dead,' he said. The screen was blank and unresponsive. 'Yours?'

'The same. Not sure I'd get a signal here anyway. So back to the old-fashioned methods. Have a look for a map.'

Blake fumbled around in the glovebox. He found a pair of oil-stained leather gloves and a set of screwdrivers. Underneath a pile of cracked CD cases he found a creased map that looked as though it hadn't been opened in years. The kind that folds up like a concertina and is almost always impossible to refold the way it's supposed to. The paper had worn and ripped where the folds had been worked open and closed too many times. He spread it out on his lap. Flicked on an overhead light and twisted it around trying to find his bearings.

'We must be here,' Mortensen said, jabbing her finger near the bottom of the map.

It was difficult to tell. The coastline looked as though it had been ripped roughly out of the sea. It was made up entirely of ragged coves, inlets, islands and fjords, like the country had been constructed of thin tissue paper and the waters surrounding it were corrosive acid that had eaten away at its edges.

'You might be right,' said Blake, holding the map to his face. 'Saetrevik,' he read.

'Can you see Mortjorna?'

'It's north east from here. I'd say less than four miles away.'

Mortensen crashed the gears into first and pulled away with a lurch. Only when they were clear of the village did she turn on the headlights.

'There's only one building on the fjord marked on the map,' said Blake, squinting to see the tiny print.

'So guide me there.'

Out of the village they turned onto a main road, followed it for less than a mile and took a narrow tree-lined track that meandered forever upwards. Progress was frustratingly slow. The Toyota chugged along obediently like a faithful old dog used to the familiar paths around its home, happiest meandering at low speed. Unsure of the roads, Mortensen approached each turn cautiously, fighting with the wheel over an uneven camber. At one point the shimmering waters of a fjord opened up through a gap in the trees, capturing the reflection of the moon but Blake urged Mortensen on.

'It's about half a mile further on,' he said, staring through the grime-encrusted windscreen.

Mortensen rolled her neck to ease the tension in her

shoulders. 'I'll be glad of a decent bath when this is all over,' she said.

'I'd settle for a warm shower and a beer right now.'

'A cold glass of Sauvignon...' She didn't have the chance to finish the sentence.

Blake grabbed the steering wheel and pulled it hard to the left. 'Pull in! Quickly!' he shouted.

Mortensen wrenched back control and crashed off the road through a bush. They came to a violent halt under a canopy of trees.

'Kill the engine and the lights,' Blake hissed.

'What is it?' Mortensen asked, deliberately stalling the engine.

'Listen.' Blake cocked his head and opened his door a fraction.

The whirling buzz of a helicopter washed through the branches overhead. Faintly at first but progressively louder. He peered at the tops of the pines towering above them and through a narrow gap that exposed the sky.

The noise grew louder until it was a deafening roar. The powerful glare from a searchlight hit them. It turned night into day for a second. The hulk of a hovering helicopter followed. It flashed overhead and was gone as soon as it had appeared. The whining drone of rotor blades and gas turbine engines tore off into the distance and silence enveloped them.

'Do you think it was looking for us?' asked Mortensen.

'They don't know we're here.'

'Unless the crew of the Princess alerted someone.'

'I doubt it. One of them's dead and I left another one out cold. As for the captain, I made sure he'll have no memory of us. It'll be a routine patrol securing a perimeter, which is good news.'

'How's that good news?'

'It means we must be close to the rendezvous point. Let's lose the truck. We're best off on foot. It looks like a short hop down through this wooded area to the edge of the fjord,' said Blake, passing the map to Mortensen. 'The cabin should be easy to locate from there.'

Blake tried to put out of his mind the thought that they were heading into the unknown with no intelligence and no back-up. It went against everything his training had taught him. A senior Iranian agent was on his way to negotiate for the Armageddon Virus which meant the place would be swarming with security. The helicopter was probably the least of their worries. He set his Browning on the dashboard and emptied his pockets. One spare magazine. Thirteen rounds. Good job he wasn't a superstitious man.

'How many rounds do you have left?'

'Two magazines and one half-full clip locked and loaded,' said Mortensen.

'Not exactly armed to the teeth are we?'

Mortensen shrugged. 'No time to call in the cavalry now.'

'We *are* the cavalry. You ready?'

The hop down to the fjord turned into a mad scramble. They slid down slick mud, trying to control their descent by clutching at sharp branches that scratched their hands. They crashed noisily out onto a narrow plateau ten metres above the sparkling blue waters of the fjord. They dropped into a crouch as they stumbled out into the open, eyes wide, scanning to see if they'd been spotted, or more likely overheard.

'Okay?' Blake mouthed.

Mortensen nodded as she straightened out her suit.

They were perched on the top of a rock protruding from the hillside. It provided a natural viewing platform to take

252

in the length and breadth of the fjord and the verdant forest that enclosed it.

'It's beautiful,' whispered Mortensen. The first glimmer of the new day had already broken the horizon although the sun remained out of sight.

Blake put a finger to his lips and pointed along the shore to a solitary building. It looked more like a Swiss ski lodge than a Scandinavian cabin, partially clad in wooden weatherboards with a grey slate roof, wide eaves and balconies on the upper floor. Just like on the cuckoo clock Blake's grandfather had owned. A wooden pier extended from a deck at the front of the house. Behind it, Blake counted at least a dozen cars. Mostly black. Highly polished. Tinted glass. Range Rovers and Mercedes mostly.

'Looks like someone's having a party,' he said.

Two men in dark suits and shirts appeared, picked out by a halogen security light. Short-barrelled sub-machine guns were slung casually across their stomachs. They walked lazily. Two bored guards on perimeter duties who looked as though they'd rather be anywhere else. Blake and Mortensen watched silently as they sauntered around the back of a squat outhouse and dropped onto a pebble beach. Their shadows disappeared under the darkness of the wood deck and eventually their voices drifted into the distance.

'The map showed a drive leading from the main road on the other side of the house. If their patrol route takes that in, it should give us at least ten minutes to find a way in before they return,' said Blake.

'What if there are more guards?'

Blake caught the edge in Mortensen's voice. 'Let's deal with that eventuality when it arises. We'll be fine,' he tried to assure her.

Blake pulled his pistol from his belt, loaded a round in the breach and prepared to move.

'Don't you ever get scared?'

Mortensen's question stopped him in his tracks. He reached out for her hand. It was icy cold. 'Keep your head down and follow me. You'll be fine,' he repeated.

'You didn't answer my question.'

'It's all a state of mind. Something in your head that needs to be controlled. The trick is to ignore what your head is telling you sometimes. Concentrate on the job.'

'Blake, we don't stand a chance if they start shooting.'

'I'm not here on a suicide mission. We get into the house, locate the virus and get the hell out.'

'How?'

'We'll find some leverage. But my biggest worry right now is that Pitts manages to offload that virus to some crackpot terrorist who'll do God knows what with it. We're the only hope of stopping that happening and I can't do it on my own. I need you, fully functioning. Understand?'

Mortensen nodded but there was sadness in her eyes. No, maybe not sadness. Fear perhaps.

'You're going to be just fine.' He squeezed her hand. 'We've got to hurry. Let's move,' he said, scrambling to his left, into the woods and down to the back of the house. His feet almost ran away from him on the steep incline and he had to concentrate hard on avoiding the craggy tree trunks that sprouted from the ground. His shins burned from the effort of staying upright.

He reached the bottom, breathing heavily, and turned to catch Mortensen as she hurtled out into the open. She narrowly avoided crashing into the rear end of a Mercedes. Blake pulled her close, feeling her ribcage rise and fall. The pounding of her heart.

'I'm okay,' she breathed.

'Keep your eyes open. I'm going to check the house. Stay here.'

He left Mortensen hidden between two vehicles while he scuttled across a gravel parking area and fell against a stone wall. It was cool. Cold almost. Moss mottled the wall where it met the ground. Four windows on the lower floor were in darkness. Made sense. Everyone would be at the front of the house with its views across the fjord. All the living areas would have been constructed around that vista. The rear of the property, where the sun rarely shone, was where the utilitarian rooms would be. Storerooms. Pantry. Kitchen. Bathrooms.

Blake stole around the side of the house, tried a door but found it locked. He snatched a glimpse through the glass into an empty hallway that told him nothing. He needed a better vantage point, somewhere to assess the layout of the house and see how many men were inside. He scooted back to Mortensen and ducked down to her level so they were concealed behind the bodywork of a gleaming Range Rover.

'I need to see what's going on at the front,' he whispered. 'We'll skirt around that outhouse, drop onto the beach and come up under the deck.'

With the sun below the horizon he figured they could snatch a look through the windows without much risk of being seen. There were lights on inside and the reflective properties of the glass should keep them from being spotted. As long as they didn't stray too close.

Blake checked for guards and seeing the area was clear, darted out of the cover of the cars. He winced as his boots crunched on the gravel. Mortensen kept close behind but froze when a bright light lit them up.

'Security light,' said Blake, pointing at a lamp above the locked door he'd tried. 'There's nobody there.' He grabbed her arm and propelled her forwards.

She stumbled, lost her footing and half-fell to the floor.

At the same moment Blake heard the drone of a helicopter somewhere in the near distance. No doubt the same aircraft that had spooked them earlier, still on its patrol loop, coming over the hill from behind the house. And closing fast. The unmistakable whump of rotor blades grew louder until it made their ears pulsate. They were caught in no-mans-land with nowhere to hide.

Blake pulled Mortensen forwards so roughly that she squealed in shock. The helicopter shot out over the trees and buzzed the roof of the house. Its powerful searchlight picked out the landscape below. Blake and Mortensen threw themselves flat on the ground. The downdraught whipped up their clothing and covered them in a cloud of dust and debris. When Blake looked up, the chopper was soaring skywards, turning a wide, slow loop over the fjord. Coming around for another pass. They must have been spotted, caught in the open under the brilliance of the security light.

It was a Hughes 500, a variant of the helicopter the military was so fond of for observational duties. Light and highly manoeuvrable with a distinctive shape that reminded him of a giant dragonfly. Its fuselage was painted matt black with no markings. No insignia. Not even a registration number. Legs dangled from each side of an opening where the rear doors had been removed. Feet propped on the skids. That wasn't a good sign. With the weak rays of morning sunshine growing stronger, he caught a fleeting glimpse of a dark figure silhouetted in the doorway. And with a sickening dread noticed the long-barrelled rifle mounted with a high-power sight.

'Get up! Run!' shouted Blake.

He was beyond caring whether his voice would be heard by anyone inside the house.

'Snipers!' he screamed.

THIRTY-FOUR

The outbuilding was less than thirty metres away by Blake's estimation. It looked like a garage but with no obvious entrance for a vehicle. It had a slate roof and walls constructed of the same grey stone used on the lodge. Whatever it was for, it was their best hope of evasion.

Blake scrambled to his feet, dragging Mortensen with him. His legs pumped in an all-out sprint, hoping Mortensen was close behind but knowing there was nothing he could do to make her run faster. He reached the far corner of the building and looked for a door. When he found one, it was locked.

Mortensen joined him a second later, panting hard. Her eyes wide and her chest heaving. Blake gave her a 'what now?' look.

'Over there.' She pointed to the upturned hull of a decrepit rowing boat. It was propped up on bricks in the middle of a scrubby lawn and partially hidden behind a barren bush. The wood had been bleached grey-green by age and exposure to the elements. It wasn't quite what Blake had in mind but, in a list of options that numbered one, it was going to have to do. Mortensen turned and ran.

Blake glanced over his shoulder. The chopper had completed its turn. It was heading back in their direction with its nose dipped. The beam of its searchlight was a translucent shaft hunting them down.

Mortensen skidded on the wet grass, deliberately falling feet first. Her body disappeared under the boat. Blake scrabbled in behind her as the growl of the helicopter swelled. They sat with their knees up to their chests, holding their breath, waiting for an explosion of gunfire to rip the boat apart. A standard .308 NATO round from a sniper rifle at close range would cut the flimsy boat to shreds as if it was balsawood. Flesh and bone would fare little better but Blake pushed the thought from his mind.

The helicopter approached so low it caused the hull to vibrate. Its downdraught kicked up through the gap they'd dived through. As Blake's vision became accustomed to the dark he saw Mortensen's eyes wide and her jaw slack. Her breathing was shallow. He tried smiling because he didn't know what else to do. It seemed a silly gesture when their lives were hanging on a thread and he gave it up.

The roar of the rotor blades enveloped them so completely that Blake sensed the aircraft was directly overhead. He braced himself for a gunshot, hoping that if this was their moment to die then at least it would be a clean shot to a vital organ. The worst he could imagine was a deep flesh wound that left them to bleed out in agony. Not that he was worried for himself. He just couldn't contemplate the thought of Mortensen suffering. Of dying an ignominious death. His grip on his Browning tightened. He contemplated rolling out onto the grass to take a shot at the chopper. A couple of well-placed rounds near the engine housing or at the windshield could be enough to bring it down. He was close enough that there was a chance he could make the rounds count. The beam of a searchlight bled under the boat and partially illuminated their pallid faces.

'Is this it?'

'No,' said Blake with as much confidence as he could muster. 'I don't think they saw us.' He wasn't sure he believed it but it might be true.

Mortensen screwed her eyes tightly closed and they waited.

But as soon as it had come, the light was gone.

The pitch of the rotor blades changed and half a minute later the sound of the helicopter had vanished completely.

'It's gone,' said Mortensen. Her face broke into a grin of relief.

'For now.' Blake peeked out from under the hull to make sure. There was no sign of it.

'Do you think it's coming back?'

'It'll keep sweeping the area at least until Khan arrives. The sooner we can get into the house the better.'

'What makes you so sure Khan's not here yet?'

'I'm not, it's only a feeling. The way the guards were behaving. They looked way too relaxed. You can usually spot a subtle change in body language when the head of an organisation arrives. It's always the same. Prime minister, president or a commander-in-chief. They all have the same effect. It's like there's a tension in the air, the moment they've been planning for and it's time to step up. My guess is Khan's expected at around first light.'

'So how do we get into the house?'

'I haven't figured that out yet. Stay here while I see if I can get a view through the front windows. I'll be a couple of minutes. No more. You'll be safe, but if anyone comes do what you have to,' said Blake nodding at Mortensen's Glock.

She lifted her gun as if realising for the first time she was holding it. 'Okay, but be quick.'

Blake pulled a wan smile and rolled out onto the lawn. He rose in a crouch, looked left and right and listened hard. He wondered how long he had before the two guards on patrol reappeared.

He jogged to the outbuilding and sidled along a wall towards the fjord where he found a slipway rolling down to the lapping waters. It spilled out from a set of double doors set into the narrow end of the building. A boathouse, he realised. He snatched a darting look around the corner and heard the dull voices of men in casual conversation. Artificial light was spilling from the house onto the wooden deck but no one was out in the open. He turned back the way he'd come and halted at a small window alongside the locked door.

Inside was in darkness but, by holding his hands to his eyes, he was able to make out the shape of a boat. It was a sleek-looking speedboat with a polished hardwood hull and a seating booth that had been cut into the body. Fixed on the far wall behind the vessel were shelves heaving with cans, bottles, boxes and tools. But what intrigued him was what he saw on the floor on the far side of the room. It looked like a quadrangular halo. Four thin lines of light each about a metre long in a perfect square. He squinted to see better and was hit by a dawning realisation.

He turned and ran back to the inverted hull of the old rowing boat.

'Alex, it's me,' he hissed, barely able to conceal his excitement.

Mortensen's head appeared followed by her shoulders and the rest of her body. She snaked her way out onto the lawn.

'What is it?'

'I've just found a way into the house,' he said.

THIRTY-FIVE

Blake pointed through the window of the boathouse. 'Do you see it?' he said.

Mortensen jammed her face up against the glass. 'What am I looking for?'

'A hatch in the floor, in the far corner.'

'Oh, right.'

Blake was deflated by the disappointment in her voice. 'There's a light on behind it.'

'So?'

'I bet that it leads to the house.'

'Or down to a basement storage room. Anyway the door's locked.' As if to make her point Mortensen grabbed the handle and tried to pull it open.

'It can't be that difficult to break in.'

'Really? With a house full of bad guys less than a stone's throw away? What are you going to do? Kick the door in? Smash the window and reach in for the key? That's a double-glazed window, by the way. Any idea how difficult they are to smash?'

'Not with this,' he said, holding up his Browning.

'So what's the plan? Shoot it out or smash it with the

stock? Either way you'll have a small army on us before we've made it inside.'

'Well, okay Miss Smartarse. Do you have a better idea?'

Mortensen gave him a withering look, reached into her hair and pulled out two thin pins. She bit off a rubber end from one and bent the other in half around her finger. She dropped to her knees and inserted the metal prongs into the barrel like a surgeon beginning a lifesaving operation.

'You pick locks too?' said Blake.

'Of course,' she said, throwing him a surprised frown. 'Basic training. It's more subtle and less likely to get us shot. Now shut up and let me concentrate.'

'I thought that only worked in films.'

'You thought wrong.' She bit the end of her tongue as she concentrated. 'It's not quite as easy as I'd hoped.'

'What's wrong?'

'Someone's left a key in the other side, but if I can just - there, got it.'

Blake heard the tinkle of a key fall to the concrete floor. Then, with her head cocked to one side listening to the tiny clicks of pins lifting in the locking barrel, Mortensen set back to work with a series of delicate pokes and tweaks. In less than twenty seconds she had the door open. She stood with a triumphant grin.

'Impressive work, Miss Mortensen. Shall we?' Blake held the door open. He ushered her inside and pulled it closed behind them.

'Wow, someone has some panache.'

An Italian-designed Saetta sat gleaming on a trailer. A modern retro-styled nineteen-foot speedboat that would have looked more at home cruising the Italian lakes. Mortensen ran a finger along its finely-varnished African mahogany hull and sucked her breath through her teeth. The grain of the timbers ebbed light and dark like the closely-clipped flank of a pedigree racehorse. It was set off against a silver trim and fixtures. Opulent leather seats had been hand-stitched and its flowing curves gave more than a passing nod to 1950s chic.

Blake was unimpressed. He gave the boat only a cursory glance as he headed for the hatch in the floor. He found a recessed brass ring-pull and heaved it open. He aimed his Browning through the gap but saw only steep concrete stairs leading into a narrow passageway lit by florescent lamps on the walls.

'Listen!' hissed Mortensen.

From the corner of his eye, Blake saw her stiffen. He froze and listened hard.

Voices. A low chatter. Drawing closer. Blake checked his watch. Eight minutes since they'd seen the two guards patrolling around the house. More than likely the same pair on their way around again.

'Get behind the boat,' Blake whispered.

Mortensen snapped into action, squeezing between the bow and the double doors at the front of the building. She took up a position crouched down behind the Saetta. Blake lowered the hatch and joined her.

The voices grew louder until they could distinguish individual tones. Blake thought he recognised the language although he couldn't understand the words. He was reasonably sure they were speaking Farsi. One man was doing the majority of the talking, as though he was telling a long story. The other was encouraging him with the odd grunt and occasional interjection. Blake peered over the top of the boat and saw their shadows through the window. A flame flared as one of the men lit a cigarette. Their conversation became more animated, both voices rising. They were close. Maybe right outside the door.

And then silence.

'Come on, move away,' Blake urged under his breath.

A face appeared in the window so suddenly that it made him jump. An unearthly visage with thick brows, dark lips and coal black pupils that swam in milky pools. A cloud of condensation from the guard's warm breath formed where he pressed his nose against the glass. He raised his hands to cover his brow and squinted into the shadows just as Blake had done.

Blake ducked behind the speedboat trying to hold his adrenaline in check. He turned to Mortensen and put his finger to his lips. He listened for the door handle opening. Seconds passed like minutes, painfully slowly. One of the voices piped up in a short burst of unintelligible garble followed by a throaty laugh. When Blake looked over the boat again the face in the window was gone.

'All clear,' he said when he was certain the guards had moved on.

He returned to the hatch, threw it open and dropped through the space in the floor. Mortensen followed. It took them into a passageway with a low roof and white painted walls that ran in the direction of the house for around thirty metres and ended in a flight of steps. Halfway along, it opened out into a small room that served as a wine cellar. Hundreds of dusty bottles were stacked on their sides in racks.

Blake stopped to grab a random bottle.

'A 1990 French burgundy,' he said examining the faded label by the weak light. 'Do you think it's any good?'

'Get us out of here in one piece and you can take one as a souvenir,' said Mortensen, pushing past. 'But for now, put it back.'

Blake returned the bottle with a reluctant shrug and followed her towards the stairs at the end of the passageway.

They were built of wood worn smooth and spiralled up to a heavy oak door pulled shut.

Mortensen went first. She put her ear against the door and listened.

'I can hear voices. But they're muffled. I don't think there's anyone on the other side.'

'Only one way to find out for sure. Ready?' said Blake.

Mortensen nodded and eased the door open a fraction. She put her eye up to the gap and looked both ways.

'It leads into a hallway. There's a flight of stairs opposite and a closed door to the right,' she relayed to Blake.

She pulled the door open and they emerged into a dark hallway, just as Mortensen had described. An unlit staircase led to an upper floor. A door to their right was pulled shut. The murmur of conversation was coming from behind it. Deep masculine voices speaking casually. Not the incessant chatter of a party but the refrained dialogue of people killing time. Like strangers chatting in an airport departure lounge. Blake put his ear to it and realised the sound was also travelling down the stairs from somewhere above. He took a step back and pondered the enigma.

Only one way to find out what was going on. He took the steps two at a time, with Mortensen following. His back brushed against one of the walls and he kept his feet away from the obvious weak points in the middle of the boards where a creak might give them away.

He wasn't surprised to find the stairs rotated through ninety degrees and led to a mezzanine floor where a line of doors opened into what he presumed were bedrooms and bathrooms. A balustrade ran along the length of the landing overlooking a lounge below. It explained how the sound had carried more clearly down the stairs than through the heavy door.

Blake counted seven men. All but one of them was

dark-skinned and dressed in cheap black suits and shirts, like the guards they'd seen patrolling outside. For the most part they were armed with sub-machine guns. Some wore them slung over their shoulders, others had set them down near to hand on tables and surfaces. Bulges in their jackets hinted they were also carrying small arms. A few were sitting, others drifted around the room aimlessly, kicking their feet on the varnished floor. They exchanged brief words as though they were waiting for something to happen.

A man who Blake immediately recognised as Elias Pitts was sitting in the middle of the room in an armchair near a blazing open fire. He looked exhausted. His skin was pale and his eyes puffy. He was absentmindedly chewing his fingernails. His shoulders were tense and his thighs bobbed rhythmically as he bounced his feet on the floor. Mortensen nudged Blake's elbow and pointed to a stippled silver case lying on a low coffee table within Pitts' reach. It was no bigger than a child's lunchbox secured closed with two clasps.

'The Armageddon Virus,' Mortensen breathed.

THIRTY-SIX

The plane dropped through the early morning haze as an indistinct blur against the low rising sun. The drone of its propeller cut through the silence like an angry mosquito in the humid heat of summer. Its wings bobbed as it glided through shifting thermals rising from the fjord. For a moment it seemed to hang in the air as if suspended on a strand of elastic. Behind the controls, a pilot in shirt-sleeves was concentrating on keeping the aircraft level. He sensed the man in the seat behind was growing restless.

Khan pulled his coat tightly around his body and stared at the icy waters below. He shuddered. He hated northern Europe for its grey, dreary days and long nights. Most of all he hated the bitter cold. Scandinavia, he thought, was the worst with its tedious snow-capped mountains, endless fjords and rolling pine forests. He wondered how anyone put up with it. He'd rather be back in Iran. At least the mountains were tempered by a climate of dusty heat, even if the cities were choked by smog.

Beside him, Tariq Shahidi was fussing with his .45 handgun.

'Put it away,' Khan encouraged with a light hand on his arm. 'Have the men secured the house?'

Shahida holstered his gun and shrugged. Khan liked to call him his PA. He thought it fitted better with his cover as a businessman. In reality Shahida was a close protection officer who knew far more about inflicting pain with his bare hands than he did about spreadsheets and appointments diaries.

'A team's had the house locked down since yesterday. Everything's okay,' he said.

The lodge appeared through a light mist at the foot of a dense forest of pines. The plane hit the water and skimmed across the surface on buoyant skis, startling half a dozen men into action. They ran from all directions like spooked sheep to take up positions around the jetty with their weapons poised. Shahidi was out of the door and onto the jetty before the plane had barely come to rest. He stood with his back to the aircraft. He crossed his hands over his stomach and scanned for threats.

Khan stood and smoothed the creases from his trousers. He had chosen one of his favourite powder-blue suits, tailored by his man in London. He set it off with an open-necked white shirt with double cuffs protruding from his jacket sleeves by a regulation half inch. He adjusted his aviator sunglasses, checked the time on a gold Rolex and ran a hand through a handsome head of jet black hair.

He bent down to pick up a briefcase from the floor and was almost knocked off his feet by the unexpected turbulence of a low-flying helicopter that rocked the plane. Khan steadied himself and scowled through a window at the aircraft banking hard over the fjord. Two snipers were hanging from the back door. He regained his composure and stepped onto the jetty. A man whose face he recognised but whose name eluded him was on hand to greet him. One of his security detail.

'Is he here?' Khan asked. He brushed past the man with barely an acknowledgement.

'He's in the house.'

Khan took long strides towards the house with his overcoat flowing behind him like a cape. A set of folding glass doors opened up into the lounge from the outside deck. He clipped his sunglasses onto the front of his shirt and saw Pitts slumped in an armchair near an open fire. He was fiddling with his fingers like a naughty child about to be chastised. His breath rasped loudly in the silence. Not what Khan had expected at all. Pitts looked up, rose from his seat and flinched as a log on the fire popped loudly. Khan suppressed a smile.

'Ricky Vaughn?'

Pitts approached Khan with his hand outstretched. 'Elias Pitts. Ricky Vaughn's been unavoidably and permanently delayed,' he said.

'Dead?'

'Yes.'

'Sit down,' said Khan. His gaze fell on the silver case. 'Is that the virus?'

'Four test-tubes. Twenty millilitres of Armageddon Virus. It's everything the laboratory has produced.'

Khan lowered himself in a chair opposite Pitts. He laid his briefcase flat on the table with its handle facing towards him.

'You'd only need a few drops to start a worldwide pandemic,' Pitts added, filling an awkward silence.

'May I?' asked Khan.

Pitts pushed the case across the table. Khan flicked the catches open to reveal four glass tubes in a protective bed of polystyrene. He prised out one of the tubes and lifted it to the light between his finger and thumb. He let the liquid roll along the glass, mesmerised by its lazy progress from one end to the other.

'It looks like water,' said Khan.

'Looks can be deceiving.'

Khan glanced over the top of the tube at Pitts. '*Is* it water?'

'No, of course not. Don't be ridiculous.'

'You're sure?'

'Of course I'm sure. It's come straight from the laboratory in Scotland, as we agreed.'

'Your brother is the bio-chemist who helped produce the virus?'

'That's right.'

'And he was working on a vaccine?'

'You're well informed.'

'How close are they to completing the vaccine?'

'It doesn't matter. That's everything the lab produced and without it they can't carry on with the research. They'd need to start from scratch and that could take years. They can't even admit it's been stolen because under international law they weren't supposed to have been developing it in the first place. It's too dangerous.'

'And you're happy to sell it? No regrets and no doubts?'

'I expect to be paid well for my efforts. We agreed twenty five million which I think is more than fair price given that it could secure Iran's place on the international stage of superpowers. If your country wants to go nose-to-nose with the US and Europe, if it wants real power, you're holding it right there in your hand. That test-tube is more potent than any nuclear weapon or army. That's world domination in twenty millilitres.'

'Once our scientists have produced a vaccine.'

'Which shouldn't take long. The British have done the hard work. As soon as the vaccine is complete and your country is inoculated, the rest of the world will be at your feet. When you threaten to unleash that virus every Western regime you despise will be on their knees begging you not to do it.'

'And my guarantee that I have the genuine virus?'

'You have my word.'

'Your word? I don't even know you. My deal was with Ricky Vaughn.'

'He was a hired hand, a bit of muscle, that's all. He was useful in helping to get the virus but he was a liability.'

'So you killed him?'

'Is that a problem?'

'And now you won't have to share the money, of course.'

'The thought hadn't crossed my mind,' said Pitts with a sickly smile.

'What about your brother. Silenced?'

'Yes, of course,' he lied.

'And I can trust you, can I?'

'Absolutely.'

'Because you know it wouldn't be wise to lie to me.'

'I understand.'

'I'm not sure do. I know all about you, Mr Pitts, and when it comes to money there's not an honest bone in your body.'

'I don't know what you mean,' said Pitts.

'You met Ricky Vaughn in prison, didn't you?'

'Yes, but that's nothing to do with - '

'What were you jailed for?'

Pitts stayed silent. A scab on the back of his hand started to itch. He fought the desire to scratch.

'I know who you are and I know what you've done. You're a conman, Mr Pitts. You trick people out of money.'

'That's not true - ' Pitts protested.

'Not so long ago you surrounded yourself with every luxury your wealth could afford. But when you lost everything you turned to crime, conning people out of their money.'

'The market crash ruined everything. One day I was earning more money than I knew what to do with, the next it was running out of my hands like sand. I was out of a job, redundant to requirements and left with nothing.'

'So you thought you'd trick people out of their money instead.'

'We do what we have to to survive. Isn't that what you do?'

'My honesty isn't in question here, Mr Pitts. You're trying to strike a deal with me for twenty five million pounds and you're fundamentally untrustworthy. That's not my opinion. That is fact.'

'This is different,' said Pitts.

'You're a born liar. I think you have difficulty knowing yourself when you're lying. So how can I be sure you're telling the truth now? You give me your word but we've established it's next to worthless. I need something more tangible.'

'One test-tube alone contains more than enough virus to cause an international meltdown. It's been engineered to be as contagious as winter flu and as deadly as the plague. One week of that in your system and you'll be drowning in your own blood. Imagine the fear that's going to cause.'

'I know exactly what the virus is capable of. That's not in doubt. What I need is proof these test-tubes contain what you say.'

Pitts wiped a sheen of sweat from his brow. 'What sort of proof?'

'Twenty five million pounds worth of proof. I need to know our investment is sound.'

'I have no proof, for God's sake.'

'So we have a problem.'

Khan let Pitts stew. He watched him squirm in his chair, scratching at the skin on his hand until his nails drew blood.

'Of course, there's one way to prove beyond any doubt whether you're lying to me,' said Khan eventually.

Pitts stopped scratching. 'There is?'

Khan slotted the test-tube back in its case, closed the lid and put it on the table. He beckoned to Shahida who was standing on the far side of the room. For a man who was more bulk than brain he moved with fluid ease. He came up behind Pitts' chair. Slipped a meaty arm around his neck and pinned him to the seat.

'What are you doing?' Pitts gasped.

'Just relax, Mr Pitts,' said Khan. He flicked open the catches of his briefcase. The box he pulled out was long and thin. Hinged on one side. He placed it on the table and plucked one of the test-tubes from the silver case. It happened to be the one second from the right. A random choice. He unscrewed the orange cap.

'What's going on?' Pitts eyes opened wide.

Khan took out a medical syringe from the box, removed a cap from the needle and plunged it into the liquid. He drew off a small quantity.

'Time to find out if you've been telling the truth.'

He grabbed Pitts' arm. Pulled back the sleeve to expose bare flesh. Traced the line of a faint vein with the syringe needle.

'For God's sake, are you crazy?' Pitts' eyes bulged in their sockets.

'It's the only way we'll be able to tell for sure if this is

273

the virus. If it's a harmless liquid you have nothing to worry about. At least from the injection.'

'If you infect me, everyone in this lodge is at risk of contracting it too. That includes you,' said Pitts through clenched teeth.

'How long's the incubation period?'

'I don't know. About the same as winter flu.'

'And how long do you think you'd take to die?' Khan applied a little pressure to the needle so it bowed the skin without puncturing it.

'Christ, I don't know! Please put the needle down. I swear to you that's the Armageddon Virus.'

'You're sure?'

Tears had welled in Pitts eyes and his body was rigid.

'Yes, it's the goddamn virus. Stick that needle in my arm and I'm as good as dead – and you'll be next. Please, don't do this. I'm begging you.'

Khan pressed the syringe a little harder. The needle punctured the skin and a drop of blood pooled on Pitts' arm.

'Okay, I believe you,' said Khan. Nobody was that good at faking fear. He stepped away and returned to his chair. 'Let him go, Tariq.'

Pitts' relief was palpable, like a smell in the air. Shahidi relaxed his grip and Pitts slumped into his seat. He rubbed his throat where his windpipe had been constricted.

'Satisfied?' asked Pitts.

'Twenty five million is a lot of money. You'll understand I had to be sure about the purity of the sample.' Khan squirted the contents of the syringe back into the test-tube and sealed the cap.

'So we have a deal?'

Khan smiled thinly. He replaced the syringe in its case and flipped open his briefcase.

'We have an understanding?' Pitts repeated.

'Yes, we have an understanding, Mr Pitts.'

Pitts didn't have time to register that Khan had produced a gun from his briefcase. A Beretta 92 with the unmistakably long barrel of a silencer. Khan squeezed the trigger and a single bullet pierced Pitts' forehead just above his right eye, killing him instantly.

THIRTY-SEVEN

There had been an inevitability about Elias Pitts' death, Blake realised, watching from the shadows of the mezzanine landing. He'd sealed his fate the moment he'd tried to strike a deal with the Iranians. No reason to let him live after he'd delivered the virus. Not that it made his execution any less shocking.

Blake nudged Mortensen's elbow and guided her down the stairs and into the underground passageway. They raced through the tunnel and bounded up the concrete stairs into the boathouse.

'See if there's any fuel in those canisters,' said Blake, indicating to a row of fuel tanks stacked against the wall alongside the Saetta.

He ransacked a workbench and found solvent in a can on a shelf. He grabbed a handful of oily rags from a drawer.

'Two of them are full,' said Mortensen.

'Throw them in the boat and look for some matches. There were some candles in the wine cellar we passed. Have a look down there.'

Mortensen vanished down the hatch while Blake doused the rags in solvent. He tossed them into the boat with the fuel tanks and poured the remains of the can over the front seats.

'Sorry, old girl,' he said. She was a stunning vessel and part of him felt a sentimental regret.

'Matches,' announced Mortensen. She reappeared out of breath. Blake caught the box one-handed. From outside they heard the whine and cough of the seaplane's engine being turned over. It stuttered three times and finally caught.

'Help me with the doors,' said Blake.

Two metal bolts that held the doors in place slid open easily. Mortensen pushed one open a fraction and risked a look outside. Two guards with weapons slung over their backs were carrying what she presumed to be Pitts' body wrapped in a sheet. It looked as if they were going to load it on the seaplane but they walked straight past to the end of the jetty and threw it into fjord. It hit the water with a loud splash and sank almost immediately suggesting it had been weighted down.

'Give me a hand,' said Blake.

He was standing at the stern of the speedboat. He struck a match and touched it to the edge of one of the solvent-soaked rags. The fumes exploded in a puff ball of fire which rapidly consumed the inside of the vessel.

'Push!' Blake yelled, putting all his weight into moving the boat.

The trailer crept forwards slowly on heavy rubber tyres. Flames that had engulfed the leather seats were giving off choking fumes. It would be only a matter of seconds before the heat caused the fuel tanks to explode. Blake pushed harder, his legs pounding on the concrete floor. He concentrated his effort through his thighs, back and shoulders. The trailer gained some momentum. Crashed through the double doors and picked up speed when it hit the ramp.

With one final effort they sent it on its way. The trailer hit the water with a surging splash and disappeared to the bottom while the Saetta bobbed onto the surface. It drifted away from the shoreline with curling fingers of flame licking the air.

Blake and Mortensen ran back inside the boathouse and dived onto the floor. The first fuel tank exploded with a roar that echoed across the fjord. It was followed by a second explosion which rattled the boathouse doors and prompted a flurry of panic-stricken shouts from the guards.

'Let's get out of here.' Blake rose to his feet and dragged Mortensen up by her arm. His ears were ringing from the blast. It was an uncomfortable sensation that left him feeling disorientated.

They ran with their heads down around the back of the house. Blake trusted the guards' attention would be focused on the front of the lodge and trying to fathom out the cause of the explosion. It gave them a limited window of opportunity.

Their luck was in. When they rounded the far side of the building they discovered Khan isolated and alone on the wooden deck with his back to them. He was watching the chaos unfold with the silver case in one hand and his brief-case in the other. Shahidi was by the seaplane. His gaze was fixed on the burning remains of the Saetta. The explosions had broken her back and her charred remains were lying half out of the water. Three guards were standing at the end of the pier shouting and waving orders to the others. Some were out of sight on the beach below. Two more had clambered onto the concrete slipway and were approaching the boathouse with weapons cocked.

As far as Blake could tell most of the guards were accounted for. He sprinted to the deck and vaulted a balustrade. He landed square on his feet behind Khan. He shoved the barrel of his Browning behind the base of his skull and wrapped a hand over his mouth.

'Quiet or I'll blow your head off,' Blake whispered in his ear.

Mortensen fell in beside Blake with her Glock trained on Shahidi. She snatched the silver case from Khan's right hand and, for good measure, wrestled his briefcase from his left.

'Start moving slowly towards the plane,' Blake instructed Khan. He encouraged him forwards with a nudge of cold steel in the bone behind his ear. 'Nice and easy. No sudden movements.'

With their bodies pressed together, Blake used Khan as a human shield. It was an added insurance in the eventuality that one of the guards should fancy taking a pot-shot. Shahidi heard their approach too late. He whirled around with his .45 drawn. His eyes popped open wide when he saw Khan with a gun to his head.

'Drop it!' Mortensen screamed.

Shahidi was momentarily paralysed. His eyes shuttled between the three figures.

'Do as she says,' said Blake, 'unless you want to see your boss die.'

Blake needed the bodyguard disarmed before he could think about his options. They were hopelessly outnumbered by the guards and there were far too many weapons in too many hands for his comfort. Shahidi released his grip on his gun. He let it swing around his finger on the trigger guard before dropping it.

'Kick it away,' said Mortensen, edging forwards. The gun skidded across the wooden planks. 'Now, down on the floor.'

Shahidi was a big man. He collapsed heavily to his knees. Mortensen stooped for his gun and stowed it in the waistband of her trousers as he lowered himself onto his stomach.

'Put your hands on your back where I can see them. If you so much as twitch I'll put a bullet through your neck,' she said.

Three guards at the end of the jetty had turned at the sound of the commotion. They held their sub-machine guns loosely in front of their bodies, unsure how to react to seeing Khan and Shahidi overwhelmed by two strangers who'd appeared from nowhere.

'Throw down your weapons,' Blake shouted at them. They glanced at each other and, after a brief hesitation, did what he asked.

In the distance, the faint drone of helicopter rotor blades grew louder in the natural bowl created by the fjord. It was no doubt on its way to circle the lodge and grounds once again. Time was in short supply.

'Who are you?' Khan asked with ill-concealed venom as Blake let his hand slip from his mouth.

'Funny you should ask. I had the same question for you. Iranian Intelligence?'

Khan said nothing.

'And you're here to buy four test-tubes of a virus stolen from a British lab? Let me know if I've got any of this wrong. The problem is the virus isn't for sale, so I'm here to collect it on behalf of its rightful owners.'

'British Secret Service?' said Khan.

'Strictly speaking I work for MI5.'

'Then I hope you're prepared to die for your country.'

'I'm not the one with the gun at my head.'

'You're surrounded and outnumbered. You have no hope of getting out of here alive, with or without the virus.'

'If they shoot, then you die. Are they trained to deal with that kind of dilemma? I didn't think so. They're here for one reason and that's to protect you. They're not going to risk your death.'

'In which case we have an impasse,' said Khan.

'I think it's more a Mexican stand-off,' said Blake, with no trace of humour. 'Get down and put your hands on your head.'

Khan fell to his knees. 'So what next? You can't kill me . I'm the only reason you're still alive.'

'I thought we might borrow your plane for a short trip.'

'And where did you have in mind for us to go?' Khan shuffled around, twisting towards Blake so the muzzle of the Browning was level with his nose.

'There are people back in the UK who'd like a chat,' said Blake. 'They have some questions about a number of attacks we have reason to believe were sponsored by the Iranian regime.'

'It's not going to happen.' Khan spoke impeccable English with barely a trace of an accent. The benefit of a Cambridge education. His eyes were emotionless. A man with a gun to his head should show some fear. But there was nothing. Maybe a touch of defiance. His expression certainly didn't giveaway what he saw behind Blake.

The first Blake knew about it was a sharp prod in his back.

'Put the gun down,' the voice said in a heavy accent. A guard who had slipped unseen under the jetty had emerged behind them. 'I said drop the gun,' the voice repeated.

Blake pressed the Browning into Khan's forehead and took up the play in the trigger.

'If I drop this gun you'll kill me. That's not going to happen so it leaves a couple of choices. You could shoot me, in which case there's a high chance the first round from that high-powered sub-machine gun in my back will pass straight through my body and kill the man you're supposed to be protecting. You could aim high but I should warn you my finger is a hair's width from activating this trigger. If you shoot, my body will tense and the weapon will fire. Your best option right now is to step away, put the gun down and I'll give you an assurance no one dies here today.'

No response. Blake let the silence hang. He'd made his offer. The ball was out of his court. Decision time for the other guy.

Khan laughed. A suppressed chortle which developed into a full-bodied howl that swelled from the pit of his stomach. He stood up and stared Blake in the eye. 'Is that the best you can do?'

The growl of the helicopter surged from behind the lodge. Blake forced himself not to blink. He held Khan's gaze until his eyes watered.

'Blake, for Christ's sake put the bloody gun down, will you?' Mortensen's voice was thick with emotion. She'd stepped away from Shahidi and was moving towards him with her back to the bodyguard.

'Alex? What are you doing?'

'Put the gun down or you're going to get us both killed.' Shahidi was picking himself up.

'Perhaps you should listen to the lady. Maybe we can come to some arrangement. Give me the virus and we can all get on our way. No harm done,' said Khan.

'No,' said Blake.

'That's the muzzle of a T9K light sub-machine gun in your back. Are you really this stupid?

'I wouldn't be so confident with a nine millimetre lined up with your frontal lobe.'

'The cards are still stacked in my favour.'

'And my finger tends to get a little twitchy when people start to threaten me.'

'But we've already established that if you pull that trigger, we'll both die. The difference is that my men will have the virus.'

'You want it that much you're prepared to die for it?'

'Of course. It's a weapon of unimaginable power. Too long we've suffered because of the West's sanctions. You treat us like a Third World country and stop us developing even basic nuclear power plants, afraid we might use the technology for weapons. But with the virus, who needs a nuclear bomb? The four test-tubes in that silver case are a thousand times more terrifying than an arsenal of nuclear warheads. That case represents more power than you can imagine.'

'You're insane. You and your country. You'd threaten the world's entire population because of a perceived slight against Iran by the West?'

'We're not insane. We're tired. And we're hungry. And we're sick of your anti-Iranian rhetoric. We have planes falling out of the sky because our airlines can't buy parts for maintenance. Inflation is out of control and meat and fruit is so expensive families can't afford them. Unemployment is rising and the economy is being strangled. All this because of the West's trade sanctions. So don't preach to me about right and wrong.'

'And you think this virus is the answer?'

'We have a team of scientists ready to begin work on a vaccine. As soon as our population is inoculated we have a rather interesting situation, wouldn't you say? Let's see how long America is prepared to maintain its stranglehold on my country when the threat of a worldwide pandemic is hanging over their heads.'

'Which is why I can't let you take it. Too many lives are at stake.'

'You can't stop me. But I know you're only trying to do your job. I'm prepared to compromise so we all might walk away from this awkward situation. Let me back on my plane with the virus and I give you my word I'll let you leave here safely.'

'I'll remind you again that I have a gun aimed at your forehead. You're not in a position to compromise.'

'Blake, it's over. Lower your gun,' said Mortensen. She was at his side with her Glock levelled at his waist.

'What?'

She gripped his wrist. Squeezed but didn't try to force his gun down. Her face was blank. 'I'm sorry it has to end this way,' she said. She jammed her Glock into the tight muscles of his neck. Blake's eyes almost popped out. What the hell was she playing at?

'Alex?'

'I'm sorry, Blake.'

'I have a new deal for you,' she said to Khan. 'Ten million pounds and I'll guarantee your safe passage home, with the virus.'

'A deal? I don't need to negotiate with you,' said Khan.

'Really?'

Mortensen's arm moved in a flash. She pulled the trigger and shot the gunman behind Blake through the temple. He dropped like a stone with his eyes rolling in his head.

'I think you do,' she said. 'I think for all your bravado you still value your life. The suit, the hand-stitched leather shoes, the Rolex watch. They all tell me you're a man enjoying his taste of Western freedom. And who's paying for it all, by the way? The Iranian Ministry of Intelligence, I suppose? Are you their man on the outside, doing the deals?'

Khan said nothing.

'And if you die? Who cares? You won't be remembered. Tehran will deny your existence. Your family will be disgraced and for what? I can offer a better way out of this for both of us.'

'Who are you?'

'My name's Alex Mortensen. I'm a field agent with British MI5. I set you up with Javid Rahimi.'

'What are you saying?' Blake took his eyes off Khan for a second to study her face.

'You don't think a prison cleaner managed to make contact with one of Iran's intelligence agents without some help, do you? He came to us when he was approached by Pitts inside Marshside. Pitts had found out about the Armageddon Virus from his brother and calculated he could sell it at a massive profit if he could find a buyer. When he discovered Rahimi's Iranian background, he figured that Tehran was as likely to be as interested as anyone else. In return, he was offering Rahimi a deal to be reunited with his family. But Rahimi got scared and had the sense to report what had happened. It was too good an opportunity for us to miss.'

'A juicy bait to hang out for one of Iran's top intelligence agents?' said Blake.

'We knew there was someone based in Europe, an Iranian-sponsored terrorist but his identity had eluded us. Khan might not have been planting bombs but he's the one orchestrating the attacks in the West. We were desperate to discover his identity. Rahimi was an unexpected Godsend. We circulated information that the virus was for sale and within days Khan's people had made contact with Rahimi, who in turn put him in touch with Ricky Vaughn. He was the front for Pitts, the guy who could arrange the prison break and put the frighteners on his brother.'

'So why are you offering me a deal to return home?' Khan asked.

'There's no other option left. My choices are somewhat

limited to death or retirement. I've had enough of dealing with scumbags like you and honestly, ten million will let me disappear. I can see out my days in the sun sipping chilled wine by the sea.'

'Alex, don't be so stupid,' said Blake.

'Shut up, Blake. We did our best but we lost. Time to adapt the plan. You might be prepared to take a bullet for your country but I don't intend to die today. Not here and not like this. We're operating illegally in a foreign jurisdiction and you know the game. The agency will deny our existence. Our lives will count for nothing.'

'Not if we can stop the virus leaving for Tehran. Think for a minute about what you're doing. You're signing the death warrant on a generation. You know what that virus is capable of. It's our duty to stop that happening. At any cost.'

'Stuff our duty, Blake. Do we have a deal?'

Khan drew a deep breath and closed his eyes.

'I need some guarantees you're not playing me. Proof of your intentions.'

'I'm not here to bargain. Straight deal, yes or no?'

'Then we all die. Prove to me you mean what you say, that you're prepared to turn your back on your country to save your skin.'

'How?'

Khan's dark eyes fell on Blake. 'If you're serious, kill him.'

THIRTY-EIGHT

The pupils of Blake's eyes grew full and round. 'Alex?'

'Put the gun down, Blake.'

'Are you serious?'

'Put the gun down!' She jabbed her Glock into his neck so sharply that he winced. His arm fell and he dropped the Browning. Khan stepped away with a victorious grin.

'Tell your bodyguard to go back to the house, then walk slowly to the plane with your hands where I can see them,' Mortensen told him.

'Alex, he'll kill you the moment you take your eye off him.'

'I don't want to hear anymore, Blake. Button it.'

Khan shouted something in Persian to Shahidi. His bodyguard shrugged and trudged off the jetty. Mortensen watched him disappear into the house.

'Good, now hands on your head and get into the plane. Tell the pilot I want to be ready for take-off in two minutes.'

'Whatever stunt you're trying to pull, you'd better start thinking again, Alex,' said Blake. 'This doesn't end well. The moment you're on that plane you're as good as dead. We can work this out. Let me come with you.'

'I'm sorry. Time to say goodbye, Blake.'

'Alex, please?'

'Let's not drag this out. Start walking.' Mortensen jabbed him in the neck to force him along the jetty.

Blake wondered if she was playing some kind of clever bluff but with every step he took, the less convinced he became. There was a deadly look in her eye. How had he misread her so completely? He considered trying to disarm her. She'd left herself vulnerable. Too close. With a flick of his elbow and a twist from his waist, he could easily knock her gun away and overpower her. But with three armed guards watching it didn't seem such a good idea. If he put her down they'd kill them both without hesitation. The only thing keeping them alive right now was their confusion. They could see she had the case with the virus and was now doing their job for them by taking care of Blake.

'Jump!' she shouted at the guards as they approached. They stared at her with puzzled expressions. 'I said jump. Get in the water.'

The three men looked at one another. They'd seen her murder one of their colleagues in cold blood so knew she was capable of violence. So when the first man plunged into the fjord, the others quickly followed.

Mortensen pushed Blake into the space they'd vacated. He stumbled forwards. Stopped at the jetty's edge and looked down at the water. It was crystal clear. A crazed pattern of rocks and stones was visible under the gentle swell. He closed his eyes and waited. The bitter stench of the smouldering Saetta filled the air and a cool breeze chilled his cheek. He took a deep breath.

'Just do it clean,' he said.

Khan leaned forwards in his seat. Through the insect-splattered windshield he watched Mortensen order his men to jump from the jetty. Fools, he thought, although he admired her audacity. He allowed the faintest hint of a smile to creep across his face. He never ceased to be amazed at the influence that could be asserted with the lure of cash and the threat of death. Individually they were seductive forces. Combined they were compulsive. How easily Mortensen had abandoned her loyalties to her country and a fellow agent when she was staring down the barrel of a bloody death. He respected her ability to change position when she realised the inevitable. Not only had she negotiated for her life but for a multi-million pound pay-off too. Not that he had any intention of fulfilling his side of the deal or sparing her life. She couldn't be trusted. Not now she knew his identity. It would have to be taken care of. Maybe when they were back in Russia.

The pilot was finishing his pre-flight checks with the single-prop engine running idly in preparation for take-off. Khan checked his watch. The complication MI5 had thrown up had delayed his schedule but not significantly. They could make up the time in the air. Right now he was more interested in Blake's execution. Mortensen had shown some steel. It was a fascinating development. His palms were moist with anticipation. He guessed Blake was ex-military. Maybe even Special Forces. He had that manner. An easy confidence in the face of unlikely odds and an icy, dead look in his eye. A man who'd faced down death before. He hadn't anticipated it would be this easy to see him off. Khan willed Mortensen to hurry.

He was on the edge of his seat when Blake reached the end of the jetty. The perverse side of his nature would have liked to have listened to the final words exchanged between the two agents. But as it was, he could only watch and imagine. Mortensen took a step backwards and raised her gun. To Khan's frustration she partially obscured his view of Blake. He was looking forwards to watching the gory detail, the sight of Blake's body crumpling as his brains were blown out.

The hollow crack of a single gunshot echoed across the water, piercing the throb of the whining seaplane's engine. Mortensen's arm jerked from the recoil of the shot and Blake's body pitched forwards into the water. A ruthless and efficient killing. Mortensen spun on her heel and marched back to the plane without a second look. Her face was deadpan. Not a flicker of emotion. She climbed in next to Khan and pulled the door closed. Khan caught the lingering trace of burning gunpowder.

'Let's get out of here,' she said.

Khan issued the order to the pilot. 'I didn't think you had it in you,' he said. 'I'm impressed.'

Mortensen settled into her seat and placed the silver case on her lap. She crossed her arm over it protectively so her semi-automatic was aimed at Khan's stomach. 'So it turns out that cold-blooded murder isn't such a big deal. And now you know I won't hesitate to kill you if you give me cause.'

Khan snatched a glance at the weapon in her hand. He liked the way her bony fingers wrapped around its curves as if she was caressing it. She was an attractive woman and he was surprised that being under her control excited him. There was nothing like a strong-willed woman who knew exactly what she wanted.

'Where are we going?' Mortensen asked. The plane bobbed into position for take-off on its inflatable skis. The fjord opened up ahead of them framed on all sides by towering green pines.

'St Petersburg,' said Khan.

The pilot increased the power to the engines and the plane accelerated over the water. The fuselage rattled with violent vibrations as they skimmed over the choppy surface and Mortensen struggled to hold her gun steady. Halfway along the length of the fjord, the pilot pulled back on his controls and the plane soared effortless into the air and calm was restored.

'Russia?' said Mortensen. She screwed up her face.

Khan stared into her eyes. Piercing pale emeralds that sparkled with a sorrowfulness. Several corkscrews of red hair had fallen loose over her forehead. He resisted the temptation to sweep them away, imagining how it would feel to brush her cheek with the back of his hand. 'Russia's always been a good ally to my country. We have a common distrust of the West.'

'My enemy's enemy? How quaint.'

'An anti-West alliance. Russia has been true to Iran while the rest of the world shunned us. They've helped us build nuclear reactors and traded with us in the face of the West's sanctions.'

'Not to mention supplying arms. From Russia I suppose you intend to fly to Tehran with the virus?'

'There's a connecting flight to Moscow where I can pick up a plane direct to Iran.'

'And the Russians are happy with these arrangements?'

Khan said nothing.

'The Russians don't know, do they? You're planning to smuggle the virus through two Russian airports. But how?'

'Diplomatic bags,' said Khan, with a knowing smile. 'The Iranian ambassador will accompany me on the flights. The virus will be stowed in his luggage.'

'Which is exempt from custom checks. What about my money? This case stays with me until the cash is wired to my account. It sounds like you're in a hurry, so you'll want to sort that out soon.'

'Don't worry about the money,' said Khan, gazing out of the window. The coast of Norway disappeared below them. 'I give you my absolute word you'll be taken care of.'

THIRTY-NINE

No one took the slightest notice of the woman who strode through Leningardsky railway station trailing a small flight case. She was tall and thin and walked with her head held high. Her lips were painted bright red and her eyes were hidden behind a pair of Audrey Hepburn sunglasses. A pure white ushanka perched on her head contrasted with the wisps of raven-black hair that spilled down her neck.

She disappeared among the bustling crowds, heading directly for the luggage lockers lined up in the shadows off a cavernous hall. She fetched a key from her pocket and rattled open one of the doors, relieved to find the silver case was still there. She snatched it by its handle. Zipped it into her flight case and walked away without a backwards glance.

It had been a long three days. Mortensen had last seen Khan in St Petersburg where she'd hijacked the private jet he'd laid on from the airport. She'd left him to make his own way to Moscow, promising to rendezvous with him in thirty-six hours. She told him she'd have the virus, assuming he'd transferred her money. She'd found a crummy hotel in a downtown area of the city and waited.

She'd done little but sleep for the first twenty-four hours having arrived in the city exhausted and with her nerves frayed. The eight-hour flight in the seaplane from Norway had been bumpy and uncomfortable. They had landed in the Gulf of Finland and been collected from a dreary coastal town by a chauffeur in a black saloon who had driven them straight to the waiting jet. It had only been a ninety-minute flight to Moscow but it had given her a head-start on Khan. Time enough to find somewhere suitable to lay low.

The hotel was as cheap and as anonymous as she'd been able to find, set between two apartment blocks with a hand-painted sign above the door. For a small cash deposit a woman with two stumps for teeth had handed over a key on a wooden fob. The building was thick with cooking smells and the sounds of raised voices and slamming doors. The room they'd given her was dirty and small, accessible by a metal lift that rattled and screeched through the core of the building. The room had hideously garish papered walls and stained carpets but the sheets had been clean even if the mattress was thin. More importantly it had had good views over the main street. Mortensen had barricaded herself inside with a chest of drawers pulled across the door. She'd kept her semi-automatic under the pillow and had spent her time listening for the creak of floorboards in the corridor.

On the second day, she'd coloured her hair with a bottle of dye from a nearby pharmacy. She'd shaded her eyebrows to match and ironed out her corkscrew curls with a clothes iron. She'd completed the look with the brightest red lipstick she could find. She'd hardly recognised the woman who stared back at her in the cracked mirror above the bath-room basin.

She'd left on the third day, wrapped in a newly-purchased overcoat over a plain, grey suit. The cut wasn't flattering but under the coat it hardly seemed to matter. The ushanka was a flamboyant touch but helped her to blend in with the locals. She'd taken a series of taxis through Moscow's congested streets, changing vehicles in the busiest parts of the city confident she'd done enough to lose any of Khan's men if they'd tried to follow her.

Mortensen walked out of the station with her heart pounding. She was more vulnerable now she had the silver case back in her possession. She hailed the first cab she saw.

'To the airport,' she said to the driver, settling into the rear seat and trying to calm her nerves.

She arrived an hour early, true to her plans. It gave her enough time to put a few details in place. Khan had suggested meeting in a cheap diner in a quiet corner of the airport. She chose a table with a chequered vinyl tablecloth near the back and sat with a clear view of the door. She ordered a Bloody Mary, with ice, and waited. She watched the natural ebb and flow of families, couples and business-men, snatching meals ahead of flights. Three men entered separately over the course of the hour and took seats at tables. Each went out of their way to avoid eye contact with her. They ordered coffees, smoked cigarettes and read news-papers. Tough looking guys with gaudy gold chains, tattooed necks and sports clothing. Killing time. None showed the unsettled impatience of passengers waiting for boarding gates to be called. They were in no rush to be anywhere. Khan's men, for sure, sent to secure the location.

Outside a rowdy gaggle of soldiers had gathered. Fresh-faced boys in grey uniforms passing around a bottle of vodka. They were in high spirits, emboldened by the alco-hol. Mortensen was caught watching by one of the men who turned to look through the window. She checked her watch pretending not to have seen them. Khan was late. She hadn't expected that.

He appeared ten minutes later in a charcoal grey suit with a sharp, white shirt and a dark tie. He drew up a seat opposite Mortensen. A waiter in a stained apron slid a menu under his nose.

'Have you eaten?' asked Khan.

Mortensen shook her head. He ordered shashlik with rice for two. The waiter gave a deferential nod, scribbled on his pad and scurried away.

'That was presumptuous,' said Mortensen.

'I'm sorry. Would you prefer something else?'

'I'm not used to other people making decisions for me,' she said.

'In Iran, a woman is grateful to be led by her husband.'

'I'm not your wife.'

A loud bang on the window. A soldier had fallen against the glass. It reduced the rest of the group to a hysteria of laughter.

'Damned drunks,' Khan muttered. He took a sip of sparkling water. 'How was your stay in Moscow?'

'You didn't find me, so I suppose it was as good as could be expected.'

'You think I was looking?'

'Of course. And if you'd have found me and located the virus, you'd have had me killed.'

'I'm disappointed you think so poorly of me.'

'You deny it?'

Khan smiled. 'I had three of my best men trying to locate you but you're most resourceful. Of course, I'd expect no less from a British MI5 agent. I almost didn't recognise you when I walked in.' He indicated to her hair. 'For my benefit I assume?'

'Sometimes a girl needs a change,' she said, running a hand over her head, feeling the straightened strands and reminding herself of her radical new look. 'Do you have my money?'

'The virus first.'

'It'll be delivered as soon as the funds clear my account.'

A flash of anger flickered across Khan's face. 'We had a deal.'

'We both know that as soon as you have your hands on that virus my life becomes worthless to you. So you'll understand I've made arrangements to ensure my safety.'

'I've given you my word. No harm will come to you.'

'Your word?'

'You don't trust me?'

'I think you're worried I'm still working for MI5, and that I've seen your face. Not great for someone who relies on their anonymity.'

Mortensen watched Khan's eyes reading her face. She worked hard to ensure her expression gave nothing away.

'You don't make a compelling case for me to spare you.'

'My death would serve you no purpose. I told you, all I want to do is disappear.'

'And if you're lying?'

Mortensen shrugged. 'Then kill me. Except you'll never see the virus again. Your choice. I'm sure Tehran will understand.' She let Khan consider that possibility for a moment. 'Let's cut the crap and do the deal. Ten million is a small price to pay. I want to live out my days in obscurity, preferably somewhere hot, where the agency can't find me. So let's get over the trust issues and move on.'

Mortensen slid a slip of paper across the table. Khan raised an eyebrow.

'Details of my account,' she said. 'The bank has instructions to confirm the moment the money has been deposited. As soon as I receive that call you'll get the virus.'

The restaurant door flew open and a man with a thick

thatch of grey hair that contrasted with his bushy black eyebrows swept into the room. He scanned the tables and picked out Khan in the corner.

'Damn traffic,' he muttered in accented English. He grabbed a chair and waved a finger to attract the waiter. He ordered a coffee and shrugged off his coat.

'I presume this is our defector,' he said. He extended a limp hand across the table.

'Less a defector and more a businesswoman with a keen eye for a deal,' said Mortensen taking his hand. It was soft and clammy. 'You must be the Ambassador?'

He regarded her across the table with penetrating eyes behind a pair of rimless glasses. His voice was barely audible above the background hubbub. 'But you *were* a British agent? Why the change of heart?'

'I've been looking for a chance to bail out. The opportunity came up in Norway when it was either die or negotiate a healthy pension.'

'How very fortunate.'

'I know this may be difficult for you to believe but I had my reasons for wanting to get out. Now, I have the virus and I'm asking a fair price. Pay the money and you can hop on the next plane home to a fanfare from the Ayatollah. Or I can walk away.'

'You've checked her background?' the Ambassador asked.

'She's an MI5 agent. There's no background to check,' said Khan, scanning her face.

'Do you trust her?'

Khan thought about the question before answering. 'Yes,' he said.

'Then make the payment. Our plane leaves in a little over an hour.'

Khan snatched Mortensen's slip of paper. 'Is the virus here, in the airport?'

'Make the transfer and you'll have it soon enough.'

Khan produced a slim laptop from a case at his side. It came to life with a chirrup. He tapped in a series of passwords while Mortensen's attention was distracted by the soldiers outside. Their mood had darkened. Earlier horseplay was developing into a quarrel. Men were squaring up to each other. Someone was shoved in the chest and sides were being taken.

Khan plugged the sequence of numbers from the paper slip into the computer.

'There,' he said, 'the money's in your account.' He showed her the screen.

'When confirmation comes through from my bank I'll fetch your case.' She gave him a wan smile and set her mobile phone on the table between them. Less than a minute later it rang. She answered, holding it to her ear without speaking.

'Thank you,' she said.

'Everything in order?' asked Khan.

'The Swiss are so efficient when it comes to banking. They've confirmed ten million pounds has been transferred from an unnumbered Lebanese account.'

'And my case?'

'In luggage storage on the underground level.' She pulled a credit card-sized token from her pocket. 'Give this to the attendant.'

The Ambassador snatched it from her hand. He rose from his seat and turned for the door. The noise of the squabbling soldiers filled the restaurant as he left. Their alcohol-fuelled shouts drowned out the sound of clattering cutlery and casual chatter.

Mortensen gathered up her hat and coat and stood to leave.

'Sit down please, Miss Mortensen,' said Khan. 'We also need confirmation you've been true to your word. You should know I have a gun under the table. You'll be free to leave when the Ambassador confirms he has the virus safely in his possession.'

Mortensen sat back down. 'Of course,' she said, forcing a smile that was belied by the fear in her eyes.

'Nothing to worry about is there?'

'Not at all,' she said.

Khan ordered coffee. It was hot and so intensely bitter that Mortensen had to drop three rocks of sugar into her cup to make it palatable. They sat in an uncomfortable silence until Khan's phone rang. He answered in Persian, listened briefly and hung up.

'The Ambassador has the case,' he said, scraping his chair backwards and pocketing a pistol. 'I hope you have a good day.'

'Good luck,' she said. She pulled on her coat but she wasn't foolish enough to think he was going to let her walk away. She'd made a fool of him. Not only had she unmasked his identity but she'd managed to negotiate a small fortune for the virus. And he hated her for that. She could tell by the way he looked at her. No doubt he intended to have her followed and killed at the first opportunity.

She let him make it half-way to the door before she threw a final taunt. 'I'll be thinking of you as I spend my money.' She couldn't help herself. The words just fell from her lips.

Khan spun around to respond. He hadn't seen the waiter coming from the other direction with a tray of drinks and whose attention was taken up by a table at the far side of the room where a couple were waving for their bill. The two men collided. Glasses spilled and drenched the front of Khan's suit.

'You idiot!' he screamed.

The waiter tried to dab Khan's clothes dry with a cloth while Khan shooed him away. A man who'd been sitting at a table alone with a newspaper since Mortensen had arrived jumped up. He shoved the waiter away and guided Khan outside. Mortensen left some cash on the table hoping it would be enough to cover the meal, and slipped out of the restaurant.

The concourse was busy but not overcrowded. Dead-eyed passengers burdened with luggage were wandering in random directions past shops, bars and cafes. Mortensen stopped in the entrance of a store selling magazines and unfamiliar-looking confectionary. She adjusted her ushanka and found her sunglasses in the bag slung over her shoulder. She made a pretence of scanning a rack of newspapers to check if she was being watched. It occurred to her that the soldiers who'd been fighting outside the restaurant had vanished. In the drama of Khan colliding with the waiter, she hadn't noticed them disappear.

On a bench across the other side of the concourse was a man she recognised. He'd been in the restaurant. He'd arrived before Khan, taken a table and ordered coffee. His arm was draped casually over the back of the bench and he was checking his phone. He never once looked in Mortensen's direction. Her pulse quickened. It was one of Khan's men. How many others were there? Her eyes darted around the hall looking for lone men. They'd be loitering, pretending not to watch her.

A languorous gaggle of students engaged in casual chatter approached the shop. All jeans and boots and greasy skin. Mortensen whipped off her hat as they passed. She turned from the newspaper stand and stepped in line with them, hoping from a distance the intermingling of arms and legs and bodies would make her invisible.

The group slowed as they approached a fast-food burger bar with its ubiquitous golden logo like a shining mecca seducing the youth. Their faces turned up to study the menu boards and Mortensen peeled away, looking for signs for the exit.

She was almost immediately surrounded by a flying fury of grey coats and noise. The soldiers from outside the restaurant had appeared from nowhere, swarming in a sweaty clamour. She couldn't make out their faces, only the blur of whirling limbs and heavy bodies, knocking her off balance as they barged their way through the concourse. A fist flew in front of her face, narrowly missing a jaw. Two men fell to the ground, wrestling like lion cubs scrapping.

Mortensen snapped to her senses. She attempted to push her way out of the throng. But the harder she tried to escape, the tighter they knitted together. Their bodies formed an immoveable barrier that held her in place.

She saw a boot fly, connecting with one of the body of one of the soldiers sprawling on the floor. He howled in pain. Hands fell on the perpetrator, clawing, grabbing and punching. The maul tightened until Mortensen couldn't breathe. Panic clouded her brain.

'Stop it! Stop it!' she yelled, but her voice was drowned out.

Her bag was wrenched off her shoulder. She'd already lost her ushanka, trodden into the ground by a dozen pairs of army boots. She was finally taken off her feet by the weight of a collapsing soldier. His legs buckled and as he dropped to the ground the group parted for a second. Mortensen went down hard. There was nothing she could do. He landed unconscious on top of her with his face in her ear. She felt the heat from his muscles and the foul stench of his breath on her skin. A heady cocktail of vodka and garlic that made her gag. She screamed. She bucked and kicked but she was pinned down by the soldier's dead weight with her ribcage compressed against her lungs.

And then everything stopped.

Short, sharp blasts of a whistle pierced the air. A stunned hush descended over the soldiers. The thud of boots running vibrated through the floor. Mortensen tried turning her head but found the stubbly chin of the soldier on her neck.

The soldiers moved apart. Men with great coats, long boots and black ushankas appeared among them. Shouting. Authority in their voices. Like policemen, she thought. Military police. A wave of panic. She had no identity papers and no passport. She was in the country illegally and that was going to take some explaining.

The body that had fallen on top of her rolled away and she took a grateful lungful of air.

'Are you okay, Ma'am?' said a voice in English.

A pair of green eyes peered down. A man offered his hand and helped her to her feet.

'Yes, I'm fine.' She smiled.

'We need to get you out of here. Come with me, quickly.'

FORTY

In a washroom near the restaurant, Khan had made the stain on his shirt look worse. He tried dabbing at it with wet paper towels but the damp patch grew larger and more distinct. He hadn't even started on the splatters on his jacket and trousers. For a man who took care of his appearance, it was a slight to his pride. He refused to turn up on a plane in Tehran looking like a tramp who'd spilled his dinner, so he'd dispatched one of his henchmen to buy a new suit and shirt.

Khan threw a pad of disintegrating wet towels into a bin and gave it a sharp kick. It resonated with a thud that masked the sound of the door opening. Two cleaners in dark overalls entered pushing a metal trolley. Khan was too caught up in his own rage to pay any attention.

The first man, broad and lean, approached the line of basins and stared at Khan in the mirror. He spoke in garbled Russian, pointing and gesticulating.

'What are you saying? I don't understand,' said Khan, turning to face him.

The cleaner spat the words out like bullets in a language Khan only had the faintest grasp of. He pointed and prodded at the wet patch on the Iranian's shirt. Khan batted his hand away.

'Get away from me,' he said. His hand wrapped around the pistol in his pocket.

The cleaner was undeterred. He grabbed a clutch of paper towels from a dispenser and tried to wipe Khan's chest.

'Stop it!' he said.

Distracted by the first man, Khan didn't see the second cleaner move silently behind him. He was a giant with a receding hairline and dashes of grey around his temples. He wrapped his arm around Khan's neck like a giant anaconda. The pressure on Khan's throat left him gasping for air and he was gripped by the horrifying terror of his windpipe constricting. His eyes bulged in their sockets and pinpricks of light danced across his vision. He wrestled with the material of his coat for his gun but it was kicked from his hand and clattered to the ground.

The arm around his neck squeezed and lifted him from his feet. He grasped at the thick muscle, rising to the tips of his toes. Eventually his feet cleared the floor. His vision faded and, as his panic set in, he became a writhing mass with his legs kicking helplessly in the air.

And then he was still.

His brain shut down. He convulsed twice before his body went limp. The cleaner dropped him to the floor in a messy heap.

They picked him up by his arms and legs and bundled him into the trolley. Covered him with a crumpled sheet, retrieved his gun and wheeled the trolley out.

Mortensen couldn't see. The Englishman with the green eyes had thrown his heavy overcoat over her head and marched her out among the soldiers. They seem to have been put under arrest but beyond that she had no idea what was going on. Boots pounded the ground and she watched her own feet scuttle along. They moved tightly together. The military policemen flanked the group. They were being herded out of the airport. But to where she had no idea. To waiting vehicles she presumed.

Her mind whirled, searching for a means of escape. She couldn't risk ending up in a Russian military prison. Not a chance. But at that moment, her situation looked grim. Her Glock was in the handbag that had been ripped from her shoulder and she was blind under the coat.

The swish of glass doors sliding open preceded a blast of icy air. Marble floor tiles disappeared under dark mats and suddenly they were outside, jogging over worn paving slabs mottled by the elements. They slowed and stopped by an enormous wheel that Mortensen guessed belonged to some kind of troop transporter. Its throbbing diesel engine was idling and she could taste the metallic fumes from its exhaust. She was guided to the back of the truck and saw the rungs of a ladder.

'Get in, quickly,' a voice said.

Someone removed the coat from her head and urged her up the ladder with a hand on her lower back. She looked left and right for somewhere to run but the light was bright and hurt her eyes. As her pupils adjusted she saw she was surrounded by stoic-looking Russians in black uniforms and fur-lined collars. The AK-103s they carried were a convincing deterrent against making a break for it. A hand shoved her forwards with an urgent insistence.

'Hurry,' a voice hissed.

Mortensen didn't have much choice. She climbed the ladder into the back of an olive-coloured military lorry with a canvas awning that provided little protection against the freezing temperatures. She sat on a wooden bench between soldiers with hand-cuffed wrists in their laps. The military policemen flanked them at the ends of the rows with their rifles between their knees.

The lorry lurched forwards. It chugged along slowly at first and stopped frequently as it negotiated its way through traffic around the airport. At last it settled into a steady speed as they moved onto an open carriageway.

The soldiers sat in silence, staring at the ground or at their hands. They shifted restlessly on the hard bench and stifled coughs. There was an uneasy tension in the air but no one paid Mortensen any attention. The presence of a foreign civilian woman rounded up with a group of drunken soldiers misbehaving at an airport should surely have elicited some curiosity. It was odd they all seemed so accepting of her presence.

She studied their faces expecting to see regular conscripts fresh out of military training. But they were much older than she'd imagined when she'd first noticed them squabbling outside the restaurant in the airport. They all had tanned, leathery skin and crows-feet around their eyes. They were broad-chested and broad-shouldered. Soldiers in the peak of physical condition.

After a little over fifteen minutes, one of the policemen stole a look through the canvas out of the back of the truck.

'All clear,' he said. His accent sounded to Mortensen like a thick Glaswegian brogue.

A collective sigh punctured the tense atmosphere. The police officers put down their guns and worked their way down the truck releasing the handcuffs. The faces of the soldiers broke into broad smiles.

'What's going on? Who are you?' asked Mortensen, as the green-eyed officer who'd escorted her from the airport stepped past.

'The rescue party.'

'You're not Russian?'

'No.'

'Special Forces?' He ignored the question. 'It's not what I was expecting.'

'If you'd have been expecting it, it wouldn't have looked so convincing.'

'What about Khan? Did you get him?'

'I can't answer your questions, I'm afraid. I'm sure they'll be a full briefing in due course. In the meantime, try to make yourself comfortable. We have a long journey ahead.'

The truck ploughed onwards until the light began to fade and it became too dark to pick out the features of the men opposite. Most were trying to sleep, their bodies hunched over with their chins resting on their chests. Mortensen's legs were numb and she was beginning to feel the chill. She pulled her overcoat more tightly around her shoulders and wished she'd managed to hold onto her ushanka.

When the truck slowed and bumped onto an uneven surface, the soldiers stirred with anticipation. It came to a grinding halt with a squeal of brakes not a moment too soon as far as Mortensen was concerned. She was cold, tired and feeling a little sick from the nauseous exhaust fumes.

Men stood stiffly, stretching their backs, arms and legs. Someone rolled up a canvas flap that had been pulled down over the back of the truck. They were surrounded by the dark outline of tall trees under a rising moon. They were at the edge of a forest.

The soldiers poured out of the truck, landing heavily on rough ground. They gathered in small pockets, exchanging jokes and cigarettes. Some used the time to check their small arms.

'Hello, Alex,' said a familiar voice. 'Fancy seeing you here.'

A distinctive figure walked towards her. She recognised his gait. A slight limp in his right leg, shoulders back, a self-confident coolness oozing from his pores.

'You're supposed to be dead.'

'You need to learn to shoot straight,' said Blake.

'I was worried.'

'That I didn't know what you were playing at?'

'I had to do something. They were going to kill us both.'

'It's okay – just next time don't shoot quite so close to my head,' he said, rubbing a hand over his ear where he'd been partially deafened by the gunshot Mortensen had fired.

'I'm sorry.'

'It was a good plan as far as it went.'

'Did you doubt me?'

'No.'

'It's good to see you again, Blake.'

She caught his smile in the moonlight. 'I'm not sure I like what you've done with your hair,' he said.

Mortensen touched her head. 'Maybe I'll shave it off when we get home.'

'That might be a little over-the-top.'

'So, what's the plan?'

Blake opened his mouth to answer but was interrupted by the arrival of a white van. It rolled into the clearing with its bright headlights bobbing over the bumpy ground. The soldiers took up positions with weapons raised.

'They're with us,' said Blake. 'Don't worry.'

The van pulled up behind the truck. Two soldiers threw open the rear doors and wheeled out a laundry trolley. They reached in and hauled out a dishevelled figure. Khan stood unsteadily with his arms tied behind his back and a strip of tape across his mouth. His suit was a crumpled mess. His hair was tousled.

Blake pushed through the soldiers. 'Khan. You remember me, don't you?'

A moment passed as Khan struggled to place Blake's face. His eyes narrowed, then widened in surprise.

'That's right, back from the dead. And no, Mortensen didn't betray her country. Far from it. She led us directly to you because we couldn't let you get away with that virus. I told you before, it doesn't belong to you.'

Khan tried to speak. Blake ripped the tape from his mouth. 'You're too late. It's already on a plane to Tehran.' Khan gave Blake a supercilious grin.

'Oh, the silver case that left Moscow with the Iranian Ambassador? I'm afraid not. We switched the test-tubes.' Khan stared at Blake with an ill-concealed hatred. 'There's no virus in that case. We filled them with vodka. Only the cheap stuff though. The problem is you really are too trusting.'

'So what now? Are you going to kill me?'

'That would be an easy way out, wouldn't it? I was thinking maybe we could hand you over to the Americans. I hear they're desperate to get their hands on you. They have quite a few questions about a number of attacks on US assets they have reason to believe you orchestrated.'

Mortensen saw the flash of fear. The idea of being gifted to the Americans appeared to hold a greater terror to Khan than death.

'I expect the President will be beside himself. They'll probably leak it to the media too. It would be a terrific coup for them. Can you imagine the headlines? Iran's secret agent exposed. Ayatollah's Armageddon Virus plot foiled.

After they've made you confess to your crimes, they'll probably let you rot in Guantanamo. That would be my guess. Meanwhile, the British Government will be able to bask in the glory of capturing you.'

'We can do a deal,' said Khan, suddenly. 'I have money. Lots of it. Name your price. She'll tell you. I transferred ten million into her account. There's plenty more. You have the virus back. You could let me go.'

'Where would you go? You've failed and humiliated the Ayatollah. They'll hunt you down. Europe's out for sure. And America. Russia would sell you back to Iran in an instant.'

'I know how to disappear. Please, I'm begging you.'

'Begging?'

'Yes.'

'Then you'd better get down on your knees.'

'What?'

'Get down on your knees and beg.'

Khan collapsed to the ground.

'Blake? You can't seriously be thinking about letting him go,' said Mortensen with a note of alarm in her voice.

'Shut up!' he barked with a venom that made her draw breath.

'Beg,' said Blake. There was a cruel edge to his tone.

'Please,' said Khan. 'I beg you, let me go.'

'Don't be ridiculous. Bag him.'

Blake nodded at one of the soldiers who lifted his rifle and struck Khan's head a glancing blow with the stock of the weapon. It knocked him out cold. The Iranian slumped to the floor and a second soldier pulled a sack over his head.

'Put him in the back of the truck,' said Blake. 'And get rid of that van. Everyone ready to roll in two minutes.'

'Where are we going?' asked Mortensen, as soldiers around them snapped into action.

'A rendezvous on the Latvian border,' he said. He turned from her with no other explanation and jogged back to the cab of the truck.

Mortensen clambered into the back with the soldiers. She was at the top of the ladder when a massive explosion rocked the night. A pluming fireball erupted in the forest. Two men came running from out of the trees. They hauled themselves on board the truck and stepped over the unconscious body of Khan to find spaces on one of the wooden benches. The engine rattled to life and they settled in for the long haul.

Blake gave the order for the driver to move on. The Russian-built Kamaz gathered speed slowly but even when it made it back onto the open road its top speed barely touched 50mph. Blake checked his watch and stared with tired eyes at the ribbon of road picked out ahead by the yellow headlights. If the driver kept his foot down they'd be at the border by the early hours of the morning. That was several hours of solid driving during which they remained vulnerable to being stopped and discovered by Russian security forces. They were going to need a lot of luck.

Not that that was at the top of Blake's list of worries. There was another big problem looming and time was running out to find a solution.

FORTY-ONE

The E22 superhighway, stretching from Dublin in the west to the Russian trading town of Ishim in the east, is one of the most strategically important roads in Europe. It's a three thousand mile narrow strip of asphalt that carries millions of tonnes of freight every year. And yet for the last thirty minutes Blake hadn't seen another vehicle.

They'd rumbled on for mile after mile catching only the occasional glimpse of headlights in the distance. Beams would appear on the horizon as pinpricks of light, dancing a hypnotic jig as they grew larger, and flashed past in a blinding glare that stung Blake's sore eyes. The weak head-lights of their own truck barely illuminated the immediate patch of road ahead and threw only a faint glow over the trees of the rolling forests around them.

Blake would have normally taken the opportunity to sleep. It was an old Army habit. Banking sleep whenever he could. But it had been impossible. His mind was working overtime. And he wanted to keep an eye on the driver. It would have been a disaster if he'd nodded off.

'How are you feeling?' Blake asked.

'Fine, thank you, Sir,' said the young corporal. He

glanced briefly at Blake before setting his eyes back on the road.

He was a quietly-spoken Liverpudlian with thick eyebrows and hairy arms. Lean and lithe. Much smaller than the tough, fighting men in the back. Not that Blake doubted his credentials. He'd trust with his life anyone who'd won the coveted winged-dagger of the SAS.

'I don't want you falling asleep on me.'

'I'm as fresh as a daisy. I only wish we could get on a bit faster.'

He'd driven for hour after hour without a hint of fatigue. Blake knew his own eyes would have been rolling into the back of his head a long time ago.

'What's your name?'

'Toller, Sir.'

'Do you have a first name?'

'Danny.'

'Volunteer for this mission?'

'Of course. Without hesitation.'

'Why?'

'Why not?'

The operation had been put together with barely twenty-four hours' notice when Blake had raised the alarm from Norway. With the Armageddon Virus heading for Russia and on to the Middle East, a plan had been hastily convened for an audacious Special Forces mission into the heart of the Russian capital, although not without resistance from some quarters of the Government. Committing troops to Russia without the Kremlin's knowledge was like waving a match at a petrol-soaked rag. It might pass off without incident, but there was a fair chance it would blow up in their faces. If the Kremlin discovered British Special Forces were operating under their noses in Moscow, it would go way beyond a diplomatic incident. Wars had been started over less. But there were precious few other options. Mortensen had presented them with a narrow window to retrieve the virus and capture Khan, and Blake had been determined to take it.

A team had been rapidly put together and dispatched into Russia in pairs to avoid suspicion. They'd posed as tourists and businessmen and travelled by plane, coach and train across the border. Their rendezvous was on the outskirts of Moscow where arrangements had been made with well-placed contacts to supply them with Russian Army uniforms and military vehicles.

So far the operation had run without a hitch. The test-tubes Mortensen had hidden at the railway station had been switched. Two of the team had taken a train to Poland with the virus, and been evacuated by helicopter back to the UK.

'No reservations? It's a high-risk mission.'

Toller rubbed his eye with the knuckle of his left hand. 'Not at all, Sir. There aren't many of us Russian language specialists in the Service.'

'You speak Russian?'

'My grandfather came from Vologda.'

'Well, what are the chances?'

They watched the lights of a truck loom large and blaze past on the opposite side of the road. The turbulence from the speeding lorry rocked the Kamza.

'Can I ask a question, Sir?' asked Toller.

'Of course.'

'How are you planning to get us across the border?'

Their rendezvous with the RAF Chinook was in a little more than ninety minutes, on the other side of the Latvian border. An airborne extraction from inside Russia had been dismissed as too risky. Latvia, on the other hand, as a paid-up member of Nato, would turn a blind eye. It had permitted an aircraft into its airspace on the condition it was on a pick-up and recovery op. But no one had resolved how to transport a lorry-load of British soldiers, an MI5 spy and their Iranian prisoner out of Russia through a fully-manned checkpoint. That detail had been left to Blake to work out on the ground and had been taxing him for the last four hours.

'Where's the next truck stop?' Blake asked.

'I'm not sure,' said Toller. He fumbled in the pocket of the door for a creased map. He tried to unfold it over the steering wheel.

'Here, give it to me.' Blake took it and spread it out on the dashboard. 'Here, in about thirty miles,' he said. He jabbed at it with his finger. 'We'll stop there. We need to lose the truck.'

'Excuse me, Sir?'

'We can't cross the border in this truck. We don't have the papers and a military Kamza packed with Russian soldiers might raise a few eyebrows on the Latvian side, don't you think? Is your Russian good enough to blag your way across?'

'Yes, Sir.'

'Then we need to find alternative transport. A service station's our best and only chance at this time of night.'

'You think it will be open?'

'Better if it's not.'

The service station appeared on their left after a gentle rise in the road. Facilities were basic. A cashier's cabin and two sets of pumps under a wide canopy. Lots of white plastic sitting starkly amid a pine forest and illuminated by the amber glow of down lighters. The cabin was in darkness apart from the strobing red light of an alarm.

Four articulated lorries with paintwork marbled with layers of dust and grime were parked in a line. Toller pulled up alongside the nearest one. Killed the engine and let the rattling die away. It was a Polish-registered truck with a plain white trailer. Ideal for what Blake had in mind. A miniature satellite dish had been mounted to the roof of the cab and curtains drawn around the windscreen.

Blake was out of the Kamza before it had rolled to a halt. Toller joined him and they approached the lorry together. Blake crept up to the driver's door. 'Hey! Hey! Wake up! Quickly!' He banged with a flat palm.

A light came on and the vehicle rocked on its suspension as someone moved about inside.

'Hey! Hey!' Blake shouted again.

The door opened a fraction and a voice heavy with sleep called out in a language Blake didn't understand. He grabbed the door and wrenched it from the hand of a startled truck driver with a looping grey moustache and an off-white vest tight over his pot-belly. His eyes grew wide when he saw Blake in his Russian military uniform pointing a pistol. Toller hauled himself into the passenger seat on the other side of the cab.

'Hello, mate,' said Toller with a cheery smile. He aimed a Sig Sauer P226 at the man's gut.

'Speak English?' asked Blake.

'Of course,' said the driver, rubbing a hand over the bristles of several days' beard growth. His brow furrowed.

'Sorry for the wake-up call but we need your truck,' said Blake. 'Move over.'

The driver looked at Blake blankly.

'What's in the back?'

'Nothing.' The driver shook his head as if he was coming to his senses. 'I carry machine parts but I made the delivery and now I'm on my way home.'

'Not ideal but we'll have to make do,' said Blake looking to Toller. He was keeping watch for approaching traffic. 'Get the men unloaded and into the back.'

Toller slipped out of the cab and when he had disappeared from view, Blake fixed the driver with a penetrating stare.

'What's your name?' he asked softly.

'Oskar Smolak.'

'Been running freight long?'

'About eight years on this route,' he said.

He'd barely managed to speak the words when Blake's left hand flashed towards his head. He tapped the driver's forehead with two fingers. 'Sleep now,' said Blake.

Smolak's eyes rolled into the back of his head and his chin slumped onto his chest. Blake intoned soothing words into the man's ear, watching his breathing slow as he relaxed into a deep trance.

From the corner of his eye Blake saw a trail of soldiers jog around the front of the lorry. He heard their boots thudding into the empty trailer. It took less than three minutes to load all the men, including Mortensen and the captive Khan, from one vehicle to the other. The rear doors clattered closed. Toller hid the Kamza behind the service station, in the shadow of the forest.

'Everything okay?' said Toller. He nodded at the slumbering driver as he hauled himself into the cab.

'Oskar, wake up. I want you drive us to the Latvian border.'

Smolak's eyes peeled open. He looked around his cab with incomprehension, as if he had no idea where he was. Blake threw him a shirt hanging in the rear of the cab and switched seats. Smolak fired up the Scania. Bright headlights illuminated the forecourt and, with a hiss of brakes, they rolled out of the service station, picking up speed as they joined the main carriageway.

The checkpoint appeared in the middle of the road out of nowhere. A blue hut with a striped traffic barrier. Smolak eased off the accelerator and a guard emerged blinking in the glare of the lorry's headlights.

'They won't be expecting me at this time of the night,' said Smolak in a flat tone. 'It will be very suspicious to them.'

Blake ducked under the dashboard. Toller followed.

'Convince them everything's normal,' said Blake. 'Remember we're not here.'

'You trust him not to raise the alarm?' whispered Toller.

'He won't.'

The lorry rolled to a halt at the barrier. Smolak wound down his window. Blake heard a woman's voice speaking in heavily-accented English. 'It's early to be travelling.' She posed the statement like an accusation.

'I'm behind time,' said Smolak. 'I had to replace a wheel and I'm supposed to be back at the depot by the morning.'

'Passport?'

Smolak handed down his documents. The guard seemed to dwell on them for an age. Longer than she might during the busy parts of the day, Blake suspected.

'Okay, come through. You know the drill.'

Smolak threw the lorry into gear and they trundled forwards.

'Good work, Oskar,' Blake whispered. Despite his concerns, their passage through the checkpoint had been remarkably easy.

'You'd better stay down,' said Smolak.

'What?'

'Keep your head down.'

The lorry was slowing again. It rolled to a halt less than twenty metres on.

'What are you doing?' asked Blake.

'I told you, he can't be trusted,' said Toller.

Smolak pulled on the handbrake and killed the engine.

'That was the first checkpoint. I need to get through customs and immigration,' he said.

'What does that entail?'

'I have to show my papers,' said Smolak. He reached into a glove box for a sheaf of documents. 'Sometimes, if they're bored, they like to search the trucks.'

'Persuade them that's a bad idea. Do you understand? You have to make sure they don't find us.'

Smolak jumped from the cab and slammed the door closed.

'Damn!' Blake cursed. It was strictly against his own code of conduct to let someone under his hypnotic control leave his sight. He considered it professional misconduct. But Smolak had gone before he had a chance to stop him.

'He's going to tell them,' said Toller.

'I don't think so, but there's a chance he might inadvertently raise their suspicions and they could insist on checking the lorry. Have your sidearm ready.'

Blake heard voices. He held his breath but couldn't make out what was being said. He checked his watch and stretched a leg where he could feel cramp setting in. Minutes passed like hours and without the heat of the engine the cab soon fell cold. Blake was grateful for his Russian greatcoat. He hoped Mortensen and the men in the trailer weren't suffering too much.

Eventually the driver's door swung open and Smolak climbed in.

'Is everything all right?'

'Yes, we're can carry on,' he said, without looking at Blake. He turned the ignition key and the truck rattled into life. Smolak raised a hand to an unseen figure and they moved forwards.

Blake risked raising his head and saw two border guards

with dark uniforms and severe expressions clutching SR-2 Veresk sub-machine guns.

'Is that it?' asked Blake.

'I told them I was in a hurry to get back and that the trailer was empty.'

'They believed you?'

'They know me,' said Smolak. His face was expressionless.

'Exceptional work, Oskar. Thank you.'

When Smolak looked down at Blake under the dashboard it was as if he was seeing him for the first time. His eyes were dead. The cab jolted forwards as he selected second gear. His foot hovered over the accelerator and he checked his side mirror.

'Halt! Halt!' One of the guards was screaming at the lorry to stop.

'What's going on?'

'They want us to stop,' said Smolak. He hit the brakes, sending Blake and Toller into the solid plastic of the dashboard with a heavy thud.

The guard caught up with the Scania and approached it with his submachine gun angled across his body. Blake's hand settled on the Browning in his pocket. He eased off the safety with his thumb. 'What do they want?'

'I don't know.'

'Act normally. Smile and get rid of them.'

Smolak wound down his window.

'We can't let you leave,' said a voice in English spoken through a thick accent.

'What's the problem?' asked Smolek.

'You know you really shouldn't be in such a hurry.'

Blake's pulse was racing and his gut tightened. He wondered how it might play out if the guards decided to check the trailer. What if they found British soldiers, dressed as Russians, hiding in the back? He thought of Mortensen and Khan. An MI5 spy and their Iranian prisoner. There was no easy way to explain any of it away.

Smolak said nothing.

'You see, I think you are forgetting something,' the guard continued.

'No, I don't think so.'

'Your passport, Oskar. You left it in the office. You wouldn't have made it far home without it.'

'I'm an idiot. Thank you.' Smolak leaned out and took the passport.

'No problem. Safe journey.'

Smolak tossed the passport onto the dashboard and wound up the window. 'We have one more barrier to clear but we shouldn't have to stop,' he said.

The truck rolled towards a third and final barrier which was raised as they approached. Smolak waved to a guard in a wooden hut and accelerated onto the open road stretching ahead.

Blake waited until he was sure they were clear of the crossing before hauling himself from the floor.

'Can I have my truck back?' said Smolak, without a hint of emotion.

'Of course,' said Blake. 'A little further on and you can pull over.'

'Where's the rendezvous, Sir,' said Toller, dusting himself down.

'Close. You'll know when we get there.'

Smolak drove at a steady 50mph, never letting his eyes stray from the road that stretched ahead straight and true for as far as his headlights would reach. The three men sat in silence until Toller spoke.

'Can you hear that?'

Blake peered through the windshield at the charcoal

sky. At first he heard nothing over the drone of the lorry's diesel engine and the hum of a dozen rubber tyres on asphalt.

'A chopper,' said Toller. 'It's close.'

'Slow down,' said Blake. Smolak eased his foot off the accelerator and changed down a gear. 'Slower,' Blake insisted.

The unmistakable throb of helicopter rotor blades resonated through the air and filled the cab. A spectral pulsating that vibrated in their chests. The bulbous hulk of an RAF Chinook materialised over the tops of the trees that lined the carriageway. It came in low and fast, swooping into their path and hovered over the road a quarter of a mile ahead.

'It's landing in the road!' said Smolak.

He jumped on the brakes, locking the wheels in a squealing cloud of burning rubber. The trailer fishtailed, threatening to slide out of control. The truck eventually came to rest with the trailer sideways to the cab.

'Get the men into the chopper,' Blake ordered Toller. 'As quick as you can. And make sure the woman is looked after.'

'Yes, Sir.' Toller nodded and vanished out of the cab.

Smolak sat with his hands on the wheel, staring at the helicopter.

'Oskar, I want you to sleep deeply now.' Blake had to shout to be heard over the noise of the Chinook. 'Let your eyes close and relax.'

Smolak's head lolled to one side and his lids fluttered shut. His hands dropped from the steering wheel into his lap.

'In a moment I want you to start counting from one hundred down to zero. When you reach zero you'll be awake and feeling refreshed. You won't remember anything about what's happened. You'll continue to drive until you find the next rest area where I want you to pull over and sleep until morning. When you wake you'll continue your journey home as if nothing has happened. Do you understand?' Blake took Smolak's slight head movement as a nod.

Through the windscreen Blake watched the soldiers scuttle towards the helicopter with their heads bowed. One of the men carried the limp body of Khan over his shoulder like a sack of flour. He kept a careful eye on Mortensen as she was escorted towards the aircraft by Toller. And when he was sure they were all safely on board, he started Smolak's countdown and jumped out of the cab.

He ran to the rear of the helicopter and up a ramp into its belly where two waiting airmen grabbed his arms to help him on board. The soldiers were strapping themselves into seats with the grins of men sensing the relief of completing a mission unscathed.

Blake sat next to Mortensen as the rear ramp closed and the engines whined into an excited frenzy ready for take-off.

'Everything okay?' he mouthed. Her skin was pallid and there were dark patches under her eyes.

She looked at him for a moment and nodded. 'Yes,' she said and let her head fall on his shoulder. They felt the pull of the giant Chinook lifting them skywards.

'Good,' he said, grabbing her hand. He squeezed it gently. 'We'll be home by morning.'

FORTY-TWO

THREE MONTHS LATER

A cooling breeze drifted off a glittering sapphire sea and ruffled Blake's hair. The tang of sea salt and the perfume of frankincense whispered through the fronds of date palms growing through squares in a wooden terrace. It was warm like an English summer. Shirt-sleeves weather. Not the stifling heat that Oman likes to cook up in the high season. The cold and wet London Blake had left behind seemed like a different world.

'Blake,' said a voice. Mortensen strode out of a stone villa. 'You came,' she said with a genuine smile.

'I was intrigued.' He was glad to see she'd rinsed her hair back to its natural colour and the tight curls had returned.

She grabbed him by the arms and offered a cheek to kiss. 'I wasn't sure you would. How was your flight?'

'Tiring.' He sipped at a cold beer someone had pressed into his hand.

She led him to a circle of Rattan armchairs around a

glass-topped table adjacent to a plunge pool cut into the terrace. They sat opposite each other, the craggy mountain the colour of lion-pelt creating a dramatic backdrop.

'This is an impressive place,' said Blake.

'Our Omani friends make sure we're comfortable.'

The villa was traditionally Arabic with its natural stone walls and soft, bleached wood but it had been designed with luxury in mind. The floors were marbled, the furniture expensive and it was kitted out with the latest technology. It was hidden behind high walls at the end of a long, private drive on the outskirts of Muscat. An expensive holiday retreat for the wealthy and privileged.

'We're handing Khan back,' said Mortensen.

Blake studied her face looking for the glimmer of a smile, a crack in her stony expression. But there was nothing. 'You asked me out here to tell me that?'

'He's no use to us any more.'

'He's a terrorist.'

'He was careful never to get blood on his hands. We know he was involved in at least half a dozen attacks on Western targets but there's nothing to link him to a single incident. We'd never make a prosecution stick. We managed to drag some useful intelligence about the regime out of him but that's it. It's too complicated to detain him in the UK. Besides the Iranians are kicking off.'

'And since when did we start worrying about what Tehran wants?'

'Since it started suiting us.'

'What about the Americans? They had their eye on Khan long before us.'

'They'd like to get him to Guantanamo but the PM's refused extradition. We've given them access in the UK but they've not had much joy either.'

'We risked everything sending a team to Moscow. How can you even think about letting him go?'

'He's already gone. A few hours ago. The Omani Government made the arrangements for the hand-over.'

'Thanks for the heads-up.'

'The Iranians know what happened in Moscow.'

'It was always a risk.'

'They're threatening to expose the operation to the Russians. We know Putin's already jumpy about the West. We don't know how he'll react if he finds out. Worst case scenario is a military retaliation. We can't risk it. The deal was we hand Khan back and they keep quiet.'

'I thought we had good intelligence on Khan? We could have saved ourselves a whole lot of trouble.'

'It *was* worth the risk. We've eliminated him from the game. He's no use to Iran now, not with his identity blown. At best he'll be punished with a desk job.' She paused for a beat. 'But there's something else I've not told you.'

Mortensen crossed her legs and picked at an imaginary hair on her knee as though she was working out how to phrase her next sentence. Blake pursed his lips.

'I was in contact with Javed Rahimi before his death,' she said. 'I was assigned as his case officer but he was killed before I had the chance to find out what was going on in Marshside.'

Blake drained his glass and watched a beery froth slide to the bottom. He set it down on the table. 'So what you told Khan in Norway was true? Why didn't you tell me before?'

'Rahimi approached the police shortly before he was murdered. The case was referred to Special Branch who alerted the agency. He was terrified about what he'd got himself caught up in. I wanted to tell you, but I needed you untainted. To draw your own conclusions.'

'So what did he say?'

'That he'd struck up a friendship with Elias Pitts.'

'Pitts was grooming him?'

Mortensen frowned at Blake's use of the word. She knew what he meant. 'I don't think so. It was more opportune than that after he found out about the project Benjamin was working on. He realised the potential of the virus as a weapon and was looking for a means to exploit an opportunity.'

'You mean he needed someone to sell it to and Rahimi was his best option?'

'Probably his only option. Rahimi told him about his past in Iran and about how he'd been tortured. He told him he'd fled the country but had to leave his wife and daughters behind. Pitts made him an offer, said he could guarantee the safe passage of his family to Britain.'

'On what condition?'

'That Rahimi found someone in Iran who would negotiate a deal on his behalf.'

'So Pitts told Rahimi about the Armageddon Virus?'

'No, I'm certain he knew nothing about it. Pitts told him he'd acquired some information that would be of interest to the Iranians. That's all. He wanted Rahimi's help to put the word out. When I interviewed him he'd already managed to make contact with someone from the Iranian Ministry of Intelligence. They'd arranged for him to smuggle a phone into the prison so they could speak directly with Pitts.'

'Khan?'

'More likely one of his subordinates. They had no idea what Pitts was offering at that stage but were intrigued enough to find out more.'

'So if you knew what was going on, why did it take the Americans to raise the alarm? You said they intercepted a call from inside the prison. But you already knew a phone had been smuggled in.'

Mortensen squinted at the sea as sunlight sparkled off its surface. 'The truth? We didn't take the threat seriously. What Rahimi was claiming seemed so far-fetched.'

'Until the Americans located the phone signal and Rahimi wound up dead?'

'Yes,' said Mortensen. When she looked back at Blake her eyes were red. 'We let him down, Blake.'

'You couldn't have known.'

'He was murdered because the Iranians found out he'd spoken to me and I did nothing to stop it.' Mortensen wiped the corner of her eye. 'As if that poor man hadn't been through enough.'

'You can't blame yourself,' said Blake, unsure what else to say. He chewed his lip while he waited for her to elaborate.

'He was really scared. He begged me not to send him home and pleaded for my help to get his family out of the country. I was due to meet him the day after his body was found.'

'If we followed up every crack-pot conspiracy theory that came our way we'd never sleep. You made the best judgement you could with the information you had.'

'I should have taken it more seriously. If it wasn't for me, the Armageddon Virus would never have been stolen and Rahimi would still be alive. I messed up. But I'm going to make amends.'

Mortensen flicked a loose corkscrew of hair out of her eyes and sniffed as she composed herself.

'How?'

'There's something I want to show you.' Mortensen rose from her seat and smoothed her skirt over her thighs.

She led Blake inside the villa and out through a main door into a courtyard he'd passed through when he'd arrived. A small group had gathered. Agency staff. All white shirts, dark suits and sunglasses. Patiently waiting among the soft plants and palms in the shade of the towering security walls that surrounded the complex.

A pair of gates buzzed open slowly letting the sunlight stream through a widening gap. A convoy of three black cars swept into the compound along a drive covered by a fine dusting of sand. They came to a halt in a semi-circle. Six men sprang from the cars at the front and rear. Omani Secret Service, Blake guessed. They all wore double-breasted suits, sombre ties and dark glasses.

A Mercedes saloon in the middle of the three was so highly polished that it reflected the stonework of the villa in its bodywork. One of the Omanis stepped up to a rear door and held it open. A middle-aged woman with a purple hijab wrapped around her head and face appeared. She adjusted her clothing and stood blinking in the bright light, staring at the faces watching. Two more women emerged. Young and slim, their eyes bright but furtive. Mortensen stepped forwards and the older woman pulled them to her chest.

'Welcome,' said Mortensen with a slight bow. 'I hope your journey wasn't too stressful.'

The women said nothing, holding Mortensen's eye with a look of distrust.

'Please, come inside and freshen up. We have a few hours for you to relax before we leave for the airport.'

The three women were ushered into the villa. Two Omani secret servicemen followed behind with bags from the boot of the car.

'Who are they?' said Blake.

'You don't recognise them?'

'Should I?'

'The older woman is Niyoosha. Her daughters are Yasaman and Alaleh. You saw their photo in Rahimi's bedsit.'

334

'His wife and daughters? What the hell are you playing at Alex?'

'Making amends for what happened to Javed Rahimi. He wanted his family out of Iran and given asylum in the UK. So, we've made it happen.'

'You exchanged them for Khan? And that's your way of fixing this?'

'Don't be so bloody righteous, Blake,' said Mortensen. She pushed past him, brushing his shoulder. She marched into the villa, Blake a few paces behind.

'Makes you feel better, does it?'

'Keep your voice down,' she said.

Blake followed her onto the terrace overlooking the Gulf.

'I can't believe this has been sanctioned. Is Patterson aware?'

'Of course he's aware. Didn't you wonder how a prison cleaner could get access to someone senior enough in the Iranian intelligence services who would sit up and take note of Pitts' claims that he had secrets to sell?'

Blake shrugged. 'I guess it was a little implausible.'

'You want to know how he did it? Well, you just met her.'

'Rahimi's wife? What do you mean?'

'No, not his wife. His daughter, Yasaman. The older girl.'

Blake's mind whirled. He tried to remember how old she was. A girl in her late teens. Maybe still at school. How could she possibly have been involved. 'I still don't understand,' he said.

'She's a chip off the old block. A computer whizzkid.'

Blake shook his head.

'Rahimi was a software engineer, in the private sector working for an oil firm. He was well regarded in the industry until he was caught up in the political unrest. It turns out Yasaman is equally adept around a computer. Except she's put her skills to less legitimate pursuits.'

'A hacker?'

'State-sponsored. She was part of an elite network of so-called black hatter hackers employed by the Iranian intelligence service to develop worms and malware to target systems in the West.'

'A cyberterrorist?'

'Tasked with probing commercial and governmental computer systems looking for weak points to exploit. But they've also been given responsibility for tightening up Iranian systems to prevent attacks like the Stuxnet worm that compromised Iran's nuclear programme.'

'Clever girl. And she was able to get access to someone who would take Rahimi's request seriously?'

'With a little digital subterfuge, we think.'

'And she's worth the trade with Khan?' asked Blake.

'I think she could be worth ten of him.'

They stood with their backs to the villa watching the dark shadow of a cormorant skim across the water, its wing tips almost touching the surface.

'I really hope so, for your sake, Alex.'

For a while they didn't speak, enjoying the warmth of the sun on their necks. The bitter remnant of hops on his tongue made Blake wonder if there was somewhere he could find another beer.

'Blake, I need your help,' said Mortensen, breaking the silence.

She was leaning on a railing on the end of the terrace peering down at the surf foaming onto the rocks below. The sun had flushed her pale skin a shade of red.

'Which is the real reason you've asked me here?'

'We want Yasaman to work for us. She's a bright kid and

her skills would be invaluable to our cyber security unit. Plus, she'll be able to give us an insight into Iran's cyber programme.'

'Will she co-operate?'

'When she finds out the truth about what happened to her father, I think we'll be able to persuade her.'

'Why do you need me?'

Mortensen angled her head upwards to look at Blake. 'I want to know if we can trust her.'

'Enough to give her access to Governmental computer systems? That's a lot of trust for someone you've only just met.'

Mortensen stared at Blake as if she was waiting for him to come to a conclusion. Those big, green eyes. Windows on the soul. He noticed a spatter of freckles across her nose. Maybe brought on by the sun. Her lips were pursed tightly, her hair scraped away from her face and cascading down her neck in tight ringlets.

'Alex, don't even think about asking.'

'Blake, please?'

He turned from her and walked away towards the villa, his feet thudding across the deck. She caught up with him, grabbed his elbow and spun him around.

'We have to be sure we can trust her.'

'Then find another way,' said Blake. 'I'm not interrogating a teenage girl. Find someone else to talk to her.'

'There is no other way. We have to be absolutely certain she won't betray us and only you can give us that certainty. You can sow the seeds in her mind that will guarantee her co-operation. I've seen you do it before.'

'No, Alex. She's no more than a girl. Her brain is still developing.'

One of the women Blake had seen earlier appeared from the villa. Another agent. More junior than Mortensen,

Blake guessed from her demeanour. She hovered at the edge of the terrace, uncertain whether to interrupt.

'Miss Mortensen, we need you upstairs,' she said at last.

Mortensen shot her a look that left her in no doubt her timing was poor.

'What is it?'

'It's Mrs Rahimi. She's working herself up into a state about everything. I think you need to come and talk to her.'

'Can't you sort it out? I'm busy,' Mortensen barked.

The woman remained rooted to the spot with a pained expression.

'All right, I'm coming.' Mortensen turned and barged past Blake. 'Stay here, I'll be right back.'

Blake watched her glide away, her hips rolling under the tight fabric of her pencil skirt, her heels clicking across the deck. He glanced up at the sky, marvelling at the deepness of blue. There wasn't so much as a wisp of a cloud. It didn't feel much like February. Voices drifted from a room upstairs and he heard muted wailing. It made him shudder. He wasn't much good with emotional women. Was there somewhere to get another beer?

He wandered casually through the villa, retracing his steps to the outer courtyard where the row of black Mercedes was parked. He stepped up to the gates and they clicked open automatically, triggered when he broke an invisible beam. He waited patiently for them to swing apart fully and reveal the sand-dusted drive ahead. They thumped to a halt against rubber stoppers and Blake adjusted his sunglasses. He glanced over his shoulder but no one was watching. He took one step forwards followed by another, onwards towards the city.

It was going to be a long walk in the heat but he knew the beer in the first bar he found would make the trek worthwhile.

Printed in Great Britain
by Amazon